Between Heaven and Hell

Am I dead . . . or dying . . . or what? Holly thought.

Evan laughed, and the sound echoed hollowly in the infinite corridor. Several of the lifeless figures in the doorways began to laugh softly. Then the sound faded.

"No, Mom. Don't be silly. You're not dead."

Holly jumped and let out a squeal when she felt something squeeze her hand. Looking down, she saw that Evan was reaching out to hold her hand. Trembling, she took his hand, surprised by the clammy, fleshy touch as his small fingers slid into her palm.

Then why am I here?

"I need you to do something," Evan said. His voice was like the rasp of sandpaper.

You know I'd do anything for you, honey . . . absolutely anything.

He looked up at her with eyes too old for his round face, and smiled.

"I want you to kill the man who killed me."

POLTERGEIST
THE LEGACY

The Hidden Saint

RICK HAUTALA
BASED ON THE TERRIFYING HIT
TELEVISION SERIES CREATED BY
RICHARD BARTON LEWIS

ACE BOOKS, NEW YORK

POLTERGEIST: THE LEGACY: THE HIDDEN SAINT

An Ace Book / published by arrangement with
Tekno Books

PRINTING HISTORY
Ace edition / October 1999

The Penguin Putnam Inc. World Wide Web site address is
http://www.penguinputnam.com

Check out the ACE Science Fiction & Fantasy newsletter
and much more on the Internet at Club PPI!

ISBN: 0-441-00645-0

ACE®
Ace Books are published
by The Berkley Publishing Group,
a division of Penguin Putnam Inc.,
375 Hudson Street, New York, New York 10014.
ACE and the "A" design are trademarks
belonging to Penguin Putnam Inc.

To Susan, Ginjer, Marty, and Larry . . .
for another chance to ride.

Thank you!

Since the beginning of time
Mankind has existed between the World of Light
and the World of Darkness.

This journal chronicles the work of our
secret society, known as
The Legacy,
created to protect the innocent
from those creatures that inhabit
the Shadows
and the Night.

ONE

Clouds as round and gray as boulders hung low over the ocean. Steel-colored waves capped with white foam rolled onto the shore and swirled around the wharf's pilings. A brisk offshore wind was blowing out over the water, making the air feel much colder than it actually was, but this late in November it would have been pretty cold even without the wind.

The crowd milling around the Plymouth Rock Monument and the wharf where *Mayflower 2* was moored, however, seemed either not to notice or not to care about the harsh New England weather. Sensibly bundled up in winter coats, woolen hats, and mittens, they were enjoying the carnival-like atmosphere of the annual Thanksgiving Day celebration in Plymouth, Massachusetts, the town founded by the original Pilgrims.

Mingling with the crowd were various folks wearing original Pilgrim and Native American clothing. Many of these folks carried their role-playing to the extreme and spoke to celebrants only within the character of the Pilgrim or Wampanoag Indian they were playing.

Alexandra Moreau was trying her best to enjoy the festivities, but she was so cold her fingers and nose were numb. Her teeth were chattering wildly as she watched the proceedings with a mixture of amusement and impatience. She had experienced cold days back in San Francisco, but New England weather seemed to have teeth that bit right through her.

The Pilgrims' Progress Parade had just finished. Like every year, there had been a small band of protesters—mostly Native Americans—who carried signs and complained that their native land had been stolen away from them by the English.

All Alex could think about was getting back to her friend's house where there was a twenty-pound turkey roasting in the oven. She was looking forward to a pleasant Thanksgiving meal and—especially—getting warm.

Holly Brown had been one of Alex's closest friends ever since they met in college. She and her son, Evan, lived in their newly constructed home in nearby Pembroke. Holly had invited Alex to Massachusetts for the holiday, but after watching the Pilgrims' Progress, touring the *Mayflower 2*, and sampling some of the local pastries and mulled cider for sale, they had pretty much seen all there was to see.

Plymouth Rock itself wasn't nearly as impressive as Alex had imagined. It was surrounded by an iron cage to protect it from vandals who otherwise would chip off pieces as souvenirs, but Alex couldn't help thinking it looked like a wild, caged beast. She had to wonder: How much can you stand around, staring at a rock?

True, it was—at least in American folklore—the place where the first settlers had stepped onto the new continent . . . that is, if you didn't count the Spanish settlers who had occupied much of Mexico and Texas for well over a hundred years before the Pilgrims arrived.

But enough was enough.

The only real fun she'd had was being with Holly and watching the events through Evan's eyes. He was brimming over with the enthusiasm that only a ten-year-old can bring to a town's annual celebration. Holly was having a tough time keeping track of him as he darted about the crowd. The only thing that helped her keep tabs on him was the bright red helium balloon she had tied to Evan's wrist. She kept a close eye on it as it weaved above the throng.

"When do you think we'll head back to the house?" Alex asked for at least the fifth or sixth time. She was trying hard not to show too much impatience.

"Well," Holly replied. Her face was beaming with contentment as she watched Evan. "We've pretty much seen all there is to see. . . . Unless you want to drive over to the Plimouth Plantation and have a tour."

"I don't think so. Maybe some other time," Alex replied, unable to stop her chattering teeth from dicing the words as she spoke them. She rubbed her gloved hands vigorously together. "Like maybe in June."

Neither one of them noticed the dark van with tinted windows as it pulled up to the curb and stopped not far from the Plymouth Rock Memorial. Tourists and townsfolk alike filled the area, and Holly was busy enough trying to keep tabs on her son.

Alex thought about giving Derek a call back at Legacy House, just to check in. She knew she was searching for any excuse so she could sit in the car and get out of the wind. She'd earned this vacation, but she still felt slightly uncomfortable about leaving the other members of the Legacy back in San Francisco.

What if something important—or dangerous—came up?

"You're really sure you made the right decision, aren't you?" Alex said as she studied the expression on her friend's face. "About leaving Roots and Branches, I mean."

"Well, I haven't really left the organization," Holly said

3

with an almost wistful look on her face. "It's just that . . . now that I've got it started and all—"

"Started?" Alex cut in. "You've got it more than started. You've done more for children of the Third World than anyone else I can think of. And almost single-handedly."

"My father did most of it," Holly said, and for just a moment, she cast her eyes downward. The tears Alex saw begin to fill her friend's eyes were not from the cold or the wind. "It's the money he left me that's done most of the work."

"Not exactly," Alex said, placing her hand affectionately on her friend's shoulder. "Because I can't imagine anyone else who would have done what you did with it."

"Yeah, well," Holly continued with a shrug, "I've got a lot of good people working for me, and now that the organization's up and running, I just thought it was time to back away a little."

"And make more time for you and Evan."

"Exactly." Holly suddenly frowned. "Speaking of whom—"

Her expression gradually shifted to one of gathering concern as she scanned the crowd, looking for Evan's balloon.

"Over there," Alex said, pointing to the big red balloon that was bobbing a foot or two above the crowd.

Holly smiled and started toward her son. Alex figured she'd take this opportunity to call Derek. She opened the passenger side door of the car and was just sitting down, the cell phone already open in her hand, when a terrible explosion ripped through the air.

The concussion hit Alex like a hammer. She didn't even hear her own terrified scream as the blast pressed her back in the car seat and rocked the car. The windshield bulged inward and then shattered into thousands of tiny shards that splattered Alex like shotgun pellets.

Alex reflexively covered her face with her arm. The only

thing she was aware of—at least right away—was the sudden pressure that filled her head.

Although it was only a second or two later, it seemed to take Alex forever to sit up and look around.

No more than a hundred feet away from where she sat, a thick, gray cloud of smoke rose from the wreck of what had been, moments before, someone's vehicle. The wind whisked the heavy smoke away as sharp tongues of orange flame licked through the debris.

She propelled herself out of the car and stumbled onto the sidewalk. Alex felt numb, as though she had pins and needles over her entire body. Her cell phone clattered as it fell to the ground, but she barely noticed it as she lurched to the grassy area beside the car and fell to her knees as if in prayer.

Her ears were still ringing loudly, even when she covered them with her hands. The scene took on a bizarre, surreal cast as she looked around and realized to her horror that she couldn't hear anything.

Then, when she looked in front of the car and saw Holly lying on her side, her legs splayed at an awkward angle, an even deeper terror struck her.

Blood was flowing from the abrasions on Holly's face where she had apparently scraped her head against the asphalt. Her eyes were open and staring wide, glazed with pain and fear.

"Holly! Oh, my God! Holly!" Alex cried, thinking in that instant that her friend was dead. She could only hear her voice inside her head; it still felt like everything—the entire world—was muffled with cotton.

She had the odd sensation that she was running in slow-motion, like someone pushing against the powerful surge of the tide as she got up and scrambled over to her friend.

Alex was only dimly aware of the activity going on around her. She could see that other people—many other people—had been dazed and wounded by the blast. She saw a kaleidoscope of torn and bloodied faces. It struck her as terrifyingly odd how she seemed to be totally isolated in a tiny bubble of silence. Her movements were tired and sludgy, but she finally made it over to Holly.

"Holly . . . It's all right, Holly . . . I'm right here with you," Alex said, not knowing if she was whispering or shouting as she cradled her friend's head in her lap.

Far off in the distance, she thought she could hear the wail of approaching sirens, but she couldn't be sure. The sound could just as well have been inside her head.

Her eyes were stinging as she looked down at her friend. Holly's face was as pale as bone; her gaze was still blank, unfocused. Already, her left eye was swelling up with a terrible prune-purple bruise that gave her face a distorted look. The blood running from her facial wounds was frighteningly red against the pale background of her skin. In extraordinary detail, Alex could see numerous specks of dirt and black grit embedded in the wounds.

She was convinced that Holly was dead, but then she saw her friend's lips begin to move. All Alex could hear was a distant, watery rattle. The muscles in Holly's body contracted and relaxed as powerful spasms shook her. Alex was suddenly afraid that she might be having a seizure or something.

"Help is on the way," Alex said.

She was positive that she was shouting, but her voice sounded to her like a reedy whisper.

"Don't move. Just stay still."

But Holly didn't stop twitching. Her lips were still moving spasmodically, like she was chewing something that wouldn't go down.

Shaking her head in an attempt to clear it, Alex leaned closer to Holly until their faces touched.

Then, suddenly, it was as if Holly was inside Alex's head. When she spoke, Alex could hear her so clearly it sent a lance of panic through her. She suspected that it was as much a psychic connection as actual communication, but

Alex heard Holly's voice as clearly as if it were her own thoughts.

"Evan!"

The voice had a razor-sharp edge of panic.

"Where's Evan? Where's my son? Tell me! Is he . . . all right?"

"Alex is in serious danger."

The words were barely a whisper, and they came out of Derek Rayne's mouth before he even realized that he was saying them out loud.

Nick Boyle was seated at the wide oak table across from Derek. He looked up from the ancient manuscript he'd been studying and stared back at Derek as though he might have imagined hearing his friend and colleague speak. He started to say something, but then fell silent.

For the briefest instant, the stab of cold in his gut made him shiver as he gazed out the picture window that framed Derek. A thick blanket of fog obscured his view of San Francisco Bay.

"How do you know that?" Nick asked tentatively. "Did she call last night?"

Derek cocked one eyebrow and shook his head as he focused on some middle distance and tried to grasp—and hold onto—the fragmented rushes of psychic contact he had just experienced.

The contact was tenuous. The images were vague and fleeting, like grainy black and white film. Derek squeezed his eyes tightly shut and concentrated.

In a rush, the images started coming so rapidly that Derek barely had time to register one before it was replaced by several others. They flashed inside his mind with strobe-light intensity, and all of the images had to do with death . . . and pain . . . panic . . . and destruction. Never in his life had he experienced such intense, detailed psychic contact.

In his mind, Derek saw a thick column of smoke—black and heavy with soot. As it rose into the sky, it was underlit

7

by wild, flickering flames. In bright silver and gray flashes, he saw dozens of faces, none of which he recognized.

But all of them were distorted as though these people were experiencing intense shock and pain.

He saw broken and bleeding arms and legs sticking out of tattered clothing . . . and faces covered with dark masks of blood . . . and the smoldering, twisted ruin of what must have once been a car or van . . . and the blank, dazed look of glassy, dead eyes, staring sightlessly up as the heavy smoke was whisked away by the wind . . . and a single, red balloon—the only color in the images Derek saw—floating above the cold, gray ocean which was flecked with white foam and charred bits of debris.

And then, in the midst of it all, he saw Alex.

Only for an instant, but the acid-sharp image filled him with fear and left him trembling.

She was kneeling down on the grass, her face contorted with pain and worry as she reached out and held . . .

A woman.

Derek let out a soft groan the instant the woman's face came into view.

He recognized Holly Brown, the friend Alex had gone back East to visit, from photos Alex had shown him before she left. Holly had short, dark hair. High cheekbones. Full lips. And dark eyes that were open wide and staring up in pain and fear.

Derek could see that Holly's lips were moving, but he couldn't hear what she was trying to say. Her voice was lost beneath a low, hollow roaring sound that filled his mind like a peal of thunder that wouldn't stop.

There was something else about the woman's face that held Derek's attention even after the image shifted and began to fade.

He could see Alex's thin, dark hands, moving in slow motion as she caressed the woman's brow. He could hear the faint echoes of Alex's voice as she spoke softly to her friend.

8

". . . Holly . . . It's all right, Holly . . . I'm right here with you . . ."

Focusing his attention on Alex made the psychic connection stronger. The vision suddenly resolved with such startling intensity that Derek propelled himself away from the table and stood up, panting. He made a low, moaning sound and covered his face with both hands to stifle the scream that was building up inside him.

In a flash, Nick was out of his chair and standing beside Derek, ready to support him if he needed help.

"Derek? Are you all right?" Nick asked, concern edging his voice.

But Derek couldn't respond.

He couldn't stop staring into the darkness of his cupped hands as the psychic images sizzled with a white-hot, acid intensity in his mind.

He had seen something . . . something written in searing white light on Holly's forehead.

It looked like a letter from a foreign alphabet . . . or possibly a number.

Derek wasn't sure what it was, but for just an instant, he had seen it. And he found the light of the marking—or the memory of it—somehow reassuring. He was aware that Alex's friend was in intense pain, but as hurt as she was, he also knew that she would survive.

But that didn't dispel the surge of panic she was feeling and transmitting to Derek through Alex as she called out.

This time, above the roaring sound inside his head, Derek clearly heard Holly's voice and what she said.

"Evan!" she shouted.

Her voice echoed in Derek's mind with an odd intensity that grew stronger before gradually fading away.

"Where's Evan? Where's my son? Tell me! Is he . . . all right?"

TWO

Alex's ears were still ringing from the concussion of the blast as she moved through the crowd, searching for Evan. She was petrified by the idea of leaving Holly alone and hurt, but she was also desperate to find out if her friend's son was alive or not. She had never experienced anything like this before, and it took her a while to figure out what must have happened.

Someone had detonated a bomb!

Someone had actually tried to blow up Plymouth Rock!

A cold, numbing dread filled her when she realized that she had last seen Evan's red balloon bobbing above the crowd much closer to the site of the blast.

Maybe too close.

She tried hard to deny it, but she was positive that unless Evan was very lucky and had been shielded, somehow, from the explosion, there was no way he could have survived it. She fought her way over to where she had last seen him, but someone snagged her roughly by the arm and held her back. She turned and looked at the person, vaguely recognizing that he was a uniformed policeman.

"I'm sorry, ma'am," the cop said.

Alex's hearing was still deadened, and she read his expression as much as heard what he said.

"You can't go any closer."

For several seconds, Alex stared at the cop, struggling hard to remember even how to speak.

"I . . . My friend's son is . . . He was over here," she finally stammered. Her voice seemed muffled, and it sounded funny, vibrating with a wasp-like buzz inside her head. "She—my friend's hurt, and she . . . she has to know if he's . . . if he's all right."

The cop regarded her sympathetically for a moment, but his grip on her arm tightened, and he turned her around, directing her back the way she had come. Alex fought against the rush of panic that welled up inside her.

"He was wearing a . . . a blue jacket . . . and a baseball cap," she said as tears filled her eyes. "A Red Sox cap . . . I-I have to know if he—"

The policeman caught her gaze and held it for what seemed like an impossibly long time. Then his expression hardened, his mouth a thin, grim line, and he solemnly shook his head.

"I'm sorry," he said, so softly Alex could barely hear him above the shrill ringing sound inside her head.

But she didn't need to hear him to know the terrible truth.

Evan hadn't survived.

Her body felt limp and drained of all energy as she started back to where she had left Holly. She was distantly aware of the flashing lights of approaching emergency vehicles and the warbling wail of their sirens. Within ten minutes, several ambulances and police cars from Plymouth as well as neighboring towns and the nearby State Police barracks filled the parking lot in front of Plymouth Rock Monument and cordoned off the blast area.

As she sat down beside Holly, Alex was distantly aware

that she must be in shock. She felt dazed, almost unconscious, and was unable to process anything that she was
seeing as she looked around at the carnage.

Dozens of people—Alex had no way of estimating how
many—were sprawled awkwardly on the grass and pavement as others, less seriously wounded or merely in shock,
knelt beside them, checking for injuries and vital signs.
Several people, looking bewildered and disoriented, wandered about, too stunned to respond to the chaos around
them. Many had splashes of blood on their faces and hands.
Some were calling out for assistance, while others were too
numb with shock to do anything more than moan or whimper.

Images of the bombing in Oklahoma City filled her with
nausea and dread. She knew it was a miracle that she and
Holly hadn't been killed outright by the blast. They certainly had been close enough to it.

Less than a hundred feet away.

Alex could see her own terror and confusion reflected
in Holly's frantic eyes. She was bleeding from the abrasions
on the side of her head, where she had smacked against the
pavement. Blood was running freely, soaking into the collar
of her heavy winter jacket.

Alex tried to convince herself that it wasn't as bad as it
looked. Head wounds bled more profusely because of the
numerous blood vessels in the scalp. Holly wasn't going to
die.

Alex's ears were still ringing with a shrill pitch, and
she experienced an oddly disassociated sensation as she
looked down at her friend as though from a great height.
All around her, people were shouting and running around
in eerie slow motion. Men, women, and children were crying . . . and bleeding.

Alex couldn't tell how many people were down.

Some—like Holly—were still moving, if barely. Some
were slumped against trees and leaning against parked cars,
too stunned to move or do anything. And others lay on the

ground with the frightening, solid inertia of the dead. Everywhere she looked, she saw bright red splashes of blood.

For a panicky instant, Alex wondered if she might already be dead.

Perhaps she was experiencing all of this with such a sense of detachment because she was a ghost who would soon fade and drift away like the thinning column of smoke that rose from the destroyed vehicle by the curbside.

"Where's Evan . . . ?" Holly asked.

Her voice was feeble. It sounded lost in the distance as she thrashed about on the ground. Her grip tightened painfully on Alex's arm as she tried to get up, but she seemed unable to control the muscles in her body, and sagged back down.

Alex went cold inside. How could she tell her friend what she suspected? How could she tell Holly that her son was dead?

"I . . . I didn't see him," Alex said to Holly, vaguely aware that she had to shout just to hear herself above the ringing sound in her ears.

Then she turned and looked out toward the ocean.

Her heart gave a single, cold thump when she saw a red balloon, weaving from side to side as it was swept out over the steel-gray water. A single spot of brilliant color against a backdrop of stark black and gray.

Evan's balloon.

Alex looked down at Holly again. She was rolling her head from side to side. Her lower lip, as pale as exposed bone, was trembling as though she were in the grip of a fever.

It took every bit of Alex's resilience to stifle the scream that surged up inside her, threatening to break out.

"I-I'm sure he's all right," she said, knowing that it was a lie as her gaze was drawn once again out over the ocean.

The red balloon was nothing more than a tiny scarlet dot—like a single drop of blood between the gray sky and

13

the darker ocean. Slowly, it drifted away, further and further until it was . . .

Gone.

In her heart, Alex knew that Evan was gone, too.

Alex choked back her tears, fighting hard for control. Holly gripped her tightly and, using her for support, struggled once again to rise. Alex gently broke Holly's grip on her arm and clasped both of her hands in hers.

"Don't move," she said, unable to moderate the volume of her voice. "You have to relax. Help is on the way."

A moment later, a paramedic came up to them—a young man who looked like he was barely out of college. He knelt down beside Holly and opened his first aid box.

"Is she coherent?" he asked, glancing at Alex.

Not positive that she had heard him correctly, Alex shook her head and watched numbly as the young man inspected the wounds on Holly's face and head.

The paramedic took a quick reading of Holly's vitals.

"She's hurt pretty bad," he said grimly. "We'll have to get her to the hospital right away."

Alex nodded and, in a low, rasping whisper, said, "Yeah . . . Her son."

"Beg your pardon?"

The paramedic barely glanced at her as he took a sterile gauze pad from the kit and opened it to apply to the most serious wound on Holly's head.

"She's worried . . . about her son," Alex said, hearing the ragged rasp of her voice inside her head.

"No! *NO!*" Holly suddenly screamed.

Spittle flew from her mouth, and her eyes widened with fright. She suddenly lurched up and grabbed the paramedic by both shoulders. Her face was white, and her dark eyes bulged from their sockets.

"You're not going to take my son away from me! You're not! *You're not!*"

She shook the paramedic viciously from side to side, then pushed him away from her. The sudden fury of the attack had caught the medic off guard. He fell backward and hit the ground with his butt, hard. Holly tried to stand up but her fury had vanished as quickly as it had come.

As the paramedic scrambled to his feet, Holly's body suddenly went rigid. She sank slowly back onto the ground, letting out a tortured groan as her eyes rolled so far back in her head all Alex could see were the whites, veined with tiny red capillaries.

When Holly spoke again, her voice was as faint as the sound a guttering candle makes just before it burns out.

"Find him, Alex. . . ." she said in a bubbly gasp. Blood flecked the foam on her lips, turning it pink. "Find Evan and . . . take care of him . . . Take care of my baby for me."

She shuddered as she inhaled sharply, held her breath a moment, then let it out in a long, hitching gasp as her body twitched and finally relaxed. Her eyes closed slowly and her head slumped to one side.

Alex was afraid that her friend had just died, but even through her panic, she noticed that Holly was still breathing. Her chest rose and fell gently, and Alex could see the rapid pulse in her neck.

The paramedic, still shaken after Holly's sudden attack, leaned over her and felt the pulse in her neck.

"She's a lot stronger than she looks," he said, as much to himself as to Alex.

Glancing at her wristwatch, Alex stood up shakily.

It was a little past twelve-thirty.

Her best guess was that the explosion had occurred a little before noon.

It was hard to believe it had been less than forty-five minutes ago. With the shock and disorientation, it was easy to lose track of the time. The world had a surreal cast as she looked around.

The carnage was beyond imagining.

Emergency workers and numerous other volunteers and survivors were now tending to the wounded and the dead. The cold November air was filled with the sounds of in-

15

jured people moaning and crying out in pain. More sirens wailed as they approached. There was a loud hissing sound as firefighters extinguished the flames that licked underneath what was left of the van. The stinging smells of hot steam, burning rubber, and singed flesh mingled with the salty tang of the ocean air.

Alex felt absolutely useless as she watched the paramedics load Holly onto a stretcher, then carry her over to one of the waiting ambulances. She was surprised by how small and fragile her friend looked beneath the thin sheet that covered her.

Still dazed with shock, Alex just stood there, watching. She had no idea what to do next. She considered following the ambulance to the hospital in her own car, but then realized that the front windshield had been blown out.

Once Holly was secure in the ambulance, the paramedic approached Alex and said, "You might want to come with us and have those cuts on your face and hands tended to."

Looking at her wrists and the backs of her hands, Alex was surprised to see several small lacerations that left thin tracks of blood on her skin.

Until that moment, she hadn't even noticed them.

Now that she knew they were there, she became conscious of their sharp sting. The pain made her feel good, though. She took it as a clear sign that she was finally snapping out of it.

"Ahh, no . . . no," she said, still unable to modulate her voice so she could hear herself above the high ringing in her ears. "I—I'll be all right."

When she shook her head, the motion sent a sharp jab of pain up the back of her neck. Maybe she was hurt worse than she realized, she thought, but she sucked in her breath and held it for a moment.

"No, I . . . I have to see if I can find—"

She almost couldn't say his name, but then swallowed hard and finished, "Evan."

Just saying his name made her heart feel cold and motionless in her chest.

She was positive that when—and if—she found him, he would be dead.

There was no doubt in her mind.

The memory of seeing his big red balloon sailing out over the stone gray water became her image for his soul, released from his body and winging its way to heaven.

Alex felt suddenly weak. Sparkling little points of light swept across her vision. Sobbing deeply, she leaned back against the side of her car and closed her eyes, but the lights were still there.

The sounds of misery all around her were muffled, but even when she blocked her ears, she knew she wouldn't be able to drown them out entirely . . . not for a long time.

If ever.

Finally, she braced herself, took a deep breath, and opened her eyes. The first several steps she took were shaky, but as she walked, she was filled with a single, burning purpose.

She had to find Evan.

If Holly was seriously hurt and ended up dying, that would be the last thing her friend ever said to her.

"Take care of my baby for me. . . ."

It was one-fifteen in the afternoon, Pacific time, when the phone rang at Legacy House. Derek was slumped on the couch in the study, still feeling physically and emotionally drained following the intense psychic flash he'd received from Alex earlier in the day. Ever since then, he, Nick, and Rachel had been watching the CNN coverage on the Plymouth Rock bombing in Massachusetts.

It was all too clear what had happened.

Nick snatched up the receiver immediately after the first ring, knowing even before he spoke that it had to be Alex. She was the only person not presently in Legacy House who had access to the private number.

17

"Alex. You're all right."

That was all Nick said. No greeting.

"Nick . . . Oh, Nick . . ."

But that was all Alex could get out before she broke down, sobbing.

Nick glanced over at Derek and Rachel, indicating that he wanted each of them to pick up an extension. Derek set aside the pad of paper that was resting on his lap. Nick noticed the strange design Derek had drawn several times on the paper, but he knew now wasn't the time to ask him what it was.

"Alex," Derek said softly, his accent sounding thicker than usual and slightly slurred. "Thank God you weren't injured. Tell us everything."

Nick listened as Alex struggled to regain her composure. Being a person of action, his first and strongest impulse was to leave immediately for the East Coast. He knew that what Alex needed right now more than anything else was a friend to be with her.

"My friend Holly was . . . was injured," Alex said in a voice that almost broke on every word. "She's pretty bad, I think. She's been taken to Mass. General in a coma, but . . . but worse than that—"

Again, her voice choked off.

Nick glanced at Derek and saw his own rising alarm reflected in his and Rachel's expressions. Even as drained as he was, Derek's concern for Alex was evident.

"The reports we're getting out here are still sketchy," Derek said. "Can you fill us in?"

"It apparently was a terrorist bomb. . . . There's talk that it was set off by a right-wing militia," Alex said.

For a moment, she seemed to be in control, but then her voice cracked again, and she added, so softly Nick could hardly heard her, "But he's dead. . . ." Her voice cracked. "Evan . . . my friend Holly's little boy . . . was . . . was too close to the blast. He . . . he didn't . . ."

"He had a red balloon, didn't he?" Derek said.

18

Nick glanced at him with surprise.

What the hell was he talking about?

"How did you know?" Alex gasped.

"I saw it," Derek replied in a low, dragging voice.

To Nick, he sounded utterly exhausted, but apparently Alex was too upset to notice.

"I knew what had happened was intense because I experienced an incredibly powerful psychic connection with you. The only color I saw in all of it was a bright red balloon drifting out—"

"—over the ocean," Alex finished for him.

Listening to all of this, Nick shivered, aware that there was still a remarkably strong connection between Alex and Derek.

"I saw it. . . . It was like his . . . his soul, drifting away . . . off to heaven," Alex said.

"I saw something else as well," Derek said.

Nick glanced at him questioningly.

"My mind was filled with images of suffering and pain, but there was something else. . . . Something about your friend Holly."

"The doctors told me they aren't sure how extensive her injuries are," Alex said. "I came back to her house. . . . I had to take the Thanksgiving turkey out of the oven before it burned to a crisp. We were going to . . . If we had only left when I first mentioned it. She wouldn't have been hurt, and Evan . . . Evan wouldn't be—"

She was unable to finish the sentence.

"You can't start thinking like that," Nick said. "What's happened has happened. That's all there is to it. Now we have to deal with it."

"Things happen for a reason," Derek added. His eyebrows shadowed his eyes as he looked over at Nick. "The fact that I received such strong psychic impressions tells me that there was more to this—that there could possibly be a dark force behind it."

"Alex," Rachel said, interrupting for the first time. "If

your friend has lost her child, it might be a good idea if I came East to be with her. After losing my son and husband, I might be able to help her.''

''Not now. Not yet,'' Alex said, swallowing hard.

For the first time, Nick detected the weariness in Alex's voice. He realized that she must still be pretty shaken by what had happened.

''I'll catch the next flight and be there tonight, Alex,'' Nick snapped. He caught the surprise in Derek's expression, but he had already decided.

Nothing was going to stop him.

''You don't have to—'' Alex started to say, but then she fell silent. After taking a deep, shuddering breath, she finished, ''I'd really appreciate that, Nick.''

''I think it's a good idea,'' Derek said. ''Rachel and I can come out in a day or two. But as for your friend, I want you to stay with her as much as possible. I'm not sure why or how I know this, but I think she's still very much in danger.''

''You said you saw or sensed something about her,'' Alex said. ''What was it?''

''I saw her face quite clearly at the same time that I saw the red balloon,'' Derek said. ''I recognized her instantly from the photographs you showed us of her. But there was something on her forehead. A mark of some kind.''

''A mark?'' Alex said, and Nick could hear the confusion and hesitation in her voice. ''She was bleeding pretty badly, but . . . no, there wasn't any kind of mark on her forehead that I remember.''

''This was something else,'' Derek said emphatically. ''Not a birthmark or an injury. It looked like something in Hebrew, either a letter or number, written in light on her forehead.''

''What—?''

''I have no idea what it means,'' Derek said, ''but I certainly intend to find out. In the meantime, I'll feel a lot better just knowing that you're with Holly, and that Nick's on his way to be with you.''

THREE

S omeone was crying.

Holly could hear a faint sobbing sound that echoed in the impenetrable darkness surrounding her.

She turned around to try to see where the sound was coming from, but everywhere she looked, all she could see was a wall of blackness so dense it seemed to vibrate and flicker. It hurt her chest, just trying to breathe.

She tried to speak. She wanted to call out, but her voice was caught like a fishhook in her throat. Her heart fluttered with an irregular beat as she moved forward into the darkness with her hands stretched out in front of her . . . grasping . . . feeling . . .

For what? she wondered.

Who's out there?

Where am I?

The crying sound seemed to Doppler oddly as she inched her way forward. It shifted around her, dancing and weaving like a teasing will-o'-the-wisp.

At the core of her being, Holly recognized the sound,

but in the sudden confusion of finding herself here—wherever *here* was—she wanted desperately to deny it.

No . . . It can't be Evan, she thought, wishing she had the courage to speak out loud, to call out to her son, if only to reassure him, to let him know that he wasn't alone.

Holly kept moving forward, cautiously sliding one foot in front of the other, all the while reaching out blindly with both hands. Her fingers slashed at the darkness, as if it were a curtain she could rip apart.

Her progress was excruciatingly slow, but she kept her rising panic in check. All she could focus on was the faint, wailing sound of someone crying.

Crying that sounded so familiar!

Please . . . please let it not be Evan!

Nearly consumed by fear, she worried that she might bump into something in the darkness, or maybe walk off the edge of a cliff or something. Her feet made dull scraping sounds as she slid them across the floor . . . or ground . . . or whatever it was. She considered kneeling down and feeling the floor to try to determine if she was inside a building or outside, but a sudden rush of fear stopped her.

She didn't want to know where she was.

All she wanted to do was find out if that really was Evan crying . . . and help him if she could.

Evan? Honey? Is that you?

She thought the words, and wanted desperately to say them out loud, but the deep, icy dread that gripped her throat made it impossible for her to breathe, much less speak.

Inching steadily forward into the well of darkness, Holly strained to get a direction on the sound, but it was maddeningly elusive. First it seemed to be coming from in front of her . . . then behind her . . . then to her left . . . and right . . . and from two directions at once.

A soft whimper escaped her when she considered that the sound might be coming from *inside* her!

No! No! There's someone out there . . . in the darkness . . . I know there is.

She hoped that she could find the courage to keep moving, to find out who it was and then do whatever she could to help.

Because that was what she was all about, Holly told herself.

She wanted to help people . . . especially children.

That's why, so many years ago, she had founded the organization Roots and Branches.

Holly's parents had died in a car crash when she was only four years old, and she'd been raised by her aunt Stephanie. Having been robbed of her own childhood, she grew up with a powerful drive to do anything and everything she could to help children—especially Third World children—who, due to social and economic and political conditions, had their own childhoods taken away from them.

Just like her.

While still in college, she had volunteered for a variety of charity work. Upon turning twenty-one, she had used the trust fund her parents had left for her to establish Roots and Branches.

And even now, as frightened as she was, just the sound of a solitary, unknown child sobbing in the darkness was enough to galvanize her. In a way, that single lonely voice represented her life's work of finding anyone who was lost, and doing what she could to help.

But how could she help anyone now if she herself was lost?

The darkness closed around her like a thick wash of India ink, embracing her, pulling her into itself. Holly was so unnerved she found it difficult even to remember who she was. She couldn't begin to imagine how she had gotten there.

Her body was rigid with tension.

She kept taking tiny sips of the damp air as she shifted

first left, then right, then turned around completely, all the while trying to get a fix on the source of the sound.

But with nothing to see, no landmarks to mark her progress, she had no idea which way to go. For all she knew, she could be moving around in circles. The sound flitted about her eerily in the dark.

"Evan?"

The sudden sound of her own voice startled her.

She listened as the single word reverberated in the darkness and then faded away.

For the briefest instant, the crying sound stopped. Then it began again, deeper, more urgent, so lonely it broke her heart.

"Evan? Is that you?"

Her voice sounded oddly muffled to her, as if thin fingers had grasped her throat and were slowly tightening, constricting the flow of air. A numbing surge of panic filled her when she imagined that she might be dead, that she might be lying in the cold silence of her coffin.

"I'm here. . . . I can help you," she called out softly.

The darkness seemed to thicken, resisting her efforts to push through it, but Holly continued to forge ahead, trying to locate whomever was crying.

She let out a strangled whimper and twisted quickly to one side when she felt . . . something . . . brush against her bare arm.

The touch, as light as it was, sent a painful jolt through her. For an instant, the mournful crying sound seemed to intensify with a rising edge of panic. Holly recognized that it mirrored her own rising alarm.

Her heart was pounding so hard she thought it might burst through her chest as she waited in the darkness for several seconds.

Then, ever so slowly, she started inching forward again.

She had taken no more than two or three steps when, again, something unseen in the darkness touched the back of her wrist. She screamed and pulled away with enough force to almost knock her over as something with a cold, damp grip clamped down on her other arm, just above the elbow.

This time, when she tried to pull away, it didn't let go.

She shrieked and thrashed wildly about, trying to free herself, but the grip was iron-tight . . . unrelenting. It clung to her, constricting the flow of blood to her hand and forearm and making them tingle.

Holly's mind was filled with terrifying images of spiderwebs as thick as ropes dangling in her face . . . and bony hands with rotting flesh reaching out, clawing at her and holding her.

Then, with surprising strength, whatever was holding her jerked her forward, lifting her clear off her feet and pitching her forward, screaming, into the darkness.

For a frightening instant, she felt herself falling . . . floating as though suspended in an endless void of black, but her fall abruptly ended when she landed on top of a soft, yielding mass that wiggled beneath her.

She imagined that she had landed in a nest of writhing snakes. Their cool, dry skin glided across her body, encircling and embracing her as they engulfed her. Her nostrils filled with the sickening stench of rotting flesh and burned hair.

Holly tried to scream, but she was suffocating and couldn't take a breath deep enough to make anything more than a tight, strangled whimper.

She was lost, sinking down . . . down into the seething, fleshy mass that gripped her arms and legs and neck and stomach, and held her there.

And then, above her raging panic, she heard it again—
The soft, faint sound of someone crying.

She had no doubt now that it was Evan, that he was lost here in the darkness, too. Fear spiked inside her when she realized that he must be even more terrified that she was.

"Evan . . ."

But the single word—her son's name—was lost in the all-encompassing darkness.

She was sinking down . . . further into the slippery, slithering mass, and knew that she was lost until faintly, just at the edge of hearing, a faint voice called out.

That voice said a single word that filled her with a violent urge to survive.

For just a moment, she ceased struggling and listened until the sound came again.

As soft as the flutter of moth's wings in the dark, she heard the voice whisper.

"Mommy . . ."

Bright incandescent lights from suspended lamps cast deep, harsh shadows across the faces of the eleven men—all members of the First Step Militia—who sat at the long table in the center of the small, pine-paneled room.

The four windows—two on the north wall of the room and two on the east—were barred and covered with inch-thick plywood that had been screwed into the window frames. The windowless door was locked with a dead bolt and an iron bar.

One man, a heavyset former professional boxer named Scott Thurston, stood by the door with an AK-47 cradled like a baby in his arms.

On the west wall of the room was a large, locked cabinet that contained a vast assortment of assault rifles and semi-automatic pistols. These weapons represented only a small portion of the illegal armaments kept within the First Step's compound. In the large, secure storage barn on the grounds, there was more than enough weaponry to arm a full company of soldiers.

And that's exactly what Adam Hunter, the leader of the First Step, considered himself and his men.

Soldiers.

Revolutionaries in a war against the United States government.

Hunter sat at the head of a wide table, flanked on either side by his two trusted assistants: Billy Morgan and Jake Williams. The meeting hadn't begun yet, but the room was filled with excited chatter as the men discussed what had happened that morning at Plymouth Rock Monument.

Hunter smiled with satisfaction, letting the conversation wash over him as he stared at the paneled walls. He could easily imagine that he could see distorted faces in the swirling wood grain patterns. Snickering softly to himself, he thought how much those imaginary faces seemed to have the terrified expressions of tortured souls, screaming in Hell.

Just like the expressions on the faces of the people he and his militia members had blown to pieces this morning.

Hunter felt a tremendous rush of satisfaction that—finally—they had taken their first step in their war against the government. He let the conversation continue a moment longer, then nodded slightly to Morgan.

"All right. All right," Morgan shouted, clapping his hands together.

The room was instantly silent.

"It's late," Hunter said, once he had the men's attention. "I know you're all exhausted, so let's get the meeting under way. First on our agenda is—"

"Hold on a second, Adam. We have to talk about what happened today."

Turning his head slowly, like a snake eying its prey, Hunter looked over at Frank McCullough, who was seated at the far end of the table. He held the man with a cruel, steady stare.

"You seem to be forgetting yourself, soldier," Hunter said, his voice low but firm. "First of all, you'll address me as befits your commanding officer."

"Fuck you . . . *Sir!*" McCullough snapped as he rose to his feet.

An excited murmur traveled around the room. All eyes turned and fastened on McCullough.

Hunter's face suddenly flushed with anger. His neck felt like his shirt collar was on fire. Forcing himself not to tremble, he clenched his fists in his lap and told himself that he wasn't about to let his men see even a moment of weakness or hesitation.

He couldn't lose control.

He had to show all of them that he was in absolute charge, and he wasn't about to let anyone challenge his authority. Especially not a sack-less dip-shit like McCullough.

"You have a problem, soldier?" Hunter asked.

He stared at McCullough steadily, without blinking, knowing that this would unnerve the man. It was something Hunter had practiced. Just one of hundreds of subtle ways he used to impose his will on weaker minds.

"Yes, *sir,* I do," McCullough said, putting a sarcastic emphasis on the word "sir."

Hunter was secretly pleased that he detected a slight quaver in the man's voice, but he didn't let it show. Now that the real war had started, they all had to be strong and united in their determination. It was incidents like this that would weed out the weak and cowardly—the kind of men Hunter didn't want in his militia in the first place.

"What we did today was . . . ill-considered," McCullough said.

Hunter noticed how McCullough scanned the men around the table as he spoke, looking for support.

It was futile.

These men were Hunter's to command. They believed as he told them to believe, and they did whatever he told them to do.

"We are at war, soldier," Hunter said, making eye contact with each man as he scanned the table. "The sooner you accept that, the better off we'll all be."

"If it means killing soldiers, yes. I agree. I'll support you on that," McCullough said tightly.

Hunter could hear how much of an effort it was for McCullough not to shout.

"But when it comes to killing innocent men, women, and children—*children*, for God's sake! Then I'm sorry. I'm not with you. I can't support an operation like that."

"We already had this discussion before the action was carried out," Hunter said icily.

"I objected to it then, and I object to it now," McCullough said. "This isn't going to win anything for any of us except jail sentences . . . or the death penalty."

Hunter noticed that two or three of the other men at the table nodded slightly at McCullough's comment. He made a mental note of the men's names, vowing to keep an eye on them as well. Dissension in the ranks was the only thing that was going to stop them. Perhaps they would see reason after he did what he knew he was going to have to do to McCullough.

But it was to be expected.

Now that they had taken action, Hunter suspected that there would be a few who would prove to be cowards under the skin—men who would chicken out at the thought of doing what, as soldiers, they had to do. It was a huge leap from talk to action, but Hunter was secretly glad this was happening tonight.

There's no time like the present to weed out those soldiers he wouldn't be able to count on in battle, though.

"We're not here to discuss the relative merits of what we've done," Hunter said, still speaking in a low, steady voice that he knew most of the men would find unnerving. "We're here to discuss our next battle action. What we did today was only the beginning. What's important is what we plan here, tonight. That's what's crucial in our battle against the illegal entity known as the United States government."

"You know what?" McCullough said, leaning over the table on clenched fists and glaring at Hunter. "I think you're full of shit. You're a pathetic, ignorant fool if you think we can effect any changes by—''

"Stand down, soldier!" Hunter suddenly barked.

He leaped to his feet and slammed both hands, palms open, onto the table so hard it sounded like a gunshot going off.

For a few tense seconds, Hunter and McCullough eyed each other, neither one backing down. Hunter knew how strong McCullough's will could be, and he knew he had to do something fast. Men like McCullough could challenge his authority, and he wasn't about to tolerate that.

Snapping his fingers underneath Billy Morgan's nose, Hunter said in a calm, measured voice, "Arrest him."

The only sound in the room was a loud *click* as Scott Thurston chambered a bullet and raised his rifle. He took a steady aim at McCullough's back as Morgan stepped forward and grabbed McCullough by the arm.

Hunter could see that, for just an instant, McCullough considered resisting. He started to twist away, but then turned and saw that Thurston's gun was aimed at him. His shoulders sagged forward, and there was a desperate look in the man's eyes that pleased Hunter. He almost laughed out loud to see McCullough wince when Morgan slipped a pair of handcuffs over his wrists.

"Take him to the stockade and let him think about what he's done," Hunter said.

He smiled slyly as he looked around the room, studying the men's faces. He could see the fear and respect reflected in their eyes, and that gave him a feeling of immeasurable satisfaction.

If these men didn't fear him, they would never respect him.

And if they didn't respect him, then he would never be able to lead them and accomplish his mission.

Of course, all of them thought that his mission was simply the overthrow of the United States government.

The fools!

His goals were much bigger even than that, and all in due time they would learn what they were. Then they would have a choice to serve him . . . or die.

FOUR

The hospital room was never quiet.

The dominant sound was the constant high hissing noise of the oxygen tank that was assisting Holly with her breathing. Below that, there were the soft electronic *beeps* and *pings* of various monitors, and the faint but steady *drip-drip* of the IV.

Every time Alex took a breath, she almost gagged on the sharp, antiseptic smells that wafted about. She was seated beside Holly's bed with a copy of *National Geographic* open on her lap, but she had barely looked at it in the past several hours, and hadn't been able to comprehend what little she had read.

She couldn't stop staring at her unconscious friend. Powerful rushes of emotion ran through her whenever she let herself register the simple but terrifying fact that Holly was in a coma and didn't even know that her son was dead. . . .

One of the sharpest images in Alex's mind was watching Evan's bright red balloon drift out over the steel-gray waters of Plymouth Bay.

Gone . . . like his soul . . .

And Alex couldn't get rid of the gnawing fear that Holly, too, was going to die from her injuries. The doctors had assured her that Holly's condition had stabilized, but she was still deep in a coma.

She looked so tiny . . . so fragile, Alex thought.

Her bandaged face looked whiter than the pillowcase on which her head rested. Thin strips of tape secured the IV needle in the crook of her elbow. The veins in her arm showed like faint blue tracing beneath her translucent skin.

The fear that Holly was slipping away from her wouldn't leave Alex, even for an instant. She was tormented by the thought that her friend, who was doing so much good work in the world, would soon be taken away from her. She found little comfort in the thought that if Holly did die, at least then she would be reunited with her son.

Leaning forward, Alex took Holly's hand and clasped it tightly with both of hers. It felt light, hollow. Alex remembered once when she was a little girl, and she had picked up a dead bird she'd found on the street. Tears streamed down her face as she leaned forward and whispered softly to her friend.

"Please, Holly . . . Please don't leave us . . . . Come back."

Alex's gaze was repeatedly drawn to the array of equipment beside Holly's bed. Spiked green lines on small monitors recorded Holly's vitals.

The signs remained steady, but in moments of rising emotion and panic, Alex would think that they were decreasing, that Holly was dying right there in front of her.

And even if Holly's vitals were strong and steady, Alex couldn't help but wonder how her friend was going to handle the terrible news about Evan.

How could she—or anyone—accept the loss of a child?

How could you go on?

Alex had always admired and respected Rachel Corrigan for the strength she'd shown over the years following the

33

deaths of her son, Conner, and husband, Patrick. But the immediacy of what had happened today gave her a deeper understanding. More than ever, she could imagine how this was a wound that would never truly heal or be forgotten.

How could it?

Alex's vision was blurred by her tears, so at first she thought she must be imagining it when Holly's eyelids fluttered.

It was just the faintest bit of movement. A subtle twitch.

"Holly?" Alex whispered, her throat dry and raw.

It was too much to hope for.

She tightened her grip on Holly's arm and shook it ever so gently, as if Holly were made of porcelain. Staring at her friend's face, she wanted desperately to see a sign—any sign of motion . . . of life!

"Can you hear me, Holly? It's me, Alex. I'm right here beside you."

Alex resisted the impulse to shake Holly's arm harder. She didn't want the shock of regaining consciousness to be too abrupt. It could possibly do more harm than good.

Leaning close to Holly's ear, Alex whispered as softly as she could, "I'm right here with you, Holly."

Once again, Holly's eyelids fluttered.

Alex could see her eyeballs rolling around behind the closed lids.

And then—miraculously—Holly made a sound.

It was low and indistinguishable, but it was a sound!

"Yes, yes," Alex whispered, fighting to contain her rising excitement. "I'm right here with you. You're going to be all right, Holly. . . . All right."

Even as she said it, though, Alex knew that it was a lie.

How would Holly ever be "all right," now that her only child was dead?

Without looking away, Alex grabbed the pager and pressed the button to summon a nurse.

Still moaning softly, Holly began to roll her head from side to side. It was only the slightest of movements, but her pillow made a loud crinkling sound. Excitement and a great feeling of weakness rushed through Alex. Her vision was still blurred. She could feel her tears—tears of joy, now—carving warm tracks down her face. She was barely aware of it when a nurse came rushing into the room.

"What's happening?" the nurse asked.

Alex was too excited to speak. She thought the mere fact that Holly was moving her head from side to side was evidence enough.

The low, moaning sound Holly was making continued, and after a moment, her mouth started to move.

"Look," Alex said, dizzy with relief as she stared at her friend's mouth. "She's trying to say something."

Holly didn't have much control of her facial muscles, but it seemed as though she was trying to form words. Alex leaned even closer, feeling the feathery touch of Holly's breath on her face.

For several tense seconds, the sound Holly was making was unintelligible, but then—ever so faintly—Alex heard a single word. . . .

A name.

"Evan . . ."

The word sent a lance of ice through Alex.

She sniffed loudly and wiped both eyes with the backs of her hand.

". . . Evan . . ." Holly said again, her voice incrementally louder and stronger.

"Don't try to speak," Alex whispered through her tears. "Just relax. You're in the hospital, but you're going to be all right. You need to rest . . . to regain your strength."

". . . No, I . . . I saw . . . Evan," Holly said.

"He's . . . Evan's not here," Alex said, glancing at the nurse, looking for guidance but getting none.

". . . I . . . I know . . ." Holly rasped. ". . . But I . . . saw him . . . and . . . and he knows. . . ."

Alex frowned and shook her head.

"He knows?" she said, confused. "Knows what?"

Holly's eyes opened to narrow slits as she looked up at Alex. Very slightly, she nodded, and before closing her eyes again, she softly muttered, "Yes . . . He knows who . . . who killed him. . . . Hunter . . . Hunter . . ."

Alex saw a dangerous glint flash in Holly's eyes as they widened and stared back at her. She felt as though Holly could see right through her, that she could see into her soul, and that she already knew that her son was dead.

"Hunter!" Holly said again, her voice raw and strangled-sounding. "He told me to find him and . . . and—"

Her body went suddenly rigid, and then, in a move that caught both Alex and the nurse off guard, she tried to propel herself up off the bed. She rolled over onto her side and was trying to rip the IV from her arm before the nurse lunged forward and pressed her back down onto the mattress.

"There, there," the nurse said, surprisingly softly as she pinned Holly's shoulders down. It wasn't much of a contest. "You just relax now. You've been through a lot today, and you can't push yourself too hard."

Holly resisted for another second or two, then went suddenly limp.

Without hesitation, the nurse took a syringe and small bottle from her jacket pocket. With a quick, efficient motion, she snapped the protective cover off the needle and stuck the tip into a bottle. Raising the needle to eye level, she slowly withdrew the plunger, filling the vial with a clear liquid. Then, with a swift, precise motion, she sank the needle into Holly's upper arm.

"This will help her relax," the nurse said, glancing at Alex, who was standing by the bedside, watching all of this with an odd feeling of helplessness.

She knew the wait was over.

Holly was out of her coma, and she was going to be all right.

But she also knew that—for her and for Holly—the terrible task of dealing with her loss was just beginning.

"Hunter . . . Hunter . . ." Holly said, her eyes going unfocused and her voice dragging as the injected drug began to take effect.

"He knows. . . . Evan knows. . . . Hunter . . . It was Hunter!"

And then, like a slowly dimming light, she faded away.

There was a soft rap on Nick's bedroom door. Nick stopped packing and turned. "Yeah. Come in," he called out.

He nodded a silent greeting as Derek entered the room. "Are you ready?" Derek asked softly.

Nick couldn't help but notice the troubled expression on Derek's face, the worry and concern. It reflected Nick's own feelings but—because of his upbringing and his training as a Navy SEAL—Nick wasn't about to let his feelings show. He had a job to do. Besides, Alex needed help, and nothing was going to get in his way.

"Almost," he said, turning back around and zipping his overnight bag shut. He was in the habit of traveling light and always kept a bag packed and ready; but he always double-checked it just before leaving, especially his weapons.

Derek hesitated at the door but didn't turn to leave. He looked confused, at a loss as to what to say or do next. Nick could see that there was something more on his mind.

"What is it?" he asked. "Something's bothering you."

"Yes, there is," Derek said.

He regarded Nick in silence for a few seconds, the look of confusion and worry deepening.

"But I . . . I'm not sure what."

Derek pressed his fingertips against his closed eyes and shook his head.

"Ever since I had that intense psychic contact with Alex, I-I've been feeling . . . I don't know. Very confused."

"That's not surprising. You're concerned for Alex. I am too," Nick said, and then waited for Derek to continue.

"True," Derek said after a moment, "but I can't help but think, especially because the contact was so intense, that there's something more to all of this."

"You mean you suspect the powers of darkness are involved?" Nick said.

Derek hesitated another moment or two, then nodded almost imperceptibly.

"There is that possibility," he said with a restrained quaver in his voice. "Just the fact that the connection I felt with Alex was so powerful makes me suspect that this is extremely serious. We have to consider that perhaps Holly and her son were the intended targets of the bombing."

"I'm not so sure about that," Nick replied. "All the news reports are attributing the blast to a local terrorist—in all likelihood, the individual who drove the vehicle to Plymouth Rock and died when the van blew up was acting alone."

"I'm not so sure about that," Derek said simply.

He still spoke with a distracted halting in his voice. Nick could see the depth of his concern. It bothered him to see Derek this worried.

"In any event," Derek said, straightening his shoulders, "I'm glad you're going to stay with Alex. It's important that we make sure she's all right. But while you're there—"

"Don't worry," Nick said, smiling as he patted his travel bag. "I'll keep my eyes open."

"Good," Derek said. "Make sure you stay in contact regularly. And tell Alex that Rachel and I will be coming out in a few days."

"No problem," Nick said.

Derek nodded, still looking troubled. Then he turned and left the room without another word.

Nick shouldered the bag and walked out into the hall, closing the door quietly behind him.

• • •

A cold, hard rain was blowing in off the Atlantic Ocean that night. Alex had spent the last several nights at Holly's home, but this was the first night she was alone in the house.

It was well past midnight.

Alex was seated on the couch in the living room, listening to the cold rain wash against the side of the house. It sounded like fine pebbles, beating against the windows.

Open in her lap was one of the photo albums Holly had shown her the other night. It was filled with snapshots of Evan, doing all the things little kids do—playing at the beach, swinging on the playground, opening presents on Christmas morning. A hollow sense of loss filled her as she flipped the pages.

There was at least one light on in every room, but Alex still felt nervous. Holly's house had been built less than a year ago, but now, without the friendly conversation of her friend and the happy sounds of Evan playing, it felt as cold and lonely and empty as any haunted house. It had its share of odd sounds, too—pipes that tapped, floorboards that creaked and snapped. Alex attributed all of these to the new wood, responding to sudden changes in temperature. Still, she couldn't help but jump whenever she heard a new sound.

Earlier that evening, Alex had watched the news reports about the Plymouth Rock bombing. It was the lead story on every channel. Numbed as she was by the day's events—she still had a high-pitched ringing in her ears and numerous tiny cuts on her hands and face—not much of what she saw made any sense. The most she gleaned was that the bomb had been detonated by a militia group calling itself The First Step. A single person—still unidentified—had driven the van into position and waited until the bomb went off.

A stupid, senseless terrorist act had claimed the lives of nearly twenty people, and close to one hundred others had been hospitalized in serious condition. The local hospital had been overwhelmed, so people had been taken to area hospitals, including Mass. General in Boston.

Through all of this, all Alex could think was that her best friend's child was dead!

It was too much to bear, but she knew that she had to be strong, if only so she could help Holly cope with her tragic loss.

Several times throughout the evening, she had talked on the phone to Derek and Rachel. That had helped some, and she felt much better, just knowing that Nick was already on his way to the East Coast.

When she had left the hospital, around nine o'clock, Holly had been sleeping comfortably. The nurse told her that the injection she'd given her would keep her out all night. Her advice to Alex was to go back home and get some rest if she could.

But right now, sleep didn't seem possible.

Alex's mind was filled with horrible images and thoughts as she tried to piece together what had happened. Try as she might to absorb everything, though, she still felt numbed by it all. The day's events had a surreal cast that Alex kept thinking—or hoping—would prove to be nothing more than a terrible nightmare from which she would soon awaken.

But that wasn't to be.

This wasn't a dream.

As tired as she was, it would be a miracle if she slept at all tonight. Even so, sometime after two o'clock, she began to nod off; but before she was fully asleep, she was startled awake by the telephone ringing.

Momentarily groggy and disoriented, Alex looked around for the phone, not finding it immediately. It rang several more times before she found it on the end table beside her. The photo album had slipped from her hand and fallen onto the floor as she drifted off to sleep.

"Hello, Alex. Sorry to be calling so late," the voice on the phone said.

40

It was Nick.

In the background, Alex could hear the roaring of the jet's engine that almost drowned out his voice.

"I wanted to let you know that this rain is holding me up some. The head winds are pretty severe, and the plane stopped in Chicago to refuel. I just wanted to make sure you were all right."

"Could you speak a little louder?" Alex said. "I can barely hear you." She figured the weather conditions were affecting communications.

"I'd been hoping to be there before midnight," Nick said.

Alex knew he was shouting to be heard, but she still couldn't make out everything he was saying. The crackling on the line sounded like a string of firecrackers going off in her ear. His voice kept warbling in and out, like someone was playing with the volume control.

"It looks like I won't make it until sometime early in the morning," he said. "I'll probably be landing around five o'clock your time."

"Did you say five o'clock?"

Nick's voice faded away. He said something else, but it was totally lost in the ozone.

"Hey! Don't worry about me," Alex shouted. "I'll be all right. You just take care of yourself, okay?"

She glanced at the clock on the mantel and saw to her surprise that it was almost three A.M.

Even so, five o'clock seemed impossibly far away.

She wanted to tell Nick how much she wished he was there with her, but immediately thought better of it.

The last thing she wanted was for him to jeopardize his own safety, hurrying to get to her.

"I'll get there as fast as I can," Nick said as though reading her mind. "I have directions to the house. I'll rent a vehicle in Boston and drive directly to Pembroke—unless you're going to be in the hospital by then."

"No, I'll still be here. It's about an hour and a half drive

41

from Boston. I'll look for you around seven o'clock. We can go to the hospital together."

"Fine. Have you learned anything more?" Nick asked.

"Nothing that hasn't been on the national news," Alex replied.

"I've been running information through the Legacy Data Network as well," Nick said. "Maybe I'll come up with something about this First Step organization that the Feds have missed."

"Maybe," Alex said, stifling a yawn behind the back of her hand. "Oh, there is one thing—"

"Yes?"

"I don't know if it's important or not, but when Holly regained consciousness, she said something that—well . . . She was still pretty delirious from the explosion and the medication and all, but she said a name—at least I think it was a name."

"A name?" Nick repeated.

His voice sounded like he was shouting from the far end of a tunnel. Alex could barely hear him.

"Yes. A name. She said she'd seen Evan, that she'd been talking to him, and he told her that he knew who had killed him. Then she kept repeating a name—Hunter."

"Hunter?" Nick said, but the connection was so bad, Alex wasn't sure she heard him correctly.

"Yes, Hunter. Nick, you're breaking up on this end. Can you hear me?"

Nick said something else, but it was totally lost in the crackling and snapping sounds that came over the phone.

"I'll see you later this morning, okay?" Alex said.

But there was no answer from Nick.

The phone was dead.

FIVE

I t wasn't really a cry.

It was more of a hitching sound ... the sound of someone's breath, catching in their throat.

Alex had been listening to it for ... she wasn't sure how long ... but for quite a while before she realized that the sound was in the bedroom with her, and that she'd better wake up.

She awoke with a start and found herself sitting up in bed and looking around. For a moment, she didn't remember where she was.

Then it came rushing back to her.

The guest room was dark. Alex didn't remember turning off any lights. In fact, because she'd been feeling so on-edge, she was positive she had left on practically every light in the house.

But they were all out now.

The bedsprings creaked beneath her as she shifted and looked around. A faint light filtered through the curtains, filling the dark room with a gauzy blue glow.

Was that the moon? Alex wondered.

It had an unearthly radiance that shimmered like sunlight seen deep underwater.

Fascinated, Alex watched as the curtains bellowed in and out on a gentle breeze. She had the crazy impression that the curtains were like lungs, breathing steadily in and out, in and out.

She shook her head, trying to clear it, but she was filled with an odd sense of unreality, as if this were a dream.

Is it? she wondered.

Then, after another tense moment, she told herself— *No . . . I'm in bed . . . at Holly's house.*

Before she could give it any more consideration, she heard the soft, hitching breathing again.

''Is . . . is someone there?'' Alex called out, surprised by the sudden sound of her own voice.

The darkness moved around her like a softly flowing current of water. Chills rippled up her arms and the back of her neck.

Was that sighing sound the sound of the darkness? she wondered.

Or was it the muffled flow of blood moving through her body?

She craned her head forward, trying to get a direction on the sound, but it seemed to be coming from several directions at once, and always behind her, no matter which direction she looked.

Has that sound always been here, and I'm just noticing it now because I'm alone in the house for the first time?

Or is this a different sound . . . something new?

Possibly dangerous?

Alex was certain that she wasn't going to be able to get back to sleep until she figured out what that sound was and where it was coming from, so with a quick, fluid motion, she tossed the bedcovers aside and stood up.

Her feet hit the floor with a sudden jolt. The hardwood floor sent a wave of chills up the backs of her legs. She shivered and hugged herself, feeling goose bumps rise on her forearms as she slowly made her way over to the bedroom door, her hands reaching out in front of her.

At the door, she briefly considered turning on the bedroom light but then decided that she would be more attuned to the sound if she remained in darkness. Her bare feet made faint scuffing sounds on the carpet as she walked out of the bedroom and looked up and down the long hallway.

Across the hall and to her left was the door that led into Holly's bedroom. The door was ajar, revealing a thick, black wedge of darkness inside the room.

Is the sound coming from in there? she wondered as a stronger current of fear ran through her.

She stared at the opening for a long time, trying to get up the courage to go to the door and look into Holly's room before proceeding downstairs. When it came again, the sound seemed to originate from downstairs, so she decided to check the stairway and foyer first.

The feeling that she was moving in a dream was further enhanced when she turned to her right and started slowly down the hall. She didn't like the feeling of turning her back to the darkness inside Holly's room as she walked away. A cool, gentle breeze wafting up the stairway made her shiver.

She wanted to call out again, to ask if someone was there, but she wasn't able to take a deep enough breath. Her chest and throat felt constricted, as if by invisible bands. Her hands were shaking as she reached out in front of her and swept them from side to side, as if the darkness were something she could brush away.

The closer she got to the stairway, the louder the sound became. At some point—she wasn't exactly sure when—Alex became convinced that it really was someone—possibly a child—crying.

Her heart filled with a cold, dull ache when she thought that it might be Evan.

But how could that be?

Evan was dead.

Could he be a poor, lost soul who had come back to his home, and was now frightened by the changes in it . . . and in him?

The hazy blue glow in the hallway shattered into thousands of tiny, bright splinters.

Alex jerked to an abrupt stop when she reached the top of the stairs and looked down into the foyer. Through her clouded vision, she saw the outline of a small figure in the darkness.

It *was* Evan!

He was huddled on the foyer's marble floor, his hands covering his face as he sobbed in fear. His thin shoulders shook with the agony of his crying.

"Evan . . . honey," Alex whispered.

In the darkness, her voice sounded like something metal scraping roughly against wood. On some deep level, she realized that all of this was impossible, that Evan couldn't be in the house, but she wanted to speak to him, nonetheless.

"Evan . . . It's me . . . It's Alex."

Evan stopped crying, the sound cutting off suddenly and leaving an eerie silence in the dark house. Moving his head slowly, Evan looked up at Alex.

In the dim light, his face looked gaunt and pale. He looked more like an old man than a child. Dark shadows filled the hollows of his cheeks and under his chin. His pallid lips were stretched thin, exposing his teeth in a terrible, skeletal grimace. A nimbus of dull light glowed around his head.

But it was his eyes that caught and held Alex.

A cold, blue light shimmered within his gaze as he regarded Alex in silence for several lengthening seconds. Alex could feel his stare boring into her, cutting through her body and mind, and reaching deep into her soul. She was filled with agony and a terrible sense of loss and loneliness.

"Oh, Evan . . . Evan," she whispered as she raised her hands and started down the stairs.

She was unable to tear her gaze away from him. She felt herself being drawn, irresistibly, toward him. A tingling shock raced up her arm as her hand brushed lightly against the banister.

But as she began to descend the stairs, she saw something else . . . something behind Evan.

At first she thought it was merely his shadow cast onto the front door. When she was halfway down, though, she realized that the shadow looked like the figure of someone else, standing behind Evan.

A huge, motionless figure that was waiting for her.

Alex hesitated, but Evan stared back at her with frightening intensity, willing her to move forward with his powerful stare.

Alex hesitated, holding her arms out, beckoning to him.

"Don't be afraid, Evan," she said in a raw, raspy voice. "I-I know that you're frightened, but I can help you."

Before she had finished saying this, the shadow behind Evan deepened and grew larger, swelling with a pulsating blackness that Alex felt was pulling her toward it to be consumed.

"No . . ." she said, her voice nothing more than a whimper.

Her body went rigid. Her feet dragged heavily on the stairs, but she was no longer in control of her own motions. Against her will, she was being pulled inexorably forward into the shadow that darkened as it grew even larger behind Evan.

No . . . That's not Evan, a small corner of her mind screamed at her, and she knew that it was true.

This isn't happening! . . . It can't be! . . . Not in reality!

She should have realized what was happening as soon as she saw that all the lights were off in the house. She was positive that she had left them on.

She should have seen that this was a trap!

Alex gritted her teeth. Her breath came in short, sharp gulps that burned her lungs as she struggled to resist the terrible force that was pulling her forward to her own destruction.

"You . . . can't . . . have . . . me . . ." she said in a burning gasp.

But there was no way out.

The thing behind Evan was gaining strength as Alex's will slowly dissolved. It seemed to gather the darkness of the night into itself, swelling with a dark and terrible power.

Alex screamed when the door behind Evan suddenly exploded inward with a terrible rush of screaming wind and the sound of splintering wood. A frigid blast of air swept over her. She knew that she was about to die or— worse— be consumed by this ghastly force of evil.

There was only one thing that she could do.

It took a tremendous effort of will, but she gripped the banister tightly with one hand and prepared to leap over the railing. If she fell and died, she thought, if she killed herself, then at least she could escape from this evil force.

It was the only way out!

And even then, she couldn't be sure.

Alex's body stiffened as she coiled up, preparing to jump, when a huge, dark shape ran past—or through— Evan's huddled form and charged up the stairs toward her.

She screamed and tried to back away, but the dark figure closed the distance fast. With cold, powerful arms, it embraced her and held her so close and so tightly she was unable to move or even think.

"Alex . . ."

She heard her name as though someone were calling to her from a great distance. The sound echoed with a hollow reverberation that gained in strength rather than fade.

". . . Alex . . . What are you doing?"

Alex thrashed in the powerful grip and tried to scream or make any kind of sound, but the darkness of the night embraced her and was absorbing her.

She couldn't breathe. All she could think was, *This is it . . . I'm going to die. . . .*

Then, in a violent, blinding flash, the room suddenly filled with painfully bright light. Alex felt herself falling, twisting and spinning head over heels as she plunged . . . plunged . . .

But not to her death.

She realized that someone was holding her.

Someone made of flesh and blood.

Squinting in the suddenly bright light, she looked around, startled to see morning sunlight pouring in through the front door windows. It filled the foyer with a warm glow that thinned the shadows to hazy gray washes.

"What the hell are you doing?" the voice asked.

It seemed to take Alex an impossibly long time to recognize Nick's voice.

The light stung her eyes, making them water as if she'd been crying. She leaned back and looked at the person who was holding her. Through the glare, she finally realized that it really was Nick, and that he had caught her seconds before she had leaped off the stairway to the marble floor below.

"Come on," Nick said calmly. "Let's go downstairs."

"Yeah," was all Alex said.

But that was all she could manage before she collapsed into his arms and started to cry.

Half an hour later, around seven-thirty, Alex and Nick were seated at Holly's kitchen table with steaming cups of herbal tea in front of them. Neither one of them had taken a sip.

Nick couldn't stop staring at Alex. He was genuinely surprised to see how shaken she was. This wasn't at all typical of her. He wasn't used to seeing someone with such strong character look so weak and vulnerable. So broken. But given what had happened to her and her friend, he could completely understand it.

"I . . . I just can't explain it," Alex said, sighing as she rubbed her eyes and shook her head.

"Well, you've been through a lot over the last twenty-four hours," Nick said. "I only wish I'd been able to get here a little sooner."

"It's not just stress," Alex said.

Nick could hear the strength and determination returning to her voice.

"I was sleepwalking . . . in a dream—or a nightmare, more likely—and that . . . that force, whatever it was . . . it was controlling me."

She looked at him, her dark eyes pleading for him to help her understand.

"I was under its power, and I—it filled me with such despair . . . such a feeling of hopelessness. I just didn't feel like I was going to be able to resist it."

"Oh, I don't know about that," Nick said with a tight grin. "I'd say trying to jump over the railing to get away from it was certainly not giving in to it."

Alex shook her head sharply.

"Yes, it was," she said, Her hands were trembling so violently she had to clasp them tightly in her lap to stop them from shaking. "Don't you see? That's *exactly* what it *wanted* me to do. It was trying to frighten me so badly that I would kill myself."

She took a shallow, shuddering breath.

"That's what it *wanted*!"

Nick nodded and stared down blankly at his cup of tea. The tendrils of steam rose and twisted like gossamer ribbons.

"We can't be certain of that," he said softly, "but I do think that you should let Derek know about this. We certainly can't leave you alone with Holly until we figure out exactly what this is all about."

Alex smiled weakly and nodded.

"And that means," Nick continued, "that either Derek

or Rachel is going to have to come out here to stay with you."

Alex looked at him and cocked an eyebrow.

"What do you mean? I thought that's why you were here."

Nick eased back in the kitchen chair, letting his gaze drift out the back door to the autumn-stripped trees. The rain had passed during the night, and now bright sunlight edged everything with a sharp, golden glow. High overhead, puffy white clouds were drifting slowly to the east across a rich, blue sky.

"You mentioned something last night," Nick said at last. "Something that I have to check out."

Alex leaned forward, prompting him with her silence. After a moment, Nick glanced at her and continued.

"You mentioned that Holly said something when she regained consciousness—a name."

Nick let his gaze drift back out to the beautiful New England autumn morning. He shivered involuntarily.

"You said that Evan told her that he knew who had killed him. That it was someone named *Hunter*."

"Hunter . . . ? Well, I don't know . . . I mean, I'm not sure that's a name, actually. It was just what Holly kept repeating. I guessed that maybe she meant the person who killed her son—the nutcase who detonated the bomb—was a 'hunter'."

Nick grit his teeth and shook his head firmly.

"No, it's a name, all right," he said. "It's the name of someone I know—or at least used to know."

Once again, Alex prompted him with her silence.

Nick shifted uncomfortably in the chair, then looked directly at her.

"It might be someone I used to know in the SEALs. A guy named Adam Hunter. He washed out right around the time I joined, but I knew him for a couple of months. A real hard case. And one thing I remember about him was that he was always spouting off about the government, especially after he washed out.''

''So what makes you think he's the Hunter that Holly was talking about?'' Alex asked. ''There's nothing to connect him to any of this. She was delirious. We can't take anything she said as truth.''

''True,'' Nick replied. ''Communications were pretty messed up by the storm last night, but I ran down what little I could about Adam Hunter on the Legacy Data Network. It looks like Hunter's got something going—a militia group with a compound. They're up in the White Mountains, in New Hampshire.''

''And you're going to go up there and check it out, right?''

Biting his lower lip, Nick nodded tightly.

''Don't you think it'd be better to pass this information along to the FBI?'' Alex asked. ''They're not going to give up on this case until they find who did it.''

Nick shook his head sharply.

''And end up with someone falsely accused, like Richard Jewel was? No, I'm not going to notify the Feds unless or until I know for certain that Hunter's the one.''

He took a deep breath and let it out slowly, letting his gaze drift back to the view outside.

''Then again . . . if it really *is* Hunter,'' he said, ''they'll never get close to him. He's much too smart.''

''And you think you can get to him?'' Alex asked.

A thin smile spread across Nick's face as he stared at her intently and nodded.

''No,'' he said, his voice as hard as iron. ''I *know* I can.''

S I X

Holly liked it where she was.
It was dark, and she was surrounded by a rich, cush-iony silence that seemed to be both inside and outside her.

She wasn't the least bit afraid.

In fact, she found it so comforting and soothing, it was disorienting, almost dizzying.

But it wasn't the least bit threatening.

She felt perfectly safe here even though she had no idea where "here" was.

She couldn't begin to guess how long she had been here, but it didn't seem to matter.

Time was of absolutely no importance to her.

And, come to think of it, neither were her body or her thoughts.

Somehow, faintly, she was still aware of her "self," but she—whomever or whatever "she" was—didn't seem to care anymore.

Wasn't able to care anymore.

She had been with Evan.

She knew that much.

She wasn't sure how they had found each other.

Had she called out in the darkness, and had he come to her?

Or had she heard him crying in the darkness and she had found him?

Ultimately, what did it matter?

Somehow, they had found each other in the dark and, although she couldn't see or hear him right now, she knew that he was with her . . . just as she was with him.

And always would be.

It was a beautiful, transcendent moment that seemed to stretch off into eternity.

With whatever spark of her own personality that was left, Holly wished and prayed that this feeling, this comfort, this sense of unity with the darkness that enclosed her would never end.

But just thinking about it made it end.

A vague stirring of uneasiness gripped her.

With wave after wave of rising panic, she became acutely aware of her own sense of self, narrowing down . . . defining her*self*.

From out of the darkness, she heard a word being spoken.

The sound drifted around her like a low, slow rumble of thunder in the distance . . . like boulders, rolling down a distant hillside.

She stared into the darkness, feeling its soft, warm pulse, and tried to will herself to drift back into it.

She wanted to become lost in it, but the sound of her name—

Yes, it was *her* name!

—came to her again . . . louder, now, and more insistent . . . a sharp, discordant wedge of sound that thrust through her sense of euphoria, pushing it aside the way she would brush unseen cobwebs from her face.

A spike of terror shot through her when she remembered—not cobwebs, but hands . . . *hands* and thick, ropey coils, like fat-bodied snakes, reaching out for her from the darkness, touching her, trying to grab her, to wrap around her and drag her down into a pit of intense suffering and despair.

"Holly . . ."

It wasn't her son's voice. She knew that much, so she resisted the voice calling her even as it lured her further and further away from that all-encompassing feeling of comfort.

A cry started to build up inside her mind, but it could find no release. A harsh, burning sensation filled her head with roaring flames. She listened to a loud hissing sound that reminded her of the sound an acetylene torch makes.

Is that sound coming from inside me? she wondered.

Or is it outside of me?

The frantic sense of imminent danger grew steadily more intense until she knew that she could bear it no longer.

As much as she wanted to stay within it, the darkness began to recede, flaking away like old paint before her eyes. Before long, Holly saw faint, flickering lights glowing all around her. Bright orange and red tongues of flame grew steadily brighter, piercing her eyes and causing intense pain.

She knew that she was crying, but she couldn't help staring into the rising flames as they blazed around her.

The voice calling to her seemed to emerge from within the flames. And then, as she watched, fascinated by fear, a face emerged from the shimmering light. Leering at her, its features contorted as though in intense, silent agony.

For a single heart-stopping moment, Holly watched. She expected to see her son's face resolve before her, but she gradually realized that it wasn't him.

It was a woman, staring at her.

The details of the woman's face were lost in the flickering chaos of flames but, unable to turn away, Holly eventually recognized Alex Moreau's features.

"Holly. Hey, you're awake," Alex said softly.

Her voice sounded funny to Holly. Low and dragging, like it had been recorded at one speed and was now being played at another, slower speed.

The brilliant light surrounding Alex's face gradually dimmed. It took a while for Holly to realize that she was lying down, looking up at her friend. After another few moments, it all came back to her. She'd been hurt and was in the hospital, and Evan was hurt, too.

No, a voice deep inside her whispered. *Evan is dead!*

Fighting back a rush of fear, Holly focused on the sounds around her and realized that the loud hissing sound she'd heard was the oxygen tank by her bedside.

She tried to blink her tears away, but her eyes felt raw and exposed. Her vision was cloudy, like she was underwater, drowning and looking up at the impossibly distant sky.

"—I—" Holly said in a strangled gasp.

That was all.

"Hey, you don't have to talk," Alex said. "Just take it easy."

There was still a sludgy drag in Alex's voice, but Holly was relieved to hear her sounding a bit more natural. She figured it must be the drugs and sleeping so long that were making her feel so groggy.

She licked her lips and carefully formed the words in her mind before attempting to say them out loud.

"How long . . . ?"

"Have you been asleep?" Alex said. "It's still early in the morning."

"What day?"

"Friday . . . The day after Thanksgiving."

"Oh," Holly said, licking her lips some more. They were rough, and had a sharp, metallic taste.

"Here. Have a sip of water," Alex said.

She brought a straw to Holly's mouth, and Holly took

a tiny sip. She was amazed at how good the ice water felt, trickling down the back of her throat.

Her vision was gradually clearing.

She looked around the room as much as she could without raising her head from the pillow. The cut on her forehead throbbed in time with her pulse, making her vision waver like she was looking through a wall of clear Jell-O.

There was someone else standing beside Alex. A man. Holly guessed that he was a doctor, checking in on her.

"I have a friend here who wants to meet you," Alex said.

She had an airy lilt to her voice that Holly thought sounded somewhat unnatural. It made her wonder just how bad off she might really be, if Alex was acting phony with her.

Am I dying? Holly wondered.

What if I'm having a near-death experience?

Holly fought to recover any trace memories of that strange frame of mind she'd been in, where she wasn't worried and didn't care about anything. But the harder she tried, the faster they drifted away from her, like sand sifting between her fingers. She knew that she had been in a good place, a comfortable place, but every increment of returning awareness drove it further away. Coming back to her senses, back to herself, made her feel a sharp pang of loss and misery.

She wanted desperately to regain that feeling.

Maybe I've already died and I'm imagining all of this just before I plunge into the eternal dark, Holly thought with a sudden, sharp flash of fear. Cold fingers ran up her back, making her shiver.

No! she thought with a forceful insistence. *I'm alive!*

"This is my friend Nick Boyle," Alex said, still cooing to her like she was a little baby. "I've mentioned him to you lots of times before."

Holly riffled her memory until the name came back to

her. She raised her head slightly, even though the motion sent a jab of pain through her.

"Yeah, sure . . ." she said in a raspy voice. "Nick . . . How are you?"

She had an impulse to raise her hand and shake hands with him, but it seemed like just too damned much effort.

"I'm just fine," Nick said. A tight smile curled one side of his mouth. "And I'm glad to see that you're doing a lot better."

Holly had no idea what to say to that, so she just grunted and let her head ease back onto the pillow.

"Look, ahh—Holly," Alex said, "I know that you're still not feeling up to par, but Nick has to ask you a few questions. Do you mind?"

"Is he a cop or something?" Holly murmured.

"No. He works with me," Alex replied simply.

Nick cleared his throat to get her attention.

"Alex told me that you said a name when you came out of the coma," he said.

Holly wasn't sure what he was talking about, and she didn't exactly like the hard edge in his voice. He seemed too brusque, all business.

"A . . . name?" she said and involuntarily shook her head in spite of the pain it caused.

"You said the word 'hunter' several times when you first came to," Alex said. "Do you remember that?"

"No, I . . . I'm not sure."

Holly squinted and stared for a long moment at the swirling darkness behind her eyes. The thoughts that came rushing back into her mind were too frightening to hang onto for long. There was nothing coherent. Just a jumble of quick, flashing images that didn't make any sense . . . except for the name *Hunter*.

"I know this is very painful for you," Nick said sympathetically, "but I really have to know everything you do if I'm going to be able to help."

With her eyes closed, Holly found that she sort of liked

his voice. It had a soft, mellow edge to it that she found soothing.

"It's very important. A lot of people were hurt and killed in the blast, you know. The FBI is going to be investigating this—"

Holly's eyes shot open, and she stared up at Nick.

"How many . . ." she asked as a cold wave of fear gushed up inside her. "How many people were . . . were hurt . . . and . . . killed—"

She almost choked on that last word, but she swallowed hard and forced herself to continue.

"—besides Evan?"

Holly felt Alex gently take her hand, and after a breathless moment, Nick said, "A total of seventeen people were killed, and more than seventy-five were hospitalized. It's a good thing the driver didn't get that van any closer to the monument. Otherwise, a lot more people would have died."

"I see," Holly said, choking back a sudden flood of tears, "but if it had been closer, maybe Evan wouldn't have—"

She didn't need to finish the sentence.

Holly indicated to Alex that she wanted another sip of water. Alex brought the straw up to her mouth, and she sipped, letting the cold water trickle down her throat.

"So," she said. "Are there . . . any leads?"

Nick shook his head tightly. "That's why I have to talk to you about Hunter."

"How do you know it's a man?" Holly said edgily. "I was out of it. Delirious. I have no idea what I might have said or why I said it. I was talking out of my head. There must've been plenty I said that didn't make sense."

"Maybe," Nick said softly. "But you said that your son knew who killed him, and then you said the name 'Hunter.' I know someone with the last name of Hunter, and I think there's a possibility that he is connected to what happened."

"And you're going to find out, no matter what I say?"

Holly stared at Nick, not knowing what to think. She felt deeply troubled that this man would just come in here while she was still only semiconscious and still trying to absorb the fact that her son was dead, and question her and talk about tracking down a lead.

A wave of dizziness swept over her. Anger flared up inside her in a way that she hadn't felt in years. If she didn't feel so weak, and if her throat didn't hurt so much, she would tell Nick to leave her alone with her grief and let her get some rest.

"I don't mean to upset you," Nick said, gently placing a hand on her shoulder and giving her a reassuring squeeze. "I just want to do what's best for you."

"And if you find this man, Hunter . . ." Holly said softly. "If you find out that he really was involved with what happened . . ."

She swallowed hard, almost choking on the hot rush of anger and hatred that was filling her.

"Will you tell me?"

She stared, long and hard into Nick's eyes until he nodded ever so slightly. She recognized that Nick was filled with a quiet, intense strength, and that he was the kind of man who could accomplish amazing things because he approached life with such focused intensity.

Holly smiled weakly and nodded, but caught herself before she said out loud what she had been about to say.

She closed her eyes and eased her head back, not telling Nick or her best friend Alex that, if Nick found this man named Hunter, and if Hunter really was involved in what had happened to Evan, then Holly wanted Nick to tell him where he was so she could go there and kill him herself . . . to pay him back for all the misery he had caused her.

"You can't do this to me, you bastard!"

Lost in total darkness, Frank McCullough crawled as far away from the wall as the heavy leg and wrist irons he was wearing would allow him. He knew that the door and single, narrow window were barred, and that both were covered with heavy burlap that didn't let in even the slightest bit of light. He wasn't sure his voice even carried outside.

But he knew exactly where he was.

He was in the stockade of the First Step compound.

The dirt floor was cold and damp from the rainstorm the night before. His wrists and ankles hurt from the hours he'd spent trying to break free from his chains, even though he knew that it was useless. He'd considered trying to dig under the wall, but he knew—having helped construct the stockade three years ago when they were building the compound—that there was a thick mesh of heavy iron chains, the kind road construction crews use to contain explosions when they're blasting, less than a foot beneath the building.

"There are people who are gonna miss me! They're gonna come looking for me!" Frank yelled. His voice sounded muffled in the closeness of the small building.

There was no response from outside.

For all the good it did him to yell, he might as well be the only person in the compound—the only person for miles around. He could shout until his voice gave out and his throat started to bleed. No one was going to hear him . . . or listen to him.

And—certainly—no one was going to help him.

Frank had no idea how long he had been locked up here. In total darkness, it was easy to lose track of time. He couldn't even count on his bodily functions to give him some idea of how long he'd been imprisoned. His bowels seemed to have shut down after not eating or drinking since being locked up.

He wasn't hungry right now, but he was terribly thirsty. His lips were dry and cracked; his throat was parched. Yelling only made it feel worse. He kept telling himself to shut up, that he was wasting his breath and energy. He should sit back and try to relax. Hunter would come back and see him eventually—if only to torment him.

Or kill him.

And what was my crime? Frank wondered, staring into the darkness.

He'd been tried, convicted, and condemned simply by opening his mouth . . . by questioning a decision his leader had made.

It struck him as ironic, at the very least, that the First Step Militia was fighting to build a new America, and here he was, imprisoned and facing certain death merely for expressing a viewpoint opposite that of his commander.

Some democracy! he thought, and he couldn't help but laugh grimly.

What kind of America would Adam Hunter make if he ever were to gain any sort of power?

Squatting in the darkness, Frank had plenty of time to think about it, and he had come to the realization that he and the other members of the militia had been absolute fools to join in with Hunter. The man was clearly a psycho-case who was using them to act out his own warped revenge. Frank chuckled to himself again, a bit louder, thinking of a term the therapist he'd seen a while ago might use.

"You have 'power and control issues,' " Frank said in a low, grating voice. "Is that your problem, Hunter?"

This was followed by another, stronger gale of laughter that made Frank think that he actually might be starting to lose his mind.

"*You bastard! You can't do this to me!*" he suddenly shrieked as he staggered to his feet and, stretching his chains to their limits, rattled them wildly. The cold metal cuffs cut like dull razors into his flesh. Warm trickles of blood flowed down his upraised arms.

After a few seconds, exhausted by the effort, Frank collapsed onto the ground, then crawled back to the wall and leaned against it.

He told himself to calm down.

This wasn't going to do him any good.

He was going to have to save his strength and try as best he could not to lose control if he was ever going to get out of there.

Moaning miserably, he slumped forward and cradled his face in his hands. Deep, burning sobs wracked his body as he started to cry. His tears ran down the length of his arms and mingled with his blood.

In his heart, Frank knew that he was a dead man.

He was never getting out of here alive.

He was going to die here because Hunter was going to have to kill him, and no one in the world would notice or care.

Killing him was the only sensible thing to do because Frank knew—and Hunter must know—that if he ever got out of here, the concern wasn't going to be that he might turn in the First Step to the authorities for the bombing at Plymouth Rock.

Hell, no!

If by some miracle he ever got free, he was going to rip Hunter's heart out of his chest and shove it, still beating, down his throat.

That is, McCullough thought, if Hunter even *had* a heart!

SEVEN

The rain had cleared the air. A brisk wind was blowing from the west, and the sky was a deep, cloudless blue later that afternoon when Nick got into his rented Jeep and started for New Hampshire.

Alex had insisted that she would be fine until Rachel or Derek arrived, hopefully in a day or two. Still, there was something in her tone that had bothered Nick, and he promised himself that he would stay in close contact with her until someone else from the Legacy House arrived.

Through his military and Internet contacts, Nick had learned that Adam Hunter's compound was on the eastern edge of the White Mountain National Forest, just north of Conway, outside a little town called Trafton.

But that was all he knew.

He had no idea of the exact location or setup of the First Step compound. It was going to take some very careful questioning and surveillance to get the information he needed.

Nick's biggest concern was to make sure he didn't tip

off Hunter that he was looking for him. In a small New England town, it wouldn't take long for word to get around that someone "from away" was asking questions. It didn't matter if the townsfolk supported Hunter or not, or even if they knew Hunter was there. If he had even half the security Nick suspected he would have, word was sure to get to him almost immediately.

Hunting season was over, so Nick couldn't use that as a cover story. He was going to have to try to pass himself off as an avid hiker who was taking one last trek into the woods before winter closed in. Once he was out in the forest, he had no doubt that he could evade anyone.

Except maybe Hunter himself.

The man had a reputation as a master of evasion and escape.

The four-hour drive from Plymouth to Conway was pleasant enough. It gave Nick plenty of time to work out his strategy. He had all the equipment he needed to find the compound and do a quick reconnaissance, and he had enough weaponry to protect himself. He hoped he wouldn't have to. If he found any indication that Hunter's group might have been involved with the bombing at Plymouth Rock, he intended to notify the authorities and let them deal with it.

A little after four o'clock, with the sun already starting to set, Nick pulled into the small town of Trafton.

It wasn't much of a town.

Main Street was lined with turn-of-the-century office buildings and houses, a post office and fire barn, a couple of "Mom and Pop" corner stores, a library, and a hardware store. That was about it. There was a small park in the center of town where children, out of school for the Thanksgiving holiday, played on rusted swing sets and slides.

Nick's first stop was the Mobile gas station on Main Street where he filled up and asked about a place to stay. The gas jockey—a tired-looking old man with heavy, beard-stubbled jowls that shook whenever he spoke—gave him directions to Mrs. Parker's Bed 'N Breakfast, about a mile out of town on River Road.

Nick thanked him and paid for the gas, then headed out of town following the man's directions. He found the place without any problem, and was glad to discover that Mrs. Parker had a vacancy. In fact, there were no other boarders, since the hunting and foliage seasons were long past, and the ski season had yet to begin.

Mrs. Parker was a rail-thin elderly woman who'd lost her husband several years ago. She proved to be a pleasant enough hostess, but Nick thought she was just a tad too curious about what he was doing up here in this "neck of the woods," as she called it. He attributed her curiosity to nothing more than her being a lonely woman, grateful for whatever company she got.

After registering, Mrs. Parker showed Nick to his room and told him that, if he was hungry, there was a nice family style restaurant called the Depot back in town. She informed him that she served a full-scale New England breakfast at seven-fifteen in the morning, and he was welcome to join her then, but no later.

Nick thanked her and closed the door, waiting until he heard her footsteps on the stairway before calling Alex on the cellular phone. While waiting for the connection to be made, he began pacing the length of the floor, pausing every time he got to the window and looking out at the cold, dark night.

After several rings, Alex answered with a chipper "Hello?"

Nick was instantly relieved to hear her voice. She sounded in a much better frame of mind than she had been earlier that day when he left.

"So how's it going?" he asked, resuming his pacing. "How's Holly doing?"

"Terrific," Alex replied. "She's doing a lot better. In fact, her doctor says she might be able to go home in a day

66

or two. I'm with her right now. D'you want to say hi?"

"No . . . no, but that's great. It sounds like quite an improvement even from this morning."

"You wouldn't believe it," Alex said. "Although . . . well, you know."

"Yeah," Nick said. "It's going to be tough."

He quickly filled Alex in on what had happened so far, which wasn't much, and then told her that he was going out for a bite to eat before getting to bed early. He was still a bit jet-lagged from the flight from San Francisco, and he wanted to get a good night's sleep before heading out in the morning to look for Hunter's compound.

"You take good care of yourself," he said.

"Don't worry about me," Alex said. "I've got it covered. You take care of yourself."

"I will. I'll call you in the morning."

He was standing by the window when he broke the connection, and couldn't help but shiver as he stared out into the thick darkness. Holly may be doing fine, he thought, but she's suffered the worst loss a person can suffer—the death of a child. No matter what, she was going to have a tough time ahead.

Nick walked over to the bed and sat down on the edge, stifling a yawn as he slipped the cell phone back in his travel bag and zipped it shut.

The mattress was soft, maybe a bit too soft, Nick thought. He wondered if he'd be able to sleep on it. As tired as he was, he considered stretching out on the carpeted floor right now and seeing if he could drift off.

Yawning again, he took a pistol from his travel bag and slid it under his pillow. Then he placed the travel bag onto the floor and, with a heavy sigh, shifted his legs up onto the bed.

His eyes closed the instant he dropped his head into the incredibly soft well of the pillow. Within seconds, he drifted off into a deep, dreamless sleep.

•   •   •

It was well past midnight. Rain was beating against the side of Legacy House, washing down the west-facing window-panes in shimmering, silver sheets.

Rachel and her daughter, Katherine, were staying in the guest room at Legacy House for a few nights while Alex and Nick were on the East Coast. Sometime before midnight Kat awoke, frightened by the storm. An hour or so later, once Kat had drifted off to sleep again, Rachel was still wide awake, lying there in the darkness and staring at the ceiling.

Thinking about Alex's friend Holly and her terrible loss reminded Rachel of her own loss of her husband and son. A wave of emotion swept through her as she reached out and gently stroked her daughter's hair. It was so smooth and silky, still so much like a baby's, even though Kat was now twelve years old.

Rachel couldn't stop thinking about how much she still missed Patrick and Conner, her husband and son who had died a few years ago.

Grief wrapped its cold hands around her heart and squeezed. Her chest filled with the same deep, aching pain that she knew would never go away. Eventually, she knew—as with all suffering—the pain would dull. Still, several times a day—usually at times like this, when she thought about how desperately she loved her daughter—no matter how strong she tried to be, the heartache would come rushing back and fill her with sadness.

Of course, Rachel was aware that thinking about everything Alex was dealing with contributed to what she was feeling. Something like that couldn't help but reopen her own wounds that had never really healed. All too easily, Rachel could imagine the pain and suffering Alex's friend must be experiencing. She hoped to have all of her obligations cleared up by Monday or Tuesday at the latest so she could fly East to help in any way she could.

A sudden gust of wind lashed rain against the window, making Rachel jump. She stared at the window for a moment and sighed. Easing her arm under Kat, she hugged her daughter tightly. It never failed to amaze her how much body heat a little girl could generate.

Leaning forward, she kissed Kat gently on the forehead, feeling her own tears running down her face. Sighing, she wiped them away.

Rachel knew that she wasn't going to be able to get back to sleep for a while. Not wanting to disturb Kat, she eased out from under the covers and got out of bed.

Maybe a glass of warm milk or a cup of herbal tea would help settle her nerves, she thought.

Without turning on a light, she made her way quietly to the bedroom door, opened it a crack, and stepped out into the hall.

The house was quiet except for the distant hiss of falling rain as she started toward the stairs. Before she started down, though, she noticed that the light was still on in the study.

Tiptoeing to the door, she cautiously peered inside.

She wasn't at all surprised to see Derek seated at one of the computer terminals. His back was to her as he hunched over the keyboard, lost in concentration.

Rachel took a step into the room and cleared her throat to get his attention. Derek glanced up and, smiling weakly, beckoned for her to enter.

"It's late," Rachel said softly. "Don't you think you should get some rest?"

Derek regarded her with a blank, tired expression. He looked dazed, almost as if he hadn't understood what she'd said. In the dim light, his face was sallow and drawn. Deep shadows lined his face, making him appear much older than he really was.

"Yes, yes . . . I suppose I should," Derek replied. His voice dragged when he spoke, making his accent sound much thicker than usual.

"What are you working on?" Rachel asked, stepping closer to the console so she could see the computer screen.

Displayed on it were some words written in a foreign language.

"It looks like . . . Hebrew," Rachel said, frowning as she studied the screen for a moment. Then she straightened up and shook her head.

"It *is* Hebrew," Derek said tiredly as he leaned back in his chair. Sighing deeply, he rubbed his eyes. Rachel felt suddenly self-conscious and wondered if he noticed that her eyes were still red from crying.

Probably not, she decided. He's much too involved in his own work to notice.

"What are you working on?" Rachel asked.

Derek didn't reply immediately. He continued to stare blankly at her, long enough so Rachel began to feel a bit uncomfortable.

"Does it have anything to do with what's happened to Alex?"

Derek cocked one eyebrow and nodded.

"I think so. I'm not sure, exactly," he said, and then fell silent.

Crossing her arms, Rachel took a step backward.

"Well, if you don't want to talk about it, I can just—"

"Oh, no, no. Please. I-I'm sorry," Derek said. "You don't have to leave. I was just— You're right. I *am* exhausted. I should get some rest. I'll be able to concentrate much better after I sleep. It's just that I-I'd really like to crack this now, if I can."

"Tell me about it, then," Rachel said. She pulled over a chair and sat down beside him. "Maybe a different perspective will help."

Derek regarded her in silence, but Rachel could tell that he was looking past her, lost in thought. Then, shaking his head, he leaned back in his chair and took another deep breath.

"Yesterday, when the bomb went off," he began, "you know that I experienced an incredibly intense psychic connection with Alex."

Rachel nodded but said nothing, silently urging him to continue. He still looked distracted, as though he were trying without success to dredge up a memory from the distant past.

"At one point, I-I saw something that I'm—that has me confused. It was only a brief glimpse of Alex's friend, Holly. Just a flash, but I knew it was her. I recognized her from the photos Alex has shown me. But I—"

He shook his head. Closing his eyes, he pinched and rubbed the bridge of his nose.

"I got a flash of her face. I saw her quite clearly, in fact, and there was something . . . something written on her forehead."

"Written?" Rachel said.

Derek nodded.

"I'm not sure I understand."

"Not like a tattoo or anything," Derek continued. "It was more like a . . . like there was something written underneath her skin. Something that glowed, as if written with light."

"And you think it was something written in Hebrew?"

"It looked like Hebrew to me," Derek said. "That was the sense I had, but I'm having trouble remembering exactly what I saw. It was just a small fragment of a quite intense flood of images."

"But you think this is important," Rachel said.

Derek nodded slowly, thoughtfully.

"Yes, I do. It was the only thing I saw that wasn't . . . natural. Everything else I saw was images of the people who were hurt and dying . . . or dead. But this . . . this was . . ."

His voice drifted off as he turned in his chair and picked up a pad of paper from the desk.

"I don't know what this is," he said as he showed the paper to Rachel. On it were three letters that, to her, looked like the letter Y, then C written backward, and a distorted W with three little dots below it.

"The closest I've come to identifying it is that it might be the Hebrew word for 'seven.' "

Rachel looked at Derek. She had no idea what to say.

"It has to be significant," Derek said emphatically. His face took on a bit of animation as he sparked again to the subject. "I've been researching books of Jewish traditions and superstitions, and I think I might have found something."

He picked up a heavy, yellowing volume with cracked leather binding and flipped through the pages until he found what he was looking for.

"Have you ever heard the Yiddish word *lamedvovniks*?" he asked, passing the book over to Rachel.

Rachel shook her head as she scanned the pages. Everything was written in Hebrew. None of it made the least bit of sense to her.

"They're known as the 'Hidden Saints,' sometimes called *nistarim*," Derek went on, adopting the tone of a lecturing professor. "Especially in Kabbalah and Hasidic traditions, there are—well, the number sometimes varies, but usually it's thirty-six; there are thirty-six righteous people in the world, and it's only because of their good deeds that God doesn't destroy the world."

Rachel raised an eyebrow as she looked at Derek, unsure of where he was going with this.

"I wonder," he said after a long pause, "if Alex's friend Holly might, in fact, be one of these *lamedvovniks*, a 'Hidden Saint.' "

"Well, I suppose that's possible," Rachel said with a shrug.

Since joining the Legacy, she had seen too many impossible things to doubt anything, but her first thought was that it didn't matter what the cause or reason for what had happened might be; the important thing, for her, at least, was that they do whatever they could to help Holly cope with her tragic loss.

"I suggested before that Holly or her son might have

been the target of the terrorist attack,'' Derek said. ''Because the psychic connection was so intense, I can't help but think that there are powerful forces of darkness at work here.''

''Have you mentioned anything about this to Alex and Nick?'' Rachel asked. ''If that's true, then they should be doubly on their guard.''

Derek nodded slowly. ''Yes, I'll do that. First thing in the morning,'' he said. ''But first, there are a few more things I need to check. I don't know what the number seven has to do with it.''

There was still a faraway, distracted look in his gaze, and Rachel was all the more concerned for him. She had seldom—if ever—seen him this distracted. It was obvious that he was working himself well past the point of endurance.

''Maybe you'll be able to figure it out after you get some sleep,'' she said. ''Let your subconscious work on the problem for a while.''

''You're probably right,'' Derek replied, but he remained where he was sitting and didn't reach to switch off the computer. Instead, his gaze was drawn back to the screen. His lips moved as he mentally translated the Hebrew that was written there.

''There's just one last thing I want to cross-reference.''

Derek remained seated at the computer terminal as Rachel made her way over to the door. She told herself that she had done what she could, and that she should get some rest herself if she was going to get done what she had to get done before she could fly back East to join Alex.

''Good night, Derek,'' she said softly before walking out the door.

The only response she got from Derek was a faint grunt as he continued to stare at the computer screen, his fingers tapping away at the keys.

EIGHT

Early the next morning, Nick awoke with a start to the quiet sounds of someone moving about downstairs. Instantly alert, he sat up in bed and swung his feet to the floor as his hand reached under the pillow and gripped the gun he'd left there the night before. He glanced around the room, looking for any source of possible danger.

After a second or two, he realized that it must be Mrs. Parker, working downstairs in the kitchen. He glanced at his wristwatch and saw that it was seven o'clock.

Breakfast was in fifteen minutes, on the dot.

Relaxing his guard, Nick looked over at the sunlight pouring in through the east-facing bedroom window. The bare branches of maple trees stood out in sharp relief against the cloudless, pale blue sky. Tiny dust motes swirled like orbiting planets in the warm yellow light that colored everything in the room.

The surroundings reminded Nick of his childhood. He smiled at the comforting sense of security it gave him. The aroma of fresh-brewed coffee and frying bacon wafted up to him, filling him with pleasant nostalgia.

Rising from the bed, he took what he needed from his travel bag and went down the hallway to the bathroom to shower and shave. Fifteen minutes later, he walked into the kitchen and saw the spread Mrs. Parker had prepared.

There was fresh-squeezed orange juice, hot buttered English muffins, a carafe of hot coffee, and an array of homemade jams and jellies.

"I heard the shower running and figured you'd make it on time," Mrs. Parker said, glancing at him over her shoulder as she stood by the stove. "How do you like your eggs?"

"Ahh—over-easy, thank you," Nick said.

He smiled as he pulled out a chair and sat down at the table. His place was already set with a plate, silverware, and a juice glass. He shook out the cloth napkin and placed it on his lap.

"Over-easy it is," Mrs. Parker said as she took three eggs from the basket on the counter and expertly cracked them on the edge of the pan. "Help yourself to the juice, coffee, and muffins." Her voice was almost lost beneath the snap and bubbling sizzle of the frying eggs.

Nick poured himself a glass of juice and took a sip. The citrus taste exploded on his tongue.

"You've got a marvelous day for a hike," Mrs. Parker said, not bothering to turn around as she tended to the frying eggs. "The weatherman said the temperatures might even reach into the sixties this afternoon. Unusual for this time of year."

"Terrific," Nick said.

He felt inclined to engage her in conversation, just to be friendly, but he was also wary of saying too much. It wouldn't pay for anyone to know that he was in town, asking around about Hunter and his militia group. He could imagine that, as innocent as she seemed to be, Mrs. Parker could easily be one of the town's biggest gossips.

"So where you headed today?" she asked, still not bothering to turn around to face him.

Nick eased back in the chair and shook his head.

"I have a stack of trail maps for this area in the Jeep," he said. "I was thinking of just taking off and seeing where I ended up."

Mrs. Parker turned and regarded him for a brief moment, then nodded slowly.

"You look to me like you can take care of yourself, Nick," she said, "but don't underestimate these mountains. No matter what the forecast says, the weather can turn on you in an instant. This time of year, it's just as likely to be snowing this afternoon as not. And, truth to tell, even though hunting season's over, there still might be some crazy fools out there in the forest."

"Hmm," Nick said, nodding thoughtfully as he took another sip of orange juice.

"You'd be best to let someone know where you're headed, just in case you don't show up when you're supposed to."

"Is there any place in particular I should avoid?"

He hoped his question sounded casual enough, but he noticed the way Mrs. Parker squinted as she regarded him for a moment, almost as though she were sizing him up. It was too much to hope that she would mention where Hunter's compound might be located.

The primary question in Nick's mind was, if Hunter was in the area, and if the townspeople had any clue as to what he was up to, would someone like Mrs. Parker be a supporter or an opponent?

It was impossible to tell.

In an instant, though, the moment passed.

A wide smile spread across Mrs. Parker's face as she turned around to the table with the sizzling frying pan in one hand, a spatula in the other. In the pan lay three perfectly cooked over-easy eggs, browned at the edges from the bacon grease. She scooped them up one by one, and slid onto the plate in front of Nick.

"Wonderful," he said, smiling as he picked up his fork. "Thank you."

Mrs. Parker smiled back at him, then turned to the counter to grab a plate that was heaped with strips of fried bacon. Nick guessed she had fried up a whole pound.

"Help yourself," she said, placing the bacon within his reach. "I'll use whatever's left to make myself a B.L.T. sandwich for lunch."

Nick was in the habit of eating low-fat bacon, but he allowed himself to indulge just this once, knowing that— with luck—he was only going to be in town for a day or two. Mrs. Parker's diet wouldn't have enough time to ruin him.

He set to eating while Mrs. Parker filled her coffee mug and sat down at the table across from him. She watched him with evident pleasure as he ate, but Nick also noticed just a hint of worry in her eyes. As much as he wanted to keep their interactions on a superficial level, to protect her as much as himself, he couldn't help but comment.

"Is something the matter?"

Mrs. Parker looked at him steadily, smiled thinly, and shrugged.

"No . . . not really," she said softly, but Nick could hear an edge in her voice that hadn't been there before.

He pretended to ignore it as he took another bite of egg and sopped up some yolk with a piece of muffin. If she had anything to say, he'd let her instigate it. He didn't want to appear too curious or too pushy. For all she knew, he was nothing more than a weekend hiker, heading off into the forest for what could be the last good weekend of the year.

"Well, I've gotta say, I'm glad I'm not staying here more than the weekend," Nick finally said, just to break the silence. "If I ate like this every morning, I'd be fat as a hog in no time."

Mrs. Parker chuckled softly and made a face when she sipped her coffee. It was obvious that she wanted to say something but—being a typical New Englander—she was keeping tight-lipped about it until he dragged it out of her.

"So, do you have any recommendations as to where I should go?" Nick said. "I'm thinking of just a day trip. Nothing too difficult."

"I should think the Sisters trail up Mount Adler would be a nice walk, although I haven't hiked it since back in the fifties. You get a terrific view of the Presidential Range from the peak."

"I'll consider it," Nick said.

He glanced at his wristwatch and tried to appear absolutely casual as he finished his breakfast and poured a cup of coffee. He wanted to ask her straight out if she had heard anything about Hunter or if she knew where he might be based. It was going to be a long, slow weekend of trial and error if he didn't get a tip from someone.

"I'd just stay to the west of town," Mrs. Parker finally said. "There's not as much to the east . . . just farms and such."

Nick nodded, wondering if she was subtly trying to warn him away from the woods to the east of town because that's where Hunter had his compound. In lieu of asking her directly, he determined to begin his search on the east side of town.

"I've gotta tell you, that's the best breakfast I've had in years," he said.

He wiped his face with his napkin and placed it on the table. Then he glanced again at his wristwatch and pushed his chair away from the table.

"Well, the day's a-wasting," he said as he stood up. "I'd better get a move on."

In spite of Mrs. Parker's protests, he carried his dirty dishes over to the sink and sunk them into the sudsy water.

"There, there," she said, rising from her chair as quickly as she could. "Let me take care of that. You're a guest in my house."

Nick smiled at her but insisted on rinsing his own dishes

at the sink. He thanked her again for the breakfast, then went up to his room to prepare his backpack for the day's hike. The first thing he did was make sure he had a pistol—a small Walther .22—in easy grabbing position at the top of the pack.

Once he was ready, he went back down the stairs, said goodbye to Mrs. Parker, and walked out to the Jeep. He was aware of her watching him from the living room window as he got into the Jeep.

The morning air was chilly. It had probably gotten down below freezing during the night, so the Jeep took a couple of tries to turn over. As he drove away, sensing that she was still watching him, Nick made sure to turn to the right, heading toward the west of town as Mrs. Parker had suggested.

After driving through the small downtown area, he turned around and started up the main road, heading east. The Maine border was no more than eight or ten miles away. He figured that Hunter's compound had to be somewhere between the town and Maine. With any luck, he'd find it today before it got dark.

As he was driving, he took out the cell phone and dialed Alex's number. He wanted to keep her posted on everything he was doing, just in case there was some trouble.

Two hours later, around nine-thirty that morning, Alex walked into Holly's hospital room. She was glad to see her friend sitting up in bed and looking a whole lot better than she had the day before. The wide bandage was still on Holly's forehead where she had banged her head, but the color had returned to her face, and Alex could see that the brightness was back in her eyes.

"You look like you had a good night's sleep," Alex said cheerily.

"As good as can be expected," Holly replied.

Her voice was low and dull-sounding, and as soon as she spoke, it was as if Alex could read her mind and hear the awful, unspoken words, *considering the fact that my son is dead!*

"I woke up a little before dawn and couldn't get back to sleep," Holly said. "I'm afraid I'm going to get too lazy, just lying around here."

Alex smiled sympathetically.

"Hey, you're supposed to get lazy in here. You have to rest up so you can get your strength back. You're going to need all the strength you have to get—"

Alex cut herself off before finishing the sentence, but Holly's eyes began to fill with tears as she finished the sentence for her.

"—to get through the next few days." She paused and swallowed noisily. "Is that what you were going to say?"

The two women made intense eye contact and held it for several seconds. Alex knew what Holly was thinking just as clearly as Holly knew what she was thinking.

Evan is dead, and—sooner, rather than later—Holly was going to have to face that fact straight on and accept it.

"We have to talk," Alex said, lowering her gaze, "about what you want to do about Evan's funeral."

Tears spilled from Holly's eyes as her expression crumbled. Her chest hitched as she tried unsuccessfully to control the flood of emotions. Alex grabbed a tissue and handed it to her.

"I know . . . I know," Holly said, her voice strained with emotion. "It's just so . . . so inconceivable that my— I can't believe that my boy . . . my little baby is . . . is . . ."

Her voice twisted off into an agonized sob as she leaned forward and covered her face with her hands. Alex stepped up close to the bed and leaned forward to hug her friend tightly.

"I know," she whispered into Holly's ear. "It's a terrible, terrible thing. I can't imagine—"

But that was all she said. The two women embraced and Holly, clinging tightly to Alex, let her tears flow.

"Go ahead," Alex whispered as she held her friend close. "Let it out. . . . Let it all out."

They remained hugging for a long time, until the morning shift nurse entered with Holly's medication. An hour later, after Holly had gotten up and taken a shower, the two women were alone again.

"So tell me what's happening with the investigation," Holly said.

Alex could see that she was putting on a brave front, and that's all it was. Inside, she was suffering.

"Do they have any idea who did it?"

Biting her lower lip, Alex shook her head.

"Nothing concrete," she said. "At least as far as I know. I've been interviewed by what seems like every law enforcement agency in the country, but they're not about to reveal anything to me."

"Yeah, they've tried to get in and see me," Holly said, "but—so far, anyway—the staff won't let them in."

"Good for them," Alex said. "But it's the only thing on the news. I've been following it as best I can. Yesterday the president made a televised speech condemning the bombing and vowing that every branch of the federal government would work tirelessly to find and convict any and all people responsible."

Holly's gaze drifted past Alex to the view outside the window. She looked numb, stunned, as she nodded slowly.

"Yeah," she said, her voice no more than a raw whisper. "Just like they did with that bombing in Atlanta."

She looked directly at Alex and added, "But even if they do find out who did it, that won't bring . . . won't bring—"

Her voice choked off, and she almost didn't finish the statement; but clenching her fists, she forced herself to continue.

"—it won't bring Evan back, will it?"

Holly let out an agonized groan and pounded the mattress in frustration. Veins and tendons stood out in her neck, and her face flushed bright red.

"It won't, will it?" she repeated. "*Will it?*"

"No, it won't," Alex said simply, forcing a calm into her voice that she didn't really feel. Her heart, too, was breaking. "And it's something we're all going to have to learn to live with."

"Right," Holly said, her voice hitching, "but when you think about it, what does it matter, anyway?" Her face was a mask of tortured emotion. "Even if they find every single person who was responsible, they'll never be convicted. They'll get off on some minor legal technicality."

"I'd like to think not," Alex replied. "Tim McVeigh didn't."

"Right, but he's still breathing, isn't he?" Holly said, her face twitching with anger and misery. All the while, she kept punching the mattress beside her.

"*The bastard should be dead!*" she shouted.

She was so enraged spittle flew from her lips, and her eyes bugged out of her head. "And those bastards who killed my son should all be dead! *All of them!*"

Alex was taken aback by the sudden fury of her friend's outburst. She had known Holly for many years, and she had never heard her express such hostility and anger.

Granted, what had happened to her and her son was appalling beyond belief, but Holly had spent all of her adult life working with various children's relief foundations around the world. She had dedicated her life and family fortune to helping innocent children who were the victims of war, famine, epidemics, family violence, land mines, and just about every other conceivable and inconceivable horror humanity has perpetrated on its young.

And through it all, Holly had remained at the core an optimistic and generous person who was utterly convinced that good people engaged in good works really *could* change the world and make it a better place for—well, if not for everyone, then certainly for more people . . . especially the children . . . "the only future we have," as Holly always said.

Even considering her appalling grief, Alex found this sudden change in Holly startling. She looked steadily at her friend, staring into her eyes, and was filled by a sudden nameless dread.

Holly Brown wasn't herself anymore.

And by that, she didn't mean that the tragedy she had experienced had changed her.

That was inevitable.

No.

Alex realized that there had been a fundamental change in Holly, in the very essence of who and what she was . . . in her soul.

Alex took a deep, steadying breath. For the millionth time, she wished she would wake up and realize that this had all been a horrible dream.

"We have to believe that the people who did this will be found and punished," she said in a low, controlled voice as she gripped Holly firmly by both shoulders and stared into her eyes.

"And even if all the feds in the country can't find the people responsible, we still have the resources of the Legacy to try to find them."

For just an instant, a gleam flashed in Holly's eyes as she looked at her friend.

"Wha-what do you mean?" she asked. "What's the Legacy?"

Alex hesitated for a moment, unsure whether or not to continue . . . and if she continued, how much she could reveal. She had spoken to Derek and had heard his theory about the "Hidden Saints." She wasn't quite sure she believed it. She didn't have the evidence she needed to draw that conclusion, but the intensity of Derek's contact with her at the moment of the explosion, and the intensity of Holly's grief and her conviction that her dead son had come to her and spoken to her indicated that there were forces far beyond their understanding at work here.

"I mean," she said, "that even now, Nick is checking out a lead."

"He's looking for that man named Hunter, isn't he?" Holly said. Her voice was as cold as steel. Her eyes flashed with a deep, simmering hatred.

Alex nodded.

Even as she spoke, she considered that she might regret revealing too much to Holly. She should let her recover and heal in peace before letting her know too much. But Holly had asked, and she was in so much pain, how could Alex refuse to answer?

"He's gone up to New Hampshire, to a little town named Trafton where someone he used to know—a man named Adam Hunter—has a militia compound."

"Trafton," Holly said.

She spoke the word with a soft lilt to her voice that made Alex suspect that—somehow—she had heard the town's name before.

"Look, I don't know if there's any connection or not, okay?" Alex said. "And even if there is, I don't think Nick's going to do anything about it other than turn over what he knows to the F.B.I."

She leaned forward and gave Holly a tight hug, but she was surprised by the stiff, unyieldingness of Holly's body, as if she were made of steel.

"We have to be patient," Alex said. "I know it may sound trite, but time really does heal all wounds."

"Not this one," Holly said through clenched teeth.

Then she pulled away, looked intently at Alex, and said, "They also say that time wounds all heels."

She leaned her head back and chuckled softly. The sound of her laughter sent a blade of ice through Alex's heart, and all she could think was, *This isn't the Holly Brown I used to know.*

NINE

Although he spent the better part of the day driving around the countryside, Nick still hadn't gotten even a hint as to where Adam Hunter's compound might be located.

Using a detailed road map of the area, he figured he had driven up and down every paved and dirt road within a thirty-mile radius at least twice, some many times more.

Along the way, he had passed numerous farms, homes, and trailers, and more dirt tracks that didn't appear on the map which led off into God-knows-where; but there were absolutely no indications that Hunter or his group was even in the area.

By three o'clock in the afternoon, with the sun slanting down behind the mountains to the west, Nick was tired and frustrated. He realized that he could easily waste the next week exploring the numerous unmapped trails and paths around town. He also knew that, before too long, he'd start arousing suspicion—if he hadn't already—if he was seen and noticed by the locals too many times.

He was beginning to think that maybe the straightforward approach might be the way to go. At least briefly, he had known Hunter in the SEALs.

Why not ask around town about the militia?

If anyone asked him why he was looking for Hunter, he could claim that he had heard about the militia and was interested in joining.

Of course, if the militia had been involved with the Plymouth Rock bombing, Hunter and his men would be instantly suspicious and protective. It could be extremely dangerous to approach them so openly.

All things considered, Nick decided that the best thing to do would be to spend another night at Mrs. Parker's Bed 'N Breakfast, then head out again first thing in the morning and hope for better luck.

He was driving along a narrow dirt road that was labeled Holbrook Stream Road on the map. Scrub pine and brush lined both sides of the road. On his right, a wide stream ran glistening and foaming as it washed over moss-green granite boulders.

A cloud of dust rose in a wide fantail behind the Jeep. Nick thought anyone within a mile or two would think the cavalry was coming if they saw it. As he negotiated a sharp turn in the road, he was surprised to see a dark green pickup truck coming straight at him.

Swearing under his breath, Nick jerked the steering wheel sharply to the right, barely avoiding the truck. The Jeep swerved hard and left the road, bouncing over the rocky terrain as it tore through the scrub brush until finally coming to a stop a few yards short of the stream. Even though he was wearing his seat belt, Nick was thrown forward with enough force to hit his head on the steering wheel. The impact was hard enough to make him see stars.

As the pickup sped past him, the driver, wearing reflective sunglasses, turned to watch Nick through his side window as he laid on his horn. Its blaring sound Dopplered as the truck roared down the road, leaving Nick behind in a swirling cloud of yellow dust that slowly drifted away like smoke on the wind.

Nick was dazed and had caught only a quick glimpse, but he was fairly certain that he had seen three passengers in the pickup truck and a dog—a German shepherd—tied in the back. Although it had happened much too fast for him to be sure, he thought that at least one of the men— the driver—was wearing a camouflage flak jacket.

Nick jammed the gear shift into reverse and backed up onto the road. The Jeep jostled and bounced, and brush scratched like claws against the under-chassis. The road maps and other supplies were scattered onto the floor, so he took a moment to organize them and consider what had just happened.

It wasn't much to go on, certainly, but at least one of the men had been wearing camouflage ... possibly all three.

That could mean they were members of the militia Nick was looking for.

It was the only lead Nick had, but he guessed maybe he was closer to the compound than he realized. He quickly opened up the detailed map of the area and located his exact position at the bend in the stream. No more than half a mile back up the road, the map showed a narrow trail or single-lane road—possibly a fire road that branched off into the forest toward the eastern slope of Mount Forester. At least according to the map, the trail cut into the woods maybe a mile or so before dead-ending.

"That's gotta be it," Nick muttered as he tapped the map thoughtfully with the tip of his finger.

He scratched his chin and considered. He was still heading back toward town, in the direction opposite to that taken by the men in the pickup truck. The more he thought about it, the more confident he was that he was in the right area.

Leaning forward over the steering wheel, he glanced up at the sky. It was turning a deep violet as evening approached. In the east, he saw a thin sickle of a moon. In the west, a few stars had already appeared.

It was getting late.

The sensible thing to do, he told himself, was to drive back to Trafton. He could have supper at the Depot, the restaurant Mrs. Parker had mentioned, and get another good night's sleep before starting out again in the morning.

His wristwatch ticked off several minutes as he sat there and considered what to do. Then, with a deep breath, he shifted the Jeep into gear and backed around slowly. The dust raised by the passing pickup truck had long since settled in the gathering gloom, but Nick had no problem finding the unnamed road. He got out and inspected the ground carefully, glad to see fresh tire tracks in the dirt.

He got back into the Jeep and drove a short way down the road. When he found a break in the brush, he shifted into four-wheel drive and drove into the brush as far as he could get. Then he grabbed his backpack and checked his equipment. After making sure the Jeep wasn't visible from the road, he took his travel bag with his cell phone, a spare pistol, and a hunting knife in it, and carried it a short distance into the woods where he hid it beneath some thick brush. It was probably an unnecessary precaution, but if Adam Hunter was around he wanted to be extra careful. He put on his camouflage poncho, strapped on his holster and pistol, and headed off into the woods, keeping a track parallel to the dirt road.

He hadn't gone more than a quarter mile in when he saw a small wooden guard station up ahead. It was manned by a solitary sentry who was wearing faded Army fatigues. The man was seated in a chair, leaning back against the wall of the guardhouse with a cigarette dangling from his lower lip and a magazine open on his lap. The light from the guardhouse cast a pale wash of yellow.

"Bingo," Nick whispered softly, smiling to himself.

Loosening his pistol in its holster, he turned and started off into the woods. Night was closing in rapidly, and he wanted at least to encircle the compound to check out its perimeter before leaving. If discipline was as lax as the guard at the front post indicated, Nick didn't think he'd have all that much trouble penetrating the compound . . . if he needed to.

He just hoped he wouldn't need to.

The tile floor was cold, and Holly's bare feet made faint mouselike squeaking sounds as she walked slowly down the darkened hospital corridor. She moved with a surprisingly fluid ease, an almost gliding motion that felt a little bit like flying, a little bit like slipping on ice.

A tingling thrill rose up within her when she considered that she might, in fact, be dreaming.

Since she'd been having those dreams—or whatever they were—about Evan, she and Alex had talked a lot about dreams. Holly realized now with a fluttery gush of excitement that she must be having what Alex had referred to as a "lucid dream."

I can't believe this is really happening, she thought/said to herself as she looked slowly from left to right. Her hair swayed back and forth, brushing her shoulders with a barely audible *swish.*

The doors on both sides of the corridor were open, and she could see into every room. Within, shadowy shapes of people were lying in bed, sitting in chairs by the windows, or standing or pacing at the foot of the bed, looking at the dark shapes in the beds. In the darkness, everyone's silhouette seemed to be outlined by a faint trace of blue light that shimmered and shifted, like something viewed underwater. In several of the rooms, one or two people turned their heads slowly and watched Holly as she passed by. Their lingering glances made her feel uncomfortable . . . exposed, almost as if they could see right through her.

Holly had no idea how she had gotten here or where she was going. It felt as though she was being swept away by a gentle but irresistible current of water, pushed along against her will.

The corridor appeared to be endless.

Both in front of her and behind her, it telescoped to a far distant vanishing point that was lost in a gray haze. Holly recalled the image of the tunnel of light that people who'd had near-death experiences had reported, and wondered if that's what was happening to her now.

Maybe she was dying!

Don't be afraid. . . . Just go with it. . . . Trust yourself, she thought/said.

She looked down at her pale, bare feet. They seemed impossibly far away, like she was balanced on stilts.

Who are these people? she wondered, looking left and right at the shadows in the various rooms.

The farther she went, the more they seemed to be aware of her. In every room, now, at least one, if not more, of the occupants watched her walk by.

Who are they? And what are they doing? she thought/said.

"Some of them are like you . . . and some of them are like me."

Holly was startled by the voice, speaking so suddenly beside her, sounding so close it was like the person was whispering in her ear.

And she instantly recognized that it was Evan.

Still moving slowly down the corridor, she turned and looked to her left.

Evan was there beside her, as if he had been with her all along. His body was curiously immobile and, although Holly still had the sensation of motion, he stayed right there beside her without any apparent effort.

What do you mean? she thought/said.

The illusion of being in a dream intensified, and Holly was suddenly afraid that if she experienced too much emotion, she might wake herself up.

And she didn't want to wake up.

She wanted to hold on to this moment and savor every second she could with her son, even though she knew that he wasn't really here with her.

"Some of them are alive," Evan said in a scratchy voice that sounded like sandpaper rasping against wood. "And some of them are dead."

She nodded her understanding, but when she passed the next room and looked into it, the figure within leered back at her. Its facial features were horribly underlit by ghastly blue light. The face was so old and ravaged that Holly couldn't tell if it was a man or a woman, but she saw the person smile at her, exposing wide, pale teeth that glowed like moonlight in the darkness.

Holly involuntarily shrank away from the person.

"You don't have to be afraid," Evan said softly. "They can't hurt you. Think of it as like watching a movie."

Only we're in the movie, she thought/said.

"Yeah . . . well, kind of," Evan said. "Think of it like all this, then . . . that all of us—you, me, and them—aren't dead or alive. We're somewhere in between."

Holly shivered.

A numb tingling spread up her back to the base of her skull.

They continued down the corridor, and at each doorway several more figures turned and glared at them as they passed by. Their eyes were sunken deep into their heads, and burned with a baleful fire. Moving like spiders that skittered in the dark, their pale, skeletal hands reached out for Holly.

She shrank away from them, but no matter which way she turned, more hands reached out of the darkness for her.

"I told you," Evan said with a sharp edge of command in his high, boyish voice. "Don't be afraid. You'll only make them angrier."

Angrier? Why would they be angry? Holly thought/said.

"Because they're here," Evan replied. "They're trapped.

They died here in the hospital, and they don't want to leave. Or they can't.''

Why is that?

''Because they haven't accepted the fact that they're dead, and they don't want to leave.''

But there are so many of them, Holly thought/said. *Where did they all come from?*

She looked down the corridor and saw that it still stretched out to an impossibly distant point up ahead. When she looked behind, she was suddenly fearful that she would never find her way back to her own room.

The fear that she would be lost forever in this corridor filled her.

Am I dead . . . or dying . . . or what? she thought/said.

Evan laughed, and the sound of his laughter echoed hollowly in the infinite corridor. Several of the figures in the doorways began to laugh softly, too. The sound echoed and then slowly faded.

''Don't be silly. You're not dead.''

Holly jumped and let out a squeal when she felt something squeeze her hand. Looking down, she saw that Evan was reaching out to hold her hand. Trembling, she took his hand, surprised by the clammy, fleshy touch as his small fingers slid into the cup of her palm.

Then why am I here? she thought/said. *What's happening to me?*

''I need you to do something,'' Evan said.

This time, when he spoke, his voice had a deep, echoing quality that didn't sound at all like him.

Holly looked at her son. When they made eye contact, for just an instant, she saw a flickering red glow deep within his eyes. Then, in an instant, his expression softened, his eyes looking dark and moist. She thought she saw tears welling up within them, and her heart nearly broke with pity for her dead son.

You know that I'd do anything for you, honey . . . absolutely anything, she thought/said.

"I know. That's why I want you to do this."

"*Do what?*"

"I want you to kill the man who killed me."

Once again, Evan's voice assumed a harsh, grating whisper that didn't sound at all like how she remembered him. She tried to pull away from him, but the grip he had on her hand was surprisingly tight.

"I want you to kill the man who set off the bomb that killed me and all those other people."

A heart-stopping chill gripped Holly.

The darkness in the corridor seemed to condense suddenly and squeeze in on her, suffocating her. The dull thump of her heart thundered in her ears so hard it was impossible for her to swallow. Her lips felt dry and cracked, and she wasn't at all sure that she could say what she had to say.

Finally, though, she managed to force it out.

I can't do that for you, she thought/said. *I know that . . . that you think whoever's responsible should be punished. I do, too, but I . . . I can't do something like that. I can't take someone else's life.*

"Oh, yes you can . . . Mommy," Evan said hollowly. "You have to!"

Too stunned to reply, all Holly could do was shake her head in denial and mumble.

She released her grip on Evan's hand, but when she pulled away from him, the dark figures in the doorways suddenly darted out at her. Their hooked, bony hands clawed at her, slicing the air with faint whickering sounds. The corridor was filled with a loud chattering that reminded Holly of the sound a nest of insects would make. She realized that it was the sound of their teeth, mashing and grinding together.

"You have to do it! . . . for me," Evan said. "That man—Alex Moreau's friend, Nick . . . He knows where they are. He's close to finding them, but he isn't going to be able to do it. He can't kill the man who killed me. *You have to do it!*''

Holly was repulsed by the heartless tone in her son's voice. She looked at him again in amazement and wondered how could this really be her boy . . . her baby.

How could such horrible, hateful words be coming out of him?

"Do you want me to be like them?" Evan said, indicating with a slow hand gesture the chattering, ghastly figures which now filled every doorway along the corridor. The sounds they made—insane laughter and angry hissing—rang painfully in Holly's ears.

Oh, honey . . . Evan . . . Don't, Holly thought/said. *Don't do this to me!*

The thought that Evan or anyone else would be trapped in such a terrifying situation filled Holly with dizzying fear.

"If you don't do it, then I won't be able to let go," Evan said. "I'll be trapped here . . . forever . . .''

When he said the word *forever*, it echoed in the darkness, reverberating from wall to wall and gaining in strength rather than fading away.

But . . . but how can I . . . I wouldn't know where to begin or how to . . . to do something like that, Holly thought/said as frantic fear swept through her.

"Don't worry about that," Evan said. "I'll help you. Whenever you need me, all you have to do is call for me, and I'll come. I'll be there to help you. All you need to know right now is that you're right. The name of the man who killed me is Adam Hunter. He's in New Hampshire, in a town called Trafton. Alex's friend Nick is there now, but if he pokes around much longer, he's going to find out the truth.''

But that's what we want. We want the truth to come out, Holly thought/said. *We want this man Hunter to be arrested and be punished for what he did.*

"Oh, no we don't! Not that way!" Evan said, his voice as cold and hard as steel. "He has to suffer because of the suffering I went through . . . and you . . . If I'm ever going to be free, *you* have to do it! *You* have to find him and kill him!''

Holly couldn't believe that she was hearing such venom from her son. She was filled with a powerful impulse to turn and run from him. But it wasn't so much Evan or what he was saying that she wanted to get away from.

It was her own thoughts.

It was the anger and bitter hatred he stirred up in her soul and the terrible pain of losing her son that she wanted to escape.

But where could she go?

The corridor wavered as it stretched out in front of her. The dark figures in the doorways were pressing closer, grabbing at her . . . reaching for her.

''We have to get you out of here,'' Evan said.

There was still a hard quality to his voice that Holly didn't like, but she nodded in agreement.

''And don't worry,'' Evan whispered.

His mouth was so close to Holly she could feel the pressure of his cold, dead lips against her ear.

''I'll be with you to help.''

Holly screamed when she turned to look at him, and saw a hideous skull face staring at her with eyes that burned like hellfire in the core of its dead eye sockets.

The scream wound up inside her, rising louder and louder until Holly opened her eyes and realized that she was sitting up in the hospital bed. Both hands were gripping her head as if trying desperately to stop it from exploding. The hospital room was dark, but Holly saw a dark figure rise up from beside the bed and reach for her.

She screamed so loud her throat almost closed off, but she couldn't stop. . . .

Not for a long time . . .

Not until she realized that Alex was there, holding her, hugging her, and whispering softly yet insistently that it was all right . . . that everything was all right . . . that it had only been a dream.

But even after she gained a measure of control and started to calm down, Holly knew that Alex was wrong.

It hadn't been *only* a dream!

TEN

Around four o'clock, having finished with her last patient for the day, Rachel left the hospital. As usual, the coast highway was congested with weekend traffic, so it wasn't until well after five o'clock that she pulled into the driveway of Legacy House and parked her car out front. She had just entered the expansive foyer of the house when the telephone began to ring.

She dropped her briefcase by the door and picked up the receiver on the fourth ring.

It was after eight P.M. on the East Coast, and she expected that this was Alex, checking in from Massachusetts. She was surprised to hear a man's voice on the line—a voice she didn't recognize.

"I want to speak with Derek Rayne, please," the man said.

There was a gruff, commanding quality to his voice that instantly put Rachel on her guard.

"May I ask who's calling?" Rachel said, glancing up the stairs to see if Derek had heard the phone ringing and had responded.

She didn't see him, and the house seemed unusually quiet. If Derek had stayed up all night, as she suspected he had, he might be asleep.

"This is Jerry Caldwell, calling from San Diego," the man said.

Over the phone, Rachel could hear the incessant chatter of voices and several other phones ringing in the background. Whoever this Mr. Caldwell was, he was calling from a busy room, perhaps a hospital or police station, or maybe the airport.

"I'll see if he's here," Rachel said.

She put the phone on "hold" and pressed the intercom button.

"Derek? Are you here?"

She could hear her voice echo faintly from the speakers throughout the house.

After a long pause, Derek's voice, sounding drawn and tired, said over the speaker, "Yes, Rachel. I've got it. Thank you."

She waited until the red light on the "hold" button stopped blinking, then shrugged off her overcoat and hung it on the coatrack by the front door.

She was exhausted after having such a bad night the night before but, curious about the call—there had been something in Mr. Caldwell's tone of voice that alarmed her—she started up the stairway. She could hear Derek's voice coming from the second floor conference room.

When she entered the room, she saw that Derek was seated at the same computer console he had been at the night before. Her immediate concern was that he'd never left it and hadn't gotten a wink of sleep since last night. He certainly looked exhausted. His face was even paler than it had been last night, and the lines around his eyes were dark and drawn tightly.

"Yes, I'll check into it immediately."

Derek glanced up at Rachel and nodded grimly as she entered the room.

"Yes. Send the fax to me right away. I'll do what I can."

Derek replaced the phone on its base and let out a heavy sigh as he slouched back in the chair.

"Bad news?" Rachel said, reading his expression and feeling a spark of concern.

Derek's lower lip tightened as he nodded curtly.

"Yes. That was the San Diego P.D.," Derek said in a low, strained voice. "Fra Felipe died this afternoon." His breath caught in his throat before he could continue. "He was killed."

"Oh, no," Rachel said in a whisper.

Her legs suddenly felt like they couldn't support her. The room started to spin, and she leaned back against the door frame for support.

"I'm afraid so," Derek said softly, "and Detective Caldwell thinks there may be an occult connection. There was evidence that he was killed in some kind of occult ritual."

"Oh, my God."

Rachel stood there, shaking her head, trying to clear it, but she was overwhelmed by a sense of absolute unreality. She could hear and feel her heart, slamming against her ribs.

"They took some photographs of the crime scene and are going to fax them to me so I can take a look. But I have to say—"

Derek looked at Rachel with concern etched deeply in every line of his face.

"—I don't like the sounds of this."

Even as he spoke, the fax machine in the corner of the room began to whine. After a few electronic beeps, a sheet of paper began to churn out of it. Derek rose from his chair with some effort and went over to the machine to receive the pictures as they arrived.

Rachel was feeling too weak to move. She was still trying to absorb the shock of the news.

"I-I just can't believe it," she said hoarsely. "Who would ever want to hurt someone like . . . like Fra Felipe?"

"They've arrested an altar boy who was found in the rectory with blood on his clothes and a bloody knife in his hands," Derek said. "Caldwell said the boy was muttering something about 'cleansing the world' so it would bring on the 'eternal night.' "

"But why Fra Felipe?" Rachel said, feeling too stunned to comprehend what Derek was saying. "He was such a kindly man. And he worked so hard, helping the homeless and the immigrants in San Diego."

"There was no one better in the world," Derek said, nodding solemnly but not looking up at her. His hand was extended as he waited impatiently for the transmission of the first photo to be completed. He frowned and squinted as he watched the hazy black and white picture slowly appear.

Rachel could tell by his facial expression that the scene was gruesome. She didn't dare go over and take a look at it. All she could think was, *Who in the world would want to harm such a nice old man as Fra Felipe?*

For the longest time, the only sound in the room was that of the fax machine as it transmitted the pictures to Derek. As each photo was completed, Derek held it up and studied it carefully. He had three or four faxes in his hand and was watching the next one come out of the machine when suddenly he let out a loud cry and staggered backward. The sheaf of faxes dropped from his hand and scattered like fallen leaves onto the floor.

In an instant, Rachel was beside him, her arm around him to support him. He was trembling beneath her touch. His face had gone ash gray.

"Sit down over here," she said, guiding him over to a comfortable chair by the window.

Derek walked beside her with stiff, halting steps, as if he suddenly had no will of his own. Rachel was convinced that he would have fallen down if she hadn't been supporting him.

Once Derek was seated by the window, she stood back and quickly assessed him. The circles around his eyes looked like soot smudges, and his lips were as pale as bone. He slouched back in the chair as though he didn't have an ounce of strength left. Rachel thought he looked like someone who was fighting a long-term, body-ravaging disease.

"What happened?" she asked, unable to disguise the panic in her voice.

"The . . . the pictures," Derek said. "I . . . It's not possible, but I . . . I saw it again."

His voice sounded raw and broken, as if he'd been shouting for a long time.

"You saw what?" Rachel asked, glancing over her shoulder at the faxes on the floor. A numbing chill wrapped its fingers around her heart.

Derek tried to speak again, but he was trembling so badly he couldn't form the words he wanted to say. He raised his hand and pointed at the fax machine.

"The one still in the machine," he rasped. "Look at the one still in the machine."

Rachel cautiously approached the fax machine. Her heart was thumping in her throat, making it difficult for her to breathe as she looked down at the grainy black and white photo.

It was a stomach-wrenching shot of Fra Felipe, lying on his back. His head was tilted to one side, and his eyes were wide open and staring. The entire left side of his cassock, from the shoulder to the waist, was black with blood.

A sick, sour taste filled Rachel's mouth as she looked at the photo of the slain priest. She reached out to pick it up but couldn't bring herself to touch it. Her heart was breaking, just remembering what a kind and gentle person Fra Felipe was . . . or had been. It seemed beyond reason that he would meet such a cruel and violent death.

"I just can't imagine . . ." Rachel said.

Her vision blurred as her eyes filled with tears.

"Look at his forehead," Derek said. His voice was so weak he sounded like an ailing, elderly man.

Rachel resisted the impulse to pick up the photo and look at it. Her gaze was riveted to the blank, staring eyes of Fra Felipe.

"What do you see?"

Through her tears, Rachel forced herself to look at the dead priest's forehead, but she saw nothing unusual—just a wide expanse beneath the Fra's thinning black hairline.

"I . . . I don't see anything," she said in a whisper, shaking her head in confusion. "There's nothing there."

"Yes, there is," Derek said.

He struggled to get up out of the chair and came over to her. He snatched the fax from the machine and held it in front of her face. With an angry, frantic jab of the forefinger, he pointed at the dead priest's forehead.

"There! Right there! It's—"

But before he could finish his statement, he caught himself. Frowning, he brought the fax up close to his face and studied it carefully. His hands started trembling so badly he dropped the fax on top of the machine.

"I saw it again," he said, so softly Rachel could barely hear him.

"Saw what?" she asked, feeling a tightening tension in her stomach.

"On his forehead," Derek rasped. "There was a symbol on his forehead. Just like I saw on Holly's forehead. I recognized it from the research I did last night."

"Derek, please. You need to rest," Rachel said, taking him by the arm and leading him back to the chair. "You can't push yourself like this."

"But I know I saw it," he said, struggling to regain a measure of composure. "It was there . . . the Hebrew word for the number *eight* was on his forehead."

"No, you imagined it," Rachel said. "You're working too hard."

Derek looked at her, nailing her with the intensity of his glance.

"I know what I saw," he said, sounding a bit more steady, now, more in control. "That has to be it. Fra Felipe must be one of the *lamedvovniks*."

He looked at Rachel and swallowed hard.

"There's no other explanation for it."

Rachel found herself at a loss for words.

"Someone . . . or some*thing* . . . is trying to eliminate all of the Hidden Saints," Derek said.

Rachel covered her mouth with her hand and fought the wave of nausea that swept through her.

She wanted to tell Derek that he was wrong, that he was past the point of exhaustion and was imagining all of this.

He couldn't have seen a Hebrew word on the dead priest's forehead.

But somewhere, deep in her heart, Rachel knew that it could be true.

"According to Jewish legend," Derek said, "if the Hidden Saints are eliminated, then God will no longer withhold his Judgment, and the Apocalypse will ensue."

Rachel shivered.

"That's exactly what the Forces of Darkness want."

"So what do we do?" she asked, hearing her own voice as if from a great distance. She was trembling inside. "What *can* we do?"

Derek stared at her, and then she saw a smile twitch at one corner of his mouth. The life and energy was returning to him.

"Why, we have to try to stop them, of course," he said simply. "That's what the Legacy is all about. And the best way to do that is to make sure that nothing happens to Alex's friend, Holly Brown."

The sun had set, and the forest was filled with a hushed silence broken only by the creaking of branches in the cold wind and the light tread of Nick's feet as he made his way carefully around the perimeter of Hunter's paramilitary compound. He was keeping a safe distance away so no one would hear him if he inadvertently snapped a twig or scuffed too loudly in the dead leaves that carpeted the forest floor.

Dim lights showed all around the compound—bare bulbs that hung from wires strung loosely onto makeshift telephone poles. When he moved closer to the compound, Nick could hear the faint hum of an electric generator. He guessed it was in one of the smaller outbuildings toward the back.

There was no wire or fencing around the complex, and Nick didn't see any guards posted. Apparently Hunter wasn't all that concerned about keeping his location a secret or deterring any intruders. He probably thought he was deep enough in the forest and far enough off the beaten track to escape the notice of any curious passersby or law officials.

Keeping to the deepening shadows of the pines, Nick studied the layout of the place from several angles as he worked his way around toward the back.

In the center of the compound was one main building, probably designated the command post. It was maybe fifty feet square, and built of rough-cut timber. Ranged around the command building were numerous other, smaller buildings. One building close to the outer perimeter of the compound had a heavily padlocked door. Iron bars and plywood covered the single window that Nick could see.

Obviously, this was the stockade.

Nick had to wonder about an operation that had to use prison—or even the threat of prison—to enforce discipline.

There was plenty of activity inside the compound.

Besides the dark green pickup truck Nick had followed out here, there were six other vehicles—an assortment of mud-splattered four-wheel-drive trucks and Jeeps—parked along the wide central avenue that led up to the command post. At least three men had arrived in the truck Nick had seen earlier. Taking that as an average number, Nick figured there could be as many as fifteen or twenty militia members all together.

Not very good fighting odds, even with the element of surprise on his side.

In spite of the deepening cold, Nick hunkered down behind a rounded boulder. Gripping his semiautomatic Walther tightly in his hand, he settled down to watch for a while.

In the space of half an hour, he counted more than a dozen men—none of whom he recognized as Hunter—moving about from one building to another. All of the men were dressed in baggy military camouflage jackets and pants and had their firearms slung casually across their shoulders. In the gathering darkness, Nick couldn't identify the exact types of weapons, but he figured, like most paramilitary militias, they had an assortment of legal and illegal automatic and semiautomatic rifles from various foreign countries. Everyone appeared to be sporting sidearms or hunting knives, as well.

Note to myself, Nick thought with a dry chuckle. *Don't try a frontal assault.*

Satisfied, he continued to encircle the compound. When he was downwind from it, he caught a strong whiff of something that he couldn't quite identify. It smelled a bit like burning manure, mixed with a tinge of overheating machinery. Some of the activity seemed to be centered around one of the smaller buildings out back, which Nick guessed was the source of the noxious smell.

Crouching low, Nick started to make his way back around to the front of the compound. Now that he had a good idea of the layout and defenses of the place, such as they were, he wanted to figure out some way to determine if, in fact, Hunter and his group had been involved in the bombing at Plymouth. The manure smell could very well be the chemical fertilizer they were using to make materials for bombs, but he wanted to have something more substantial than that before going to the authorities.

To the west, the land sloped gently down from the compound. In the darkness of the forest, Nick had to move very slowly. His plan was to go back to town, spend the night at Mrs. Parker's, and then come back out here first thing in the morning, before daylight, and have another look around. He wasn't sure how many—if any—of the men stayed at the compound overnight, but the number of vehicles compared with the number of soldiers he'd seen indicated that not many of them were permanent residents.

Then again, the stockade building indicated that at least a few of them might be semipermanent residents.

Nick was about a hundred yards from the front, having almost completed his encirclement of the compound, when the door to the command post opened, and a man stepped out into the night.

Nick dropped to the ground, concealing himself behind a spray of low scrub pines.

He immediately recognized Hunter. He was wearing a cap with a wide brim that seemed to shadow his eyes from the feeble glow of light, no matter which direction he turned. Hunter was followed by two heavily-built men who maintained a respectful distance behind him.

Hunter walked with a cocky swagger down the central avenue toward the building that Nick guessed was the stockade. The two men accompanying him, obviously his personal guards, carried automatic rifles at the ready. Their heads continually turned from side to side as though they were sweeping the area for imminent danger.

When they arrived at the guardhouse, one of the men stepped forward. After selecting a key from the heavy ring hooked to his belt, he unbolted the padlock on the door and threw the heavy door open. Nick heard the throaty groan of the rusted hinges.

Inside, the building was a dense wall of darkness, but none of the men entered. Instead, Hunter turned around and, for a few seconds, scanned the area. Cocking his head from side to side, he seemed to be focusing beyond the lighted compound and into the night-drenched forest.

Even at this distance, Nick could hear a faint chuffing sound, as though Hunter was sniffing the night air like a bloodhound.

Then Hunter raised one arm and pointed directly at the spot where Nick was crouching. His voice was faint with distance, but Nick clearly heard what he said and was struck with disbelief.

"Morgan . . . Williams," Hunter said.

His voice filled the night.

"Go out into the woods there and get our new guest."

Nick knew that there was absolutely no way Hunter could have seen him beyond the lighted area of the compound, but the man was pointing directly at where he was hiding.

"Tell him that we have his new quarters ready for him."

ELEVEN

That evening, around eight o'clock, Alex had needed a break. She left the hospital and went back to Holly's house to relax and have a late supper. She was relieved to see that Holly was recovering so quickly.

Recovering *physically*, anyway.

Alex knew that *emotionally* her friend was in for a long, slow, agonizing recovery.

And no matter what, Alex thought, Holly was going to be a changed person from now on. Losing a child under any circumstances was something that you never truly got over.

But it turned out to be just as stressful back at Holly's house. Alex was looking forward to being alone, without the TV news on or any other reminders of the tragedy that had happened. She had just settled down in the dining room to eat a light supper when two F.B.I. agents—a man and a woman—showed up at the door. They had been out to the house the day before and wanted to ask her a few follow-up questions.

Without inviting them in, Alex stood in the doorway and willingly answered their questions, but she couldn't really add anything to the statements she had already given. Although she tried to get some indication from the agents as to how the investigation was going, they had remained stereotypically "perfect" agents—tight-lipped, clipped, and emotionless. They didn't tell her a thing. The evening news had reported no leads in the case, but Alex knew that wasn't necessarily so. The feds often misled the media and fed it disinformation in order to follow their leads without interference and to avoid alerting the suspects.

Of course, Alex was sure that Nick was close to finding the people who had planned the bombing. Although she knew Nick could take care of himself, she couldn't stop worrying about his safety.

The agents left after less than five minutes. Alex finished her meal standing at the kitchen counter. She considered lying down for a nap, but then decided instead to head back to the hospital. Derek had told her that, at least until he had investigated his "Hidden Saint" angle a bit more, it was crucial for her to stay with Holly as much as possible.

On the drive back to the hospital, Alex thought about what had been uppermost in her mind all day. She mentally rehearsed what she planned to say to Holly because she couldn't stop thinking about what Holly had told her, about the dreams—or hallucinations—she'd had about her dead son.

It bothered her that, at least according to Holly, Evan was filled with such a terrible rage and hatred for the person who had killed him—this man named Hunter.

Throughout her years of working with the Legacy, Alex had seen and experienced many strange phenomena, so she didn't automatically discard the possibility that Evan's soul—caught in the limbo between life and death—could be angry at having his life terminated so abruptly. That could be why he was appearing to his mother and urging her to hurt the people who had hurt him.

It was entirely possible.

But it didn't make sense.

Why or how could a small child like Evan have such venomous hatred festering in his soul?

Holly had raised Evan to be a loving, caring child, and in the little time Alex had spent with them, that's all she had ever seen—a ten-year-old boy who was the product of a loving, nurturing upbringing. Alex considered herself to be extremely intuitive, and in all of her interactions with Evan, she had never sensed even the slightest bit of hostility or evil inside Evan.

So why was he appearing to his mother now, demanding vengeance?

Is that what sudden death did to people?

Could the remorse of losing their life fill someone— even an innocent child—with such bitter spite?

Alex didn't think so, and the more she thought about it, the more convinced she became that the figure Holly had encountered might not even be Evan, just as she doubted the figure she had seen at Holly's house had really been Evan.

Perhaps Holly's terrible dreams were just that—terrible dreams that revealed more about Holly than they did about Evan's spiritual state of being in the afterlife.

That thought bothered Alex even more deeply because of what it might reveal about her friend.

As long as Alex had known Holly, and as close as they had been as friends, she now began to wonder if she really knew who Holly Brown was.

It was unsettling to consider that, beneath the surface, maybe Holly wasn't the loving, caring person she seemed to be. Perhaps it was all pretense, and everything Holly did—all the work for international children's relief, even founding the Roots and Branches organization—was a cover for a terrible, raging darkness in her soul.

Alex was so lost in thought that she almost missed the exit for the hospital. When she saw it up ahead, she considered—for just an instant—going right past it and just driving for a while.

She could use a little more time alone to consider what she was going to say to Holly.

There was so much she could and maybe should say, and she was afraid that something she might say would do permanent damage to their friendship.

There was no doubt about it, Alex thought grimly, the pressure was starting to get to her.

The burden of waiting and watching with Holly was compounded by the stress of being interviewed by law enforcement agencies every spare minute and wondering when and if Derek or Rachel were going to come East to be with her.

But as she approached the exit, Alex snapped on her turn signal and slowed down for the turn.

No matter how stressful it was, no matter how bad things got, she knew that she had to be there for Holly. She trusted and loved Holly as one of her closest, dearest friends. If she had something to say to her, she didn't need to rehearse it. No matter how painful anything she had to say might be, Holly would know that Alex had nothing but her well-being at heart.

But that didn't make it any easier for Alex to face some of the thoughts she was having.

The closer she got to the hospital, the more nervous she became. Her face was slick with sweat, and she was gripping the steering wheel so tightly it hurt her hands as she slowed down and pulled into the hospital parking lot. She was trembling as she got out of her car, locked the doors, and went inside the hospital. Her throat felt dry and raw as she rode the elevator up to the third floor.

The slick coil of tension inside her only got worse when she saw a staff doctor standing in the corridor outside of Holly's room. The doctor was talking to one of the shift nurses, who looked up as Alex approached.

"Ahh, here she comes now," the nurse said, and the doctor turned to look at Alex.

"What's going on?" Alex asked, a slight tremor in her voice betraying her hot rush of nervousness. She saw the doctor's name—Dr. Alfred Hardy—on the name badge above the pen-filled breast pocket of his blue hospital shirt.

"Well, Ms. Moreau," Doctor Hardy said, "it seems as though your friend has decided to take off."

"What?" Alex shouted.

A jolt of panic went through her as she pushed past them and looked into Holly's room.

It was empty.

The sheets were hanging over the side of the bed and draped onto the floor. The monitors had been turned off, and Holly's hospital gown and paper slippers were in a rumpled bunch on the floor.

"Does anyone know—" Alex began, but Dr. Hardy cut her short.

"No one saw her leave," he said, sounding a bit edgy. "We're just now trying to determine exactly when she left."

"I just started my shift at eight o'clock," the nurse said. "Helen, the floor nurse on duty before me, says she checked in on her just before I got here, and Ms. Brown was sleeping soundly at that time."

"I left around seven-thirty," Alex said, shaking her head and trying to remember exactly what they had said when she was leaving. "She didn't mention that she was feeling tired. In fact, I remember thinking that she seemed fairly rested and alert."

The lighting in the hallway seemed unusually bright. It brought out sharp details that Alex had never noticed before, and she was filled with an unnerving sense of unreality. She had to convince herself that this wasn't all a bad dream; that this was really happening.

"I have no idea how she got past us," the nurse said, shaking her head in wonderment. "There's been someone sitting right there at the nurses' station since four o'clock.''

"She couldn't have gotten very far on foot, could she?" Alex said. "Have you checked the area?"

Both she and the doctor shook their heads, no.

"We just now discovered that she was missing," Doctor Hardy said. "We know that she changed into her street clothes before she left. She could have taken off in any direction."

Alex shook her head in disbelief, still trying to absorb this new development. What she didn't like was the feeling that Holly had planned all of this. As she recalled, it had been Holly who had told her that she looked exhausted and had suggested that she go back to the house to rest.

"So she's had close to an hour lead," Alex said after checking her wristwatch.

She still couldn't believe that Holly had taken off like this, but she wasn't quite prepared to suggest that something worse might have happened.

Not yet, anyway.

"She couldn't have gotten very far in that time," she said. "Do you think she'd go back to her house first?"

"Your guess is as good as mine," Dr. Hardy said. "Of course, she's here voluntarily and is free to leave whenever she wants, but for insurance and liability purposes, it's preferable for a patient to be formally discharged."

"I understand," Alex said.

She cocked an eyebrow at him, and couldn't help but wonder if he knew something he wasn't telling her.

"Do you have any idea where she might be headed other than home?" the nurse asked.

Alex bit her lower lip and shook her head. She didn't like the way the nurse and the doctor were looking at her, as though they were positive she knew exactly when and where Holly had gone, and that maybe she had even helped her leave.

But why think in such paranoid terms? Alex wondered. Holly didn't have to *escape* from the hospital. Like the

113

doctor said, she was a patient here, not a prisoner.

And then a thought hit Alex so hard she let out a gasp. Feeling weak in the knees, she had to take a few steps back and lean against the wall for support.

She's going after Hunter!

It was so obvious, Alex was amazed that she hadn't thought of it the instant she heard that Holly was missing.

That's why she had shown so much interest in what Nick was doing, where he was going. She was going to try to find Hunter—

And kill him!

Just like her dead son wanted her to.

"Are you all right?" Dr. Hardy asked.

He stepped forward and grasped Alex by the upper arm. She could feel the strength of his grip as she closed her eyes and nodded.

"Yeah," she whispered, "I'm just . . . the last couple of days have been really terrible. And I-I'm worried about my friend."

"Don't worry. I'm sure she'll show up," Dr. Hardy said.

"Umm—I sure hope so," Alex said, but she didn't dare say out loud what she was thinking.

What she had been about to say was, *I hope I can find her before she finds the man who killed her son!*

The two men started toward Nick's hiding place and fanned out, one sweeping to the left, the other to the right to encircle him. In spite of their size, they moved with amazing speed and confidence, as if they could see exactly where he was hiding.

Nick looked around, his grip tightening on his pistol as he quickly assessed the situation and calculated his odds.

Basically, he had three options: He could either evade these men, fight them, or give himself up.

Trying to escape wasn't a very likely option.

It was as much intuition as objective knowledge, but

Nick was certain that these men would be able to catch him. They obviously knew the area and terrain better than he did, and they moved through the woods with an uncanny ease and stealth, like trained hunters.

Nick still couldn't figure out how Hunter had known he was out there in the first place. It was almost as if the man could see in the dark as easily as he could in the daylight. So with Hunter directing them, his two bodyguards would no doubt run him down and kill him before he got very far.

Fighting also seemed to be out of the question.

Hunter's goons were armed with automatic rifles, and both of them looked to be in peak physical condition. With the light from the compound behind them, their shadows stretched out over the uneven terrain, looking menacingly huge. Nick had a fleeting impression that their eyes gleamed with a green, reflective shine, like jungle cats.

They already knew where he was, and they were closing fast.

Nick knew they'd rip him to pieces with gunfire before he got off half a dozen shots. The cover here was too thin, and the terrain and darkness only made it worse. Also, fighting with the light from the compound shining in his face, not behind him, only gave his enemies another added advantage.

So as much as he didn't like it, it looked as though he was going to have to give himself up and hope he could talk his way into Hunter's confidence.

Nick dropped his pistol to the ground and, standing up slowly, raised his hands high above his head.

"Don't shoot," he called out.

Without looking down, he kicked some dead leaves onto the pistol to cover it. Having a gun hidden out here might come in handy later, he thought, if he was forced to make a run for it.

The two men stopped a short distance away. Nick heard

the distinctive click of their rifles as they each chambered a round.

"I don't want any trouble," Nick said.

He knew he couldn't let these men or Hunter see even a shred of hesitance or nervousness in him. Like savage animals, if they knew he was weak or afraid, they'd swoop in for the kill.

"I want to talk to your commander . . . to Hunter," Nick called out.

"We'll do the talking around here," one of the men said. His voice wasn't much more than a low, animal-like growl.

"Bring him to me," Hunter commanded.

The two guards moved closer, stepping behind Nick.

"Move," one of them snarled, and the butt end of his rifle slammed hard into Nick's back, just above the left kidney.

The pain and the force of the blow staggered Nick. He had to take a few quick steps forward to keep from falling face-first onto the ground. One of the men stepped up behind him and, after quickly patting him down, relieved him of the hunting knife that hung in the sheath on his hip.

"What do you intend to do with this little toothpick?" the man said, and his companion chuckled softly as the man touched the back of Nick's neck with the sharp tip.

"Get the pistol he dropped onto the ground, too," Hunter called out.

Once again, Nick was amazed by the man's uncanny perception.

With the guards pushing and jabbing at him with the muzzles of their rifles, Nick made his way out of the brush and into the compound. As he approached Hunter, he fastened his gaze on the man, quickly running through what he should say.

Nick recognized Hunter from the short time they had been together in training many years before, but the man seemed to have changed in subtle, yet important, ways.

Although not physically large, Hunter seemed to be much bigger than Nick recalled. With the backdrop of the night behind him, he had an imposing physical presence that made Nick feel small and weak.

"So do you mind telling me what you're doing out here at this time of night, Boyle?" Hunter snapped.

His voice had a deep resonance that was oddly both pleasing and vaguely disturbing.

"I came out to see what kind of operation you have going on out here," Nick replied evenly. "I was thinking of maybe joining up."

"Oh, you were, were you?" Hunter said with a chuckle.

His eyebrows lowered, dark and dangerous. No matter what the angle of light, Hunter's face seemed to be cast in perpetual shadow, but Nick could see that he was smiling a thin, feral grin.

Nick nodded, knowing it was best to say as little as possible. Like the guard had said, let *them* ask the questions.

"Well, you found us," Hunter said, clapping his hands together and rubbing them vigorously. He glanced back and forth between Nick and his bodyguards, who were still standing behind Nick with the tips of their weapons digging into his back.

"You penetrated our defenses. What do you think we should do about it?"

Without missing a beat, Nick replied, "Well, I think you should tell Mutt and Jeff here to put their weapons away, and then I think we should sit down and talk."

"Talk? About what? About old times?" Hunter said with a humorless laugh. When he smiled, his wide teeth gleamed like pearls in the moonlight.

"No," Nick said quickly. "About the future."

"Oh, I see. The future," Hunter said.

He laughed again softly, and the sound of his laughter gave Nick a chill as it echoed in the darkness that surrounded them.

"And what is it about the future that you'd want to discuss with me?"

Caught off-guard by the question, Nick had to take a moment to think. Then he said, "What we're going to do about it."

"Oh, I see . . . I see. What we're going to do about it," Hunter replied coolly. He cupped his chin in his hand and nodded deeply. "Well, I'm not sure there's any point in doing that."

Nick was suddenly positive now that he should have chosen either option one or two.

"You see, I already know the future."

Hunter's voice had a hollow, almost metallic ring to it that Nick found unsettling. He was sounding like a crazed fanatic who thought he knew the truth.

"I know who you are, and I know why you're here," Hunter said. "I can also tell you that you won't succeed in stopping me. In fact, I can safely predict that, come morning, you won't even be breathing."

He snapped his fingers once. The sound was like a gun going off close to his head, and Nick couldn't help but flinch.

"Take him to the stockade," Hunter said to his goons.

"Hey! Wait a minute!" Nick said. "You don't understa—"

Before he could finish, one of the guard's rifle butts slammed hard into the back of Nick's head. An explosion of white light filled his vision as he dropped down to his knees, fighting hard to retain consciousness.

"Oh, but I do understand," Hunter said smoothly.

To Nick's hearing, his voice had now taken on an even stranger quality. It rose and swelled with an odd distortion that sounded electronically produced.

"It's you who doesn't understand," Hunter continued. "Sadly, however, you won't be alive long enough to figure it out. But you did try. I'll grant you that."

Hunter laughed again, but there wasn't a trace of humor

in the sound. Then he said to the guards, "Go on. Get him out of here."

The two men grabbed Nick roughly under the arms and started dragging him toward the small, barred building at the far end of the compound. Nick's body felt light, like a child's. He wanted to resist, but he was too weakened by the blow to the head. It was hard enough just to stay conscious.

Once they arrived at the stockade, one of the men held the door open as the other raised him from the ground just high enough to propel him forward into the waiting darkness.

Nick stumbled forward, unable to control his fall until he slammed into the opposite wall and then dropped, hard, onto the frozen ground. He was about to cry out in protest, but the heavy door slammed shut behind him, and he was plunged into total, silent darkness.

TWELVE

This is much too easy, Holly thought.

But with Evan seemingly close beside her whispering into her ear and telling her what to do, she passed like a ghost through the hospital.

No one saw or recognized her or, if they did, no one spoke to her or tried to stop her.

Wearing the street clothes Alex had brought in for her, Holly walked past the nurses' station, down the corridor, and into the elevator, which she took to the first floor. Her stomach was twisted up with tension, but she walked out the front door just as bold as could be.

As soon as she stepped out into the night, she was grateful that she had her winter coat. The frigid November air froze her throat and lungs. She breathed a sigh of relief that sent out puffy clouds of steam that were whisked away on the wind.

Moving furtively and feeling all the time as though unseen eyes were watching her, she started down the road toward the distant, brightly lit corner, where she could see a gas station and convenience store. The night was filled with an eerie sense of unreality as she walked along the littered roadside, moving as if in a dream.

But she knew this was no dream.

There were too many sensory clues to remind her that she was awake. Cars zipped past her, the wind and exhaust of their passing blowing into her face and raising her hair. Her feet crunched on the frozen gravel and turf of the roadside. She had to step gingerly to avoid the broken bottles and other trash that drivers had carelessly thrown away.

At the corner store, she asked for change and used the phone booth to call for a taxi. Twenty minutes later, a battered yellow cab pulled up, and she got in.

"Where yah headed?" the cabby asked.

He was chewing a wad of gum or chewing tobacco that made him difficult to understand. Fortunately, after Holly told him she was going to Pembroke, he said little else to her.

Her first impulse was to go straight home. She figured she could get her car and anything else she might need before heading out to do what she planned to do . . . to do what Evan wanted her to do.

On second thought, however, she decided that it would be much too risky to go home.

Alex might still be at the house, and as soon as she and the hospital staff realized that she'd taken off, they'd no doubt be looking for her. And if Alex figured out her plan to kill Hunter, she might get the police involved as well.

She couldn't take any chances of being found.

Not yet, anyway.

Besides, there wasn't anything at home that she *really* needed for what she was going to do tonight.

The most important item was a gun, and she didn't have one.

Everything else she might need, she could buy on the way as long as Evan kept whispering to her, telling her what to do.

Holly gave the cabbie an address in Duxbury. It was the home of Ted and Sylvia Martin, friends of hers who she knew were vacationing in Aspen for the Thanksgiving weekend. Ted was an avid hunter, so Holly knew there were plenty of guns in the house. In the past, when the Martins had gone away on vacation, Holly would go over to water their plants, pick up their mail, feed their fish, and keep an eye on things. She knew where the house key was hidden, where Ted kept the guns, and where to find the car keys.

She smiled to herself as the cab zipped silently through the night. The heater was on high, and before long she was starting to feel sleepy. The cabbie had the radio tuned to a classic rock station that played several Beatles tunes in a row. She closed her eyes and leaned her head back against the seat, enjoying ''Strawberry Fields Forever.''

Yeah, she thought, smirking to herself, *this is almost too easy.*

Lulled by the motion of the cab, she started to drift off to sleep. She didn't open her eyes again until she felt the cab lurch to a stop. Looking out the window, she was momentarily confused as to where she was.

Then she remembered.

She shifted forward in the seat and read the fare on the meter. She reached into her purse and took the money from her wallet.

The cabbie said something that sounded like an offer to wait until she got into the house, but Holly told him no, thanks, as she handed him two twenties, opened the door, and stepped out into the night. The sudden cold, after the warmth of the cab, made her shiver wildly.

''Keep the change,'' she said before slamming the door shut.

She pulled her collar up tightly around her neck and waited on the curb until the car drove away. She let out a faint sigh of relief when its taillights disappeared around a curve in the road a short distance away.

When she turned and looked at the Martins' house, Holly felt a sudden rush of nervous anticipation.

She couldn't believe that she was actually thinking about breaking into her friends' house and stealing a gun, but the wind blowing in her ear—or was it Evan, whispering softly to her?—told her that everything would be all right as long as neither Alex nor the police found her before she did what she had to do.

The night was eerily quiet. Off in the distance, she heard a dog barking, but that was all. After casting a furtive glance up and down the street to make sure no neighbors were watching, she made her way around to the back of the house.

On the slate patio beside the cast-iron picnic table and chairs was a large flowerpot, under which was the key to the sliding glass door. The clay pot made a loud grinding sound as Holly pushed with all her strength and, finally, managed to lift and roll it just enough to expose the key. It was covered with dirt and cobwebs, which she brushed off on her coat sleeve.

The key was cold to the touch and sent a numbing chill up her arm all the way to her elbow as she considered what she was doing.

This is absolutely crazy, she thought. *I could go to jail if I get caught doing this.*

But after only a brief hesitation, she slid the key into the door lock and turned it.

The lock clicked, and a blast of warmth hit her in the face as she slid the door open just enough to step inside. As soon as she was in, she closed the door, snapped on a light, and went to disarm the security alarm.

She had only a minute to do that. A mild rush of panic ran through her when she wondered if Ted might have changed the code, but she tapped in the numbers she had used before, and was relieved to see that the alarm was deactivated.

"All too easy," she whispered out loud, thinking for an instant that it was Evan's voice, not her own that she heard.

Smiling, she walked boldly from the kitchen into the living room. Off the living room was the small, paneled den where Ted kept his rifles and guns. Holly switched on the light in the den. Her smile widened as she looked at the confusing array of weapons in their locked cabinets.

A small part of her mind nagged her about what she was doing. She had never had much use for guns. In fact, over the years, because of her work with children's advocacy groups working to ban the use of land mines, she had done a bit more than tease Ted about owning guns.

But—at least tonight—she was glad that Ted was a gun devotee, and that he and Sylvia were out of town.

Of course, looking at the armament, Holly had no idea which gun to select. She wandered from cabinet to cabinet, carefully studying each weapon as if—somehow—she would know intuitively which one to take.

They all looked scary to her, and she wasn't at all confident that she would even know how to use a gun once she picked one—especially if, as Evan kept whispering to her, she was going to have to go to a town named Trafton, New Hampshire, find a man she had never met before, and kill him.

"Who the fuck're you?"

The voice, coming so suddenly out of the darkness, startled Nick as he lay sprawled on the ground where he had fallen. He was trying to get his bearings and not doing so well. The pain in the back of his head was intense.

The small room was pitch black, and the voice seemed to be all around him.

"My . . . my name's Nick. Who are you?"

This was followed by a short silence, just long enough for Nick to start thinking that maybe he had imagined hearing the voice.

Then it came again.

"You ain't a member of the militia. What the fuck're you doing here?"

Nick didn't answer immediately. He wanted to think carefully about how much he would reveal to this unseen person. For all he knew, this might be one of Hunter's men, set up to entrap him into revealing his real reason for coming out to the compound.

"I've known Hunter for years," Nick finally said, trying to sound casual about it. "I thought I'd stop by and see what he was up to these days, and this is what I get."

The only response was a faint, sniffing chortle.

"So tell me who you are," Nick said, once the laughter stopped. "Who are you? Why are you in here?"

"What the fuck's it to you? We're both gonna die, anyway."

"I don't know about that," Nick said with a shrug, knowing that the motion was wasted in the darkness. "But we're in this together, so we might as well know a little something about each other."

"I already know something about you," the man said.

Now that he was a little more oriented, Nick realized that the man was sitting on the floor in the far corner, over to his left.

"Yeah? What's that?"

"Yesterday morning," the man said. "Did you see the sunrise?"

Confused for a moment, Nick said, "You know, as a matter of fact I did."

"Well, then—"

The man's rough laughter filled the darkness again, sounding much more menacing this time.

"I hope to Christ you enjoyed it, 'cause it was the last sunrise you're ever gonna see."

"Is that a fact?" Nick said calmly.

He guessed by the man's voice and attitude that he, like Nick, was Hunter's prisoner; but he still wasn't ready to reveal any more than he had to . . . just in case.

"My name's Nick . . . Nick Boyle. I'd shake your hand, but I can't see where you are in the dark."

"I'm Frank McCullough. And I'd shake your hand, too, but you see—"

The loud sound of rattling chains filled the darkness.

"I'm a bit tied up at the moment."

"They've got you chained in here?" Nick said.

"Yeah, and if there was another set of manacles in here, you'd be locked up beside me."

"Lucky me," Nick said. "So why are you here? What'd you do wrong?"

Again, McCullough sniffed with laughter that this time ended in a raw rumbling in his throat as he hawked up some mucus and spit.

"I didn't do anything wrong," McCullough said, "except maybe question a decision my commanding officer made."

"You mean Hunter?"

"Yeah, I mean Hunter," McCullough said with a growl, and then he spit again as if the name was a bad taste in his mouth that he could get rid of. "That arrogant, no good son of a bitch!"

Nick realized that, if McCullough was chained up in here, then he couldn't be a plant for Hunter. There wouldn't have been time from when Nick was first spotted until he gave himself up for this to be set up. On the spot, he decided that if McCullough was right—that Hunter intended to kill them both before morning—then they'd better start thinking and working together to get out.

"How long have you been in here?" Nick asked.

Even though he had been in the small building for a while now, and his eyes should have adjusted, he still couldn't see anything except a solid wall of darkness. The prison had obviously been carefully constructed to keep out any hint of light, at least at night. Maybe in the daytime some stray rays of sunlight would find their way in, but if

126

McCullough was right, they'd both be dead by then, anyway.

"About a day or so," McCullough replied. "Christ, I can't tell. It's hard to keep track of time in the darkness like this, you know?"

Nick grunted his agreement.

"Well," he said, "first things first. Let's get those chains off you."

"You think you can do that?" McCullough said, and for the first time, Nick noticed at least a trace of hope in the man's voice.

Nick took off his belt and, feeling his way over to McCullough in the dark, felt around until he found one of the iron cuffs on the man's hand. They didn't appear to be overly sophisticated handcuffs.

Using the narrow prong of his belt buckle as a lock pick, Nick fiddled around until he felt something click inside the cuff, and the cuff opened up and fell away.

"Oh, man. Thanks a million," McCullough said with genuine gratitude in his voice.

Nick heard a flapping sound as he shook his hand to restore the circulation. He didn't say a word as he set to work on the other handcuff and, after a bit of effort, managed to spring that lock, as well.

McCullough heaved a deep sigh of relief as he stood up and, clasping Nick's hand, shook it vigorously.

"I don't know how to thank you, man," he said. "We may not make it out of this shit-hole alive, but at least I won't be bound up like a pig, waitin' to die."

"We're not going to die," Nick said, keeping his voice low and steady. "The first thing we've got to do is check every inch of this place to see if we can find some weakness in it."

"You're wasting your time there," McCullough said.

Once again the tone of resignation tinged his voice.

"You won't find anything. I helped build this place. There's three or four feet of concrete below us, and the walls are lined with inch-thick blasting net. There are bars over the window, and the door is made with three-inch-thick oak boards. It'd take a couple of sticks of dynamite to crack this place open.''

"There's gotta be a way," Nick said, still feeling around the walls in the dark. He wondered why Hunter hadn't had him handcuffed, too. He hoped Hunter wouldn't think of it and return . . . at least not until he'd made a plan of escape. Try as he might, though, he couldn't find even the slightest weakness in the walls to exploit.

"I'm tellin' yah, man, you're wasting your time," McCullough said. "The best we can hope for is, when— not if—they come for us, we can get the drop on them. Of course, what they'll probably do is just leave us here to starve to death. From what I heard, they're clearing out of here.''

"You mean they're abandoning the compound?"

"That's the rumor," McCullough replied. "After what we did in Plymouth on Thursday—"

"So it *was* Hunter. You were involved with the bombing at Plymouth Rock?"

"Yeah, maybe just a little," McCullough said. "But I didn't want anything to do with that.''

Nick could hear the agitated edge in the man's voice, which only reinforced his opinion that he had a true ally here.

"And that's what you questioned him on?" he said, "whether or not the militia should be doing operations like that?''

"Who are you, Sherlock fucking Holmes?" McCullough replied bitterly. Then, after a short pause, he said, "Yeah. I challenged him on that. I told him it was counterproductive to our cause to injure civilians, but he maintained—still maintains—that civilian deaths and injuries are an inevitable result of war.''

"Sometimes, maybe," Nick said. "So you're at war with the United States?"

"Not against the *people* of the United States. Just the damned government."

Again, Nick heard the agitated edge in McCullough's voice and he realized that, although he felt betrayed by his leader, McCullough was still invested in his cause. In the long run, that could prove a liability and make him dangerous. Their primary concern right now should be to get out of this prison. Nick was about to say that when, through the thick walls, he heard the muffled sound of voices as someone approached the stockade. He couldn't make out what they were saying, but then a fist pounded heavily on the door.

"Hey! You fellas nice and comfy in there?"

"That's Morgan," McCullough whispered. "A really twisted son of a bitch. If he's out there, his buddy Williams is there, too."

Nick didn't say a word.

He was hoping that—maybe—Morgan would open the door, and he and McCullough could fight it out with them.

"Weatherman says tonight's gonna get a bit chilly," Morgan called out. "Might even snow 'fore morning. We was thinking maybe you fellas could use a little extra heat."

While Morgan was saying this, Nick heard another sound that came faintly through the thick walls.

At first he wasn't exactly sure what it was—a splashing sound and scuffing footsteps as someone walked around the outside perimeter of the stockade. As soon as the stinging odor of gasoline fumes hit his nose, Nick knew what they intended to do.

Morgan was going to set the stockade on fire with them in it.

"Have a toasty little evenin'," Morgan called out, followed by a laugh that was entirely without humor.

Then Nick heard a faint, metallic click that sounded like a Zippo lighter being opened. This was followed by a rough scratching sound as Morgan or his accomplice struck the flame.

Nick's question about whether or not any light could get into the building was soon answered when he saw a slim, orange glow of flames flicker beneath the edge of the heavy oak door.

"See you in hell," Morgan shouted, and again he followed it with a gale of laughter as he and his accomplice walked away from the burning building.

THIRTEEN

"She's heading north on Route 16," Hunter said softly, almost dreamily. "She just passed through the Dover toll booth and should arrive in Trafton within the hour."

Morgan, who was driving Hunter's jet black Lincoln Continental, glanced into the rearview mirror. All he could see was a faint silhouette—dark black outlined against the black of the tinted windows. For just an instant, inside that dark silhouette, he thought he saw two small, pulsating points of amber light. It spooked him, the way Hunter's eyes sometimes seemed to collect whatever light there was in the night and reflect it back.

Smiling his approval and secretly amazed at his commander's uncanny way of knowing things, Morgan nodded slightly.

He didn't dare say what he was really thinking.

Over the years, ever since joining the First Step militia, he'd found that it was dangerous—possibly even worse than deadly—to question anything Hunter said or did.

Look at what had happened to McCullough.

He'd been thrown into the stockade and was probably even now burning to a crisp simply because he had the audacity to question the actions the First Step had taken at Plymouth Rock.

Repressing a shiver, Morgan shook his shoulders and settled back in the seat, letting his hands play lightly with the steering wheel. The car zipped silently through the cold night, weaving effortlessly along the narrow turns of the twisting road almost as if driving itself.

It wasn't his job to think, Morgan told himself.

All he had to do was drive and do whatever his commander told him to do.

No questions asked.

"I know what you're thinking."

Hunter's voice issued from out of the darkness in the backseat like the low growl of a hungry predator.

Morgan glanced over at Williams, who was in the passenger's seat beside him. He urgently hoped that Hunter was talking to Williams, not him.

"Morgan . . . ?"

When Hunter said Morgan's name, it seemed to ride on a gentle breeze that carried with it the rotting stench of death.

"Ye-yes, sir," Morgan replied.

His grip on the steering wheel tightened. He tried to make his mind go blank as he gazed straight ahead at the twin pools of light from the headlights on the road. The effect was mesmerizing.

"I know you're thinking that, perhaps, I made a little mistake," Hunter said. "You're thinking that maybe we shouldn't have left the compound with the possibility that those two men might escape before the building burned them alive."

"I—ahh, well, I just don't like leaving things to chance, is all," Morgan stammered, trying hard to fight the tremor in his voice but, ultimately, unable hide it.

He glanced again into the rearview mirror and saw that

132

Hunter's eyes were indeed glowing like orange coals that were being fanned by the wind and were about to burst into flame.

"Oh, but you see," Hunter said smoothly, "that's where you're wrong."

He hesitated and snickered softly as if in response to a private joke.

"Because no matter how well you plan anything, even if you plan it down to the last, tiniest detail, things can always be altered by chance. Chance is the one random factor in this boringly mundane universe that, otherwise, simply ticks along with the dull stupidity and precision of clockwork."

"Well, a bullet in the back of the head certainly would eliminate any chance of them getting out of there."

The words were out of Morgan's mouth before he could stop them.

He braced himself, waiting for something terrible to happen. The pleasant hum of the car's engine jacked up his nerves until it sounded like a whirring dentist's drill inside his head. A cold sweat broke out on his forehead, and his heart did a couple of crazy little skipping beats.

"True . . . true," Hunter said with a soft sigh.

The pleasant, genial tone in his voice allowed Morgan to relax, at least a little bit.

They drove on for a while in silence, but all the time, Morgan was aware that his shoulders were hunched up, and every muscle in his body was tensed. He was sure that he could feel Hunter's gaze boring into the back of his head like a laser beam.

"The thing of it is," Hunter finally said, his voice breaking through the silence like claws savagely ripping apart the night, "there are other, more important things that I need to attend to."

"Oh, I'm sure there are," Morgan said. "I never questioned that."

Once again, he silently cursed himself for continuing the

conversation. What he should do, he told himself, is just keep his goddamned mouth shut and let Hunter do all the thinking and talking.

"This Holly Brown . . . she's nothing . . . nothing whatsoever to me, really," Hunter said. His voice had taken on a more thoughtful tone, as if he was thinking out loud as much as talking to Morgan and Williams.

"But she has friends . . . some very powerful friends."

"Like that guy we caught snooping around the compound?" Williams said.

Morgan was grateful that his partner had spoken up, if only to take Hunter's attention off him.

"Yes. He's one of them," Hunter said.

"He didn't seem like much to me," Williams said. "It wasn't all that hard to catch him."

"True, but he's a member of an organization that I wouldn't mind seeing destroyed entirely."

"Yeah? What's that?" Williams asked. "Another militia group?"

As far as Morgan could tell, Williams wasn't picking up on any of the tension he was feeling, so he allowed himself to relax just a bit more. Hunter wasn't going to do anything to either one of them.

"It's an organization called the Legacy," Hunter replied.

When he said the name, it seemed as though his voice suddenly lowered and resonated with a dangerous hollow tone. Even Williams seemed to pick up on it this time. He glanced over his shoulder into the backseat.

"If things go according to plan, Holly Brown will arrive at the compound before long. Once there, she will either discover two charred corpses . . . or else she'll find two living men . . . one of whom will look surprisingly like me, and whom she will shoot and kill with the shotgun she has in her possession. If, by chance, one of them happens to kill her . . . ? Why, then, I lose the chance for a small victory. But there are other, larger battles to fight."

He took a deep breath and let it out slowly.

"In the meantime, however, we have to go to Holly Brown's home in Massachusetts and deal with her friend who's staying there."

"Is she a member of this Legacy, too?" Williams asked.

"Yes, she's a member . . . and the next rung up on the ladder which will eventually bring me to the head of the Legacy. A man you've never heard of before, but whose demise is earnestly anticipated and will be greatly celebrated . . . A man named Derek Rayne."

Morgan licked his lips nervously and started to say something but checked himself. Instead, he simply stared straight ahead at the winding road, trying hard not to think about anything.

The headlights seemed small and feeble in the dense night. The darkness that lined both sides of the road pressed in against the car. The sky above the fringe of the forest was overcast, and Morgan could see no hint of starlight.

Worse than that, Morgan felt a cold emptiness emanating from the backseat. It washed over him like the frozen vacuum of outer space. He could feel it pulling him, tugging at him, threatening to suck him into it.

"But there—there's always chance, isn't there?" he said, cursing himself for a fool for saying anything.

"Of course there is," Hunter replied with a menacing resonance in his voice. "That's what gives existence its edge . . . knowing that there are forces and powers beyond your control with which you have to contend and, ultimately, master and control."

Morgan bit down hard on his lower lip before he could say aloud what he had been thinking—

Master and control . . . or else be destroyed.

He took a shuddering breath.

No! Just drive! he told himself, forcing himself to relax the tense grip he had on the steering wheel and settle back in the seat.

The winding road unspooled in front of the car like a

silver ribbon in the night. The wheels hummed with a pleasant, lulling sound. Morgan told himself that he would drive Hunter to wherever he wanted to go, and he would do whatever Hunter demanded.

That was his job . . . his duty.

"Pull over up ahead here," Hunter said, his voice low and soothing in the darkness. "Just around the corner."

Morgan experienced a sudden cold tightening in his groin as he nodded his agreement. His foot lifted off the gas pedal, and he allowed the car to lose momentum without touching the brake pedal.

The car swung easily around the turn.

Up ahead, Morgan saw a small clearing beneath a row of pine trees by the side of the road.

Now he tapped lightly on the brake, and the car silently glided to a stop beneath the trees that overhung the road.

Morgan jumped when he heard a *click* as Hunter undid his safety belt. Then the door snapped open, and Hunter said softly, "I want you to get out, Morgan. Williams . . . You wait here."

"Sir, yes, sir," Williams said, sounding like he didn't have the faintest clue as to what was going on.

The pit of Morgan's stomach was knotted like a fist as he opened the driver's door and stepped out into the night. A chilling gust of wind blew into his face, making him shiver after the warmth of the car. He shut the car door easily and watched as Hunter walked away from the car, heading into the dark woods that lined the road.

"Come over here with me," Hunter called out once he was entirely lost in the darkness. His voice seemed to come from close behind Morgan. Like a robot, Morgan started walking toward where he had last seen Hunter.

The inky shadows of the trees embraced him like a wash of ice-cold water. His breath caught painfully in his throat, and his heart was slamming like a jackhammer in his chest.

"I . . . What do you want, sir?" Morgan asked in a high, trembling voice.

"What do I want?" Hunter replied, his voice echoing oddly in the darkness.

Looking around, Morgan tried to see where Hunter was, but he was confused by the subtly shifting shadows. The night moved around him with hallucinatory slowness, twirling like a dark kaleidoscope.

"What I want is simple," Hunter said. "I want your obedience . . . your absolute, total obedience."

And then he laughed, the sound rising and falling in the night like a distant siren.

"You have that, sir," Morgan said, barely able to speak.

Shadows danced and loomed around him, and it seemed as though Hunter was in several places at once.

"No, I'm afraid that I don't," Hunter said, his voice still vibrating with a menacing resonance. "Not if you're going to question me and what I do."

"I . . . I wasn't questioning you," Morgan stammered. "I was ma-making convers-s-sation . . . We were just ta-ta-talking . . ."

"No. We weren't," Hunter said.

From out of the darkness, Morgan saw two burning points of light deep within the shadows. He knew they were Hunter's eyes, watching him, staring at him, their cold gaze plunging into him like a drill.

"You have your doubts," Hunter said, "and I can't afford that. I can't have anyone with me who has any doubts whatsoever. And now I'm afraid you'll have to pay for your lack of faith and confidence."

"P-p-pay . . . h-h-how?"

Morgan heard sniffing laughter from out the darkness, and the two glowing points of amber light pulsed and brightened.

"You'll pay with your soul, as all of us must."

The words hit Morgan like a sudden clap of thunder.

He tried to take a breath and found that he couldn't. The night pressed in against him, squeezing him, making him feel like he was several feet under water and descending.

"No . . . I," he gasped, but that was all.

The pressure surrounding him continued to build until he felt a hot straining in his chest. Intense pain spiked through every inch of his body. He saw tangled threads of red fire ripple like lightning across his arms, legs, and chest. In a shattering instant, he felt like he was falling . . . plunging backward, turning head over heels into a cold, silent, weightless vacuum.

The pain that gripped him continued to increase until he was sure that he couldn't bear it any longer, but it continued to grow even more intense, burning and freezing him at the same time.

He wanted to scream out loud but couldn't.

Sizzling pressure continued to build in the center of his chest until, suddenly, it burst out of him. A hot spray, which he distantly recognized as his own blood, exploded from his chest, and he pitched forward, falling face-first onto the ground.

His body started twitching with agonizing spasms.

He couldn't see or hear Hunter, but he knew that his commander was standing close by, watching him writhe in agony on the ground. He was vaguely aware that he should feel a lessening of the pain as he died—because that's what he was doing—dying.

But the pain seemed only to grow worse, ratcheting up past any possible level of tolerance. A rich, deep darkness embraced him as he thrashed about. He didn't so much see or hear Hunter leave as he felt a lessening of the man's presence.

Then, distantly, like he was listening to voices whisper in the next room, he heard Hunter say something.

The words came to Morgan, low and slurred, like a tape recording being played at the wrong speed.

". . . You're . . . going . . . to . . . have . . . to . . . do . . . the . . . driving . . . now . . . Williams . . ."

Morgan concentrated hard, trying to will himself to dissolve into the ever-deepening darkness where, he thought,

138

he would find refuge from the excruciating pain of dying.

But then, to his horror, he saw the rich, red glow of flickering flames rising up all around him, and he was falling . . . falling into those flames, each one of which was like a pitchfork that tossed him back and forth with ever-increasing pain and torment.

As Holly drove north into New Hampshire on Route 16, she made sure to keep an eye on the speedometer. The last thing she needed was to be pulled over for speeding in a stolen car and have the cops find the gun she had taken from the Martins' house.

The night was dark, with no moon. The road seemed curiously deserted.

Throughout most of the drive, she was absolutely convinced that Evan was sitting beside her in the passenger's seat. She couldn't stop imagining that she and her son had been talking and laughing together on the drive north, and now, because it was getting late, he was quiet, perhaps taking a nap.

But then, whenever the thought sank in that Evan was really dead, an immense sadness gripped her.

Tears filled her eyes, blurring her view of the road ahead. Every now and then, when she glanced over at the passenger's side to convince herself that Evan truly wasn't there, she would catch a fleeting glimpse of a shadowy, transparent figure beside her. And she would see Evan smile at her, his features underlit by the soft glow of the dashboard lights.

"You're my co-pilot, right?" she said out loud, fighting against the rising swells of emotion that swept through her.

She was convinced that, very faintly, just on the edge of hearing, she could hear Evan whisper to her, "You know I am, Mom."

Holly knew that she didn't have much time.

The Martins were due to return from Aspen in a day or two. They would, of course, report their car as stolen as soon as they realized it. Holly figured she had twenty-four hours—maybe a little bit more—to find Hunter's compound and—

"And kill him."

Evan's voice whispered in the dark, barely audible over the high whining of the tires on the road.

A small, rational corner of Holly's mind told her that this was insane, that it was foolish and dangerous to think that killing Hunter or anyone else was going to satisfy anything.

Her grief was and would remain deep.

It was something she would have to learn to live with, even knowing that it was a scar that would never heal or go away.

If she were caught, even for attempted murder, she might spend some time in jail. All the humanitarian work she had done with Roots and Branches would have been for naught.

"But he killed me," Evan whispered to her from out of the darkness. His voice cracked with emotion, bordering on tears.

"He killed me . . . so you have to kill him."

"Yes, I-I know, honey," Holly replied.

Fresh tears filled her eyes. When she rubbed them away with the back of her hand, it only made her eyes burn all the more.

"And I know where he is," Evan said softly. "I'll tell you where to go."

"I know."

"And once we get there," Evan said, his voice lowering until it sounded unnaturally deep, "you can't hesitate. You have to do it right away, or else he might kill you."

"I know . . . I know that," Holly said, nodding emphatically.

She gritted her teeth and gripped the steering wheel so tightly her hands ached; but she drove on, her gaze fixed steadily on the road ahead.

She drove north for another hour or so until, up ahead, she saw a small sign on the roadside that read:

WELCOME TO TRAFTON

Even then, the winding tension in her body didn't release. She knew that she couldn't rest—she would *never* rest until the man who had killed her son was dead!

FOURTEEN

Within seconds, the small room became an inferno as flames licked up the outside of the building and quickly sucked most of the available oxygen from the room. Heavy smoke laced with the sting of gasoline fumes started to fill the room, choking Nick and McCullough in the darkness.

"We're . . . dead meat," McCullough said between coughing fits. He was down on his knees with his hands covering his face, looking wild-eyed with fear.

But Nick wasn't about to give up until every possibility was exhausted.

Ignoring McCullough, he made his way over to the door. Sitting down so he'd be low where the smoke wasn't yet quite as thick, he positioned himself so he could bring his feet up against the hard oak boards. Gasping for breath, he leaned back on his haunches and then, grunting viciously, kicked the door as hard as he could with both feet.

It was like slamming into a stone wall.

The shock reverberated all the way up to his shoulders

and wrenched his neck, but he tried several more times, all with the same result.

Sweat streamed down his face, blinding him and turning the thin, flickering line of flame beneath the door into a hazy orange glow that rapidly intensified.

The air in the room was almost gone.

Nick felt as helpless as a drowning man as the heat toasted his throat and lungs with every breath he took. The cloying stench of burning hair and singed flesh filled his nostrils. He knew that he and McCullough had only a few seconds left to live if the door didn't give.

"Get over here and help me!" Nick called out, struggling to mask any fear he might be feeling. He was a trained soldier who had faced death—and some things much worse than death—many times before in his work with the Legacy.

If it was his time to go, then that was it . . . He would go without giving in to fear.

But not without a fight.

"Come on!" Nick said.

He was trying to shout, but his voice wheezed thinly as his lungs struggled to pull any trace of oxygen from the air.

He heard McCullough move over beside him. Together, they positioned themselves so they could both hit the door with maximum force.

"Okay, on three," Nick gasped. He shook his head hard, trying to clear it, and counted, "One . . . two . . . *three*."

In unison they kicked as hard as they could, connecting solidly with the door. Above the roaring sound of the flames, Nick heard the satisfying splintering of wood as the door started to give way.

But not enough.

"Again," Nick said, barely able to speak.

The skin on his face and arms was prickling painfully. His vision was swirling so badly he could hardly see which way he was facing.

"One . . . two . . . *three*!"

Nick let loose a savage yell that tore at his throat as he and McCullough slammed their feet against the door.

There was another, louder sound of splintering wood. Amazingly, the door shuddered and sagged open at the top, revealing a wall of orange flame that instantly filled the room with dazzling light.

Wave after wave of intense heat washed over them. Nick was weak and dizzy from lack of oxygen, and he knew that McCullough was no better off. He staggered to his feet and, grabbing McCullough by the arm, started dragging him toward the narrow opening.

"We've got . . . one . . . last . . . chance," he said, each word ripping like claws through his throat.

"No . . . I . . . can't," McCullough said weakly, then he made a funny gurgling sound in his throat and slumped face-first onto the floor.

"The hell you can't!" Nick shouted.

Shielding his face from the flames with one arm, he wrestled McCullough to his feet again and then, turning around quickly, ducked his head and rammed his shoulder hard into the door, like a football player making a desperate tackle.

The hinges snapped and pulled out of the burning wood, and the heavy door fell to the ground, raising a shower of sparks that corkscrewed up into the night sky and created a momentary gap in the wall of flames.

The blaze reached like a huge hand into the prison and swatted the two men, but first Nick, then McCullough, darted through the opening, diving over the fallen door and through the fire before plunging into the cool evening air.

Nick took a few staggering steps, just enough to get safely away from the blaze, and then collapsed onto the ground. Not far behind him, he heard McCullough grunt loudly as he, too, hit the ground. The intense heat of the fire singed Nick's back, but the cold air flooding into his lungs with every breath he took felt like powerful gushes of ice water. In spite of the pain, he rolled over onto his back and took several more deep, wrenching breaths.

The fire was roaring and crackling like a raging beast in the night as it quickly consumed the prison building. Weak and trembling inside, Nick got up and crawled farther away from the inferno, grateful to feel the gradual lessening of heat on his back.

"McCullough . . ." he called out, surprised to hear the ragged croak of his voice.

He looked around but didn't see him.

"Where are you?"

For a tense moment, there was no reply.

Then he heard a low, guttural groan and, turning, saw McCullough facedown in the dirt several yards away.

"Talk to me, man. Are you all right?" Nick called as he crawled on his hands and knees over to the fallen man.

McCullough's shirt and pants were black and smoldering. Tendrils of blue smoke rose from his back, and he was surrounded by the stench of singed flesh and hair.

Nick rolled McCullough over onto his back and quickly inspected him. The skin on his face and hands was charred, but not as badly as it might have been. Nick figured he must look about the same, although—at least for right now—he didn't feel any pain . . . only relief to be out of that building.

They had both been lucky.

"We're not dead yet," Nick said, and this time when he spoke, he thought his voice sounded a bit more normal.

McCullough looked at him with glazed, terror-filled eyes. Then, very slowly, the faintest trace of a smile curled his upper lip.

"You are one tough son of a bitch. You know that?" McCullough said. He followed this with a brief snort of laughter.

"Yeah . . . I guess so," Nick said.

McCullough continued to chuckle, and before long Nick also found the situation quite humorous. He sat back on his heels and started to laugh. Within seconds, both he and McCullough were swept away by gales of out-of-control laughter.

In the back of his mind, Nick knew that this was the result of feeling such immense relief after coming so close to dying; it was the aftereffect of the adrenaline rush that had given them the strength to kick open the stockade door and run through a wall of flame; but it was such a miracle to be alive that Nick quickly gave himself over to it.

As the stockade blazed away in the night, the two men sat side by side a safe distance away from it, both of them laughing like absolute lunatics. If anyone had seen them there with their faces and clothes blackened and smoldering, they might have mistaken them for cackling demons who had just escaped from hell.

"Rachel, can I speak with Derek?" Alex said.

Her voice was trembling with agitation, and she had the cell phone pressed tightly against her ear as she paced back and forth across the living room floor. All the lights were on in the house, but her gaze kept being drawn to the living room windows and the deep night beyond.

"He's not here right now," Rachel said. "He's in San Diego, investigating what happened to Fra Felipe."

Alex sighed heavily and shook her head with frustration. "I think I should drive up to New Hampshire and find her."

"No," Rachel said. "If Holly's in New Hampshire looking for Hunter, I'm sure Nick will find her and watch out for her. Derek thought it'd be best if you stayed at her house, in case she comes back home."

"I know, but I just don't like sitting around here. I'm worried about her, and I don't like feeling so useless. There's got to be *something* I can do."

"You've done plenty," Rachel said with a calm, reassuring tone in her voice "You've been there for Holly when she's really needed you."

"What if she's in trouble now?"

"You have to trust that she's all right," Rachel said. "She will be once Nick finds her."

"I know. I just hope that she doesn't find Hunter before Nick finds her," Alex said. She stared out at the night, wishing more than anything that she was already in her car and driving north.

"You know Holly better than I do," Rachel said. "Do you think she's capable of violence?"

"She told me that she'd seen her dead son, and that he told her—practically demanded—that she find Hunter and kill him to avenge his death. I just—"

A sudden prickling sensation gripped Alex. She shivered and glanced over her shoulder as though sensing that someone unseen was watching her. She almost dropped the phone and had to grip it hard against her ear as a deep tremor shook her body.

"What is it?" Rachel asked, her voice still measured and calm.

Alex could feel the blood draining from her face as she looked around the brightly lit living room. The darkness outside the large windows seemed suddenly threatening, fraught with danger. The feeling that she was being watched intensified.

"What if she really did see Evan?" Alex said in a low whisper. "I didn't really believe her when she told me. I said I thought she might have imagined it because of the grief she was feeling. But knowing Holly the way I do, I just can't believe that she would actually follow through on anything violent like that. She's spent her whole life, her entire inheritance and more, working to make the world better."

"We can't even be sure she's gone to New Hampshire to find this man Hunter," Rachel said calmly. "For all we know, she just needed time to be alone, to think things through and absorb her grief. She could be on a city bus or in a cab somewhere and show up at home any time."

"No, I don't think so," Alex said, shaking her head. "She would have contacted me by now if she was all right . . . but not if she was going to do something crazy like this."

"Well, as hard as it is for you, I think the best thing is for you to stay right where you are," Rachel said. "And I'm sure Derek would agree. If she shows up in New Hampshire, let Nick handle it. I've got a seat booked on the first flight out in the morning, so make sure you wait at Holly's house until I get there. And don't worry about Nick—"

Before Rachel could say any more, Alex's phone beeped.

"Hold on a second," she said. "That's my call waiting."

Without waiting for Rachel to reply, Alex hit the flash button.

"Hello?" she said, hearing the tension in her voice.

She held her breath as she waited for the person on the other end of the line to speak.

"Hey, Alex—"

It was Nick!

Alex was instantly flooded with relief even though she registered that his voice sounded oddly raspy and strained.

"—it's me."

"Nick! Where have you been? I was getting worried! Why didn't you call?" The words tumbled from Alex. But before Nick could say anything else, she said, "Wait a second. I have Rachel on hold."

Alex quickly switched back to Rachel and told her that Nick was on the other line and that he sounded all right and that she'd call her right back; then she flipped back to Nick.

"So what's going on up there? I was worried sick," Alex said, unable to hide the agitation in her voice.

Nick's speech was rough and halting, but—typically— in as few words as possible, he told her about finding the compound and everything that had happened after that.

He concluded by saying, "So I have no idea where Hunter might be headed. He left the compound and, for all I know, has disappeared."

"Are you coming back here tonight?" Alex asked.

"Yeah, I thought I would," Nick said. "McCullough says he wants to come along, too. Says that if we're going to try to find Hunter, he wants to be in on it."

"Do you think we can trust him?" Alex said. "How much does he know about the Legacy?"

"Nothing, as far as I can tell," Nick said, "but he might be useful to us. He might have some idea where Hunter would go."

"Okay, I guess," Alex replied. "But you're sure you're all right? You don't think you need to see a doctor first?"

"I'm fine, believe me," Nick said. "McCullough and I are at my Jeep right now. We're going back to the compound first to do a quick search. Then we'll head out. With luck, we should be in Pembroke in—I'd say four or five hours, but if it's going to be longer, I'll be sure to call you."

"Maybe you should notify the authorities first," Alex said. "If Hunter really was responsible for the bombing at Plymouth Rock—"

"Oh, he was. There's no doubt about it. McCullough will testify to that. First we have to find him, though. After we have a look around, I'll give the F.B.I. a call and get them out here. McCullough says there are still explosive materials in the workroom that they'll be able to match with the chemicals used in the Plymouth Rock bombing. They'll be able to connect Hunter directly to it."

"Well, you just be careful," Alex said. "Remember how that guy in Montana had his cabin booby-trapped when the authorities went in."

"Don't worry," Nick said.

He chuckled, but Alex thought it sounded a bit strained. "I think I know what to look for."

"Yeah, well, if I'm right, Holly's on her way up there, too," Alex said.

"She's coming to Trafton? How does she even know where to go?" Nick asked.

"She's been in contact with her dead son, and from what she's told me, he might be directing her, so she may know exactly where to go."

"This compound isn't the easiest place to find, even in daylight," Nick said.

"If you see her . . . well, I don't know if she's dangerous or not, but I suspect she's in pretty bad shape."

"I said don't worry," Nick said emphatically, and then he laughed again. "I'll take care of her if I see her. See you soon."

"Yeah . . . See you soon," Alex said.

She depressed the cut-off button with her thumb and called Rachel back. She reassured her that she would stay put until tomorrow morning, when Rachel would arrive from San Francisco, and Nick got back from New Hampshire. Then the three of them could figure out what to do next.

After saying goodbye to Rachel, she just sat there on the couch for a long while, listening to the deep silence of the house and staring blankly at the dark night outside the window. The feeling that she was being watched hadn't passed entirely, and she still felt uneasy.

But Nick is safe, she thought with a measure of relief. *That, at least, is good.*

Still, it bothered her deeply that Holly was out there . . . somewhere in the night.

And something deep inside Alex told her that this wasn't over yet.

In fact, she was filled with a cold, dread certainty that it was far from over.

FIFTEEN

Nick broke the connection on the cell phone, then slid it back into his travel bag, which he'd retrieved from the brush where he'd hidden it earlier. He figured that Alex was worried about him enough already, so he hadn't given her any more details about what had happened. After breaking out of the stockade, they had high-tailed it into the woods and run back to Nick's rented Jeep, hoping to get away.

No one had been alerted or had chased after them, but before leaving, Hunter and his goons had destroyed the Jeep.

Exasperated, Nick stepped back and surveyed the damage once more.

All four tires were slashed, and a good-sized boulder from the side of the road was now resting in the bird's nest of broken glass that used to be the front windshield. The hood was raised, and the distributor cap had been yanked out and thrown onto the ground. Numerous loose wires hung over the engine block, and Nick was sure that more, unseen damage had been done to make sure the Jeep was totally out of commission. The gas cap had been removed, and someone had poured sand into the gas tank.

"I guess we're lucky they didn't do a more thorough search of the area," Nick said, opening his travel pack and withdrawing the .22 caliber pistol he kept in reserve. He chambered a round.

"Shows they don't think of everything," he added dryly.

"Or didn't have time before lighting out," McCullough said.

Straightening up, Nick scanned the dark trees that surrounded them. The road leading back to Trafton glowed sheet-metal gray in the night.

"So," he said, "should we start walking back to town, or do we go back to the compound and see if any of the vehicles there are still operable?"

McCullough was silent for a moment as he considered. His eyes held a dull, unnatural glow in the night. Finally, in a voice that sounded raw and thick with phlegm, he said, "To tell you the truth, I'm curious as hell to see what's going on back there."

He indicated the road back to the compound with a quick nod of the head.

" 'Sides, I'd prefer to drive back to town 'stead of walk, if possible. It's gotta be at least ten miles."

"Sounds good to me," Nick said, so side by side they started down the road to the compound.

It was a little after midnight. A cold wind was blowing out of the north, making the high treetops sway and creak in the darkness. Frost crunched underfoot, setting Nick's teeth on edge. A low raft of clouds obscured the moon and stars, so it was difficult to see more than a few feet in front of them. The wind sighing in the branches overhead only added to the desolate feeling. They kept hearing sounds from the forest that made them tense, but Nick figured they were just overreacting.

As they approached the outer perimeter of the compound, Nick was positive the area was deserted, and that no one was waiting in ambush for them. If anyone was still around, they would have responded when he and McCullough broke out of the stockade and made a break for the Jeep.

"That's my Ford truck over there," McCullough said, indicating the last vehicle in the line of parked vehicles. It was the dark pickup truck that had run Nick off the road earlier that day.

"Wait a second," Nick said.

He snagged McCullough by the arm and caught him up before he could walk over to it.

"Where the hell is everyone?"

He and McCullough scanned the deserted grounds.

"All of their trucks and cars are still here, so where'd they go?"

McCullough frowned as he looked around. Then he shrugged and shook his head.

"Beats the shit out of me," he said. "Look, I just want to get the hell out of here, okay? I need a hot shower and a couple of beers to soothe my throat. Then maybe I'll feel like trying to figure out the rest of this."

"Let's just have a quick look around," Nick said. "To be on the safe side."

A shiver ran up his spine as he turned away from McCullough and started down the central avenue, heading toward the large building in the middle of the grounds.

It was like walking through a ghost town.

Out back, at the edge of the compound, the stockade building was still burning. It had been reduced to a pile of blazing coals and blackened timbers. A thick column of smoke rose into the night sky and was quickly whisked away by the wind. The flickering light of the flames, along with the few outside lights still on, cast an eerie orange glow over the scene. The shadows of the trees and remaining buildings seemed as dense as ink.

Nick looked at the destroyed building and shuddered.

He couldn't help but imagine that, except for a bit of luck on their part, right now he and McCullough would be charred corpses buried beneath that pile of smoldering rubble.

As parched as their throats were, both men decided that it would be best not to drink any water from the compound, just in case Hunter had poisoned the well before leaving.

"I've got a feeling Hunter's the kind of man who's not going to leave many loose ends," Nick said. "Did he ever reveal any plans about evacuating the compound?"

McCullough thought for a moment, then shook his head.

Nick suddenly realized that, although they had been through a lot together in a short time, he still knew next to nothing about the man. He wondered if—and how far—he could trust McCullough.

"I don't like this," Nick said, tightening the grip on his pistol. "We should try to find some better weapons first. I don't like walking into any situation so poorly armed."

"Most of the members kept their weapons in the commons, although I doubt Hunter would leave anything behind, even if he was bailing out fast."

Nick stopped at the front door to the building and stared at it.

There was a light on inside. Its dull yellow glow filled the shaded windows but did little to push back the surrounding darkness. The commons building certainly appeared to be deserted, but if this was a booby trap, they'd be walking right into it.

"Cover me," McCullough said, and before Nick could stop him, he stepped up to the door, grasped the doorknob, and gave it a quick turn.

"What the hell are you doing?" Nick cried out as the door latch clicked, and the door opened a crack.

McCullough looked back at him with a perplexed expression.

"That could have been booby-trapped," Nick said. "Jesus, let me check these things out before you go barrelling ahead, okay?''

He let out the breath he'd been holding and smiled grimly.

''Sorry,'' McCullough said sheepishly. Then he gave the door a shove with his foot and flattened himself against the outside wall as the door swung open the rest of the way.

They heard it bang against the inside wall. For a few tense seconds, they waited to see if that would trigger a response from inside, but nothing happened.

All was quiet.

Nick heard McCullough let out a slow, whistling breath, but he didn't let himself relax. As soon as you let your guard down, he thought, trouble happens . . . especially when you're dealing with someone as smart as Hunter.

''Think it's safe?'' McCullough asked as he edged around the doorjamb so he could peer inside the building.

Nick hesitated, still wary. After taking a quick look around the compound, he went up to the door and stood next to McCullough.

''I don't like it,'' Nick whispered, frowning deeply. ''A man like Hunter's not going to leave any loose ends. This is much too easy.''

He scanned the edges of the door frame, but—as far as he could tell—there were no wires on the outside indicating that the door had been rigged.

With his gun at ready, Nick sucked in a breath, then stepped into the building, dropping down into a defensive crouch.

It took a second or two for his eyes to adjust to the dim lighting inside; then another moment for his brain to register what he was looking at.

When he realized what he was seeing, he gasped in shock and amazement.

He jumped and spun quickly around, ready to fire, when McCullough noisily entered the room behind him. McCullough stopped a few feet behind him, his face a mask of absolute horror at what he saw in the room.

Strewn randomly across the floor, sprawled in awkward postures and lying in puddles of their own blood, were the bodies of nearly a dozen men. All were clad in military fatigues, and all were dead. All of them had been shot in the back of the head, at point blank range.

Drying splashes of blood and chunks of brain and bone were splattered across the floor and walls. The stench of death was thick and cloying. It clawed at Nick's parched throat and made his stomach flip. He heard a loud droning sound and realized that, already, flies were busy feasting on the slaughtered carrion that had once been men.

"What the hell happened?" McCullough said in a low, shattered whisper. His eyes were wide with shock as he tried to take in the scene. "What were you saying about Hunter not leaving any loose ends?"

"Jesus, I can't believe this," Nick said, still stunned as he surveyed the carnage.

Before either of them could say anything else, a soft *popping* sound drew Nick's attention.

He turned and saw a small puff of blue smoke rising from behind a stack of square metal containers that were piled up in the far corner of the room. When he looked back at the door they'd entered, he saw the thin wire running down the edge of the frame.

"Get out! Now!" Nick shouted as he turned and pushed McCullough toward the doorway. They both dove for the opening just as a roaring blast ripped through the building.

A ball of flame exploded out like a fist and punched them in the backs, propelling them out into the night. Carried by the shock wave of the explosion, they flew several feet through the air until they landed—hard—on the ground.

As both Nick and McCullough scrambled for safety, the commons building behind them blossomed in flames. Thick, oily smoke mushroomed into the starless sky. The crackling sound of fire filled the night like strings of firecrackers going off as it consumed the wooden structure.

The first explosion was followed by three more. In less than thirty seconds, the entire building was engulfed in a wall of flames. The explosion had been rigged to go off in sequence.

"You all right?" he shouted to McCullough, who was huddled facedown on the ground, shielding his head from the terrible heat of the blaze.

"Yeah," came the reply, muffled by McCullough's arm.

After a moment, McCullough rolled over and sat up, wincing as he watched the flames lick the night sky.

"Good reaction time," McCullough said, then he chuckled crazily. Shielding his face from the heat of the blaze, he shook his head.

"I can't believe I fell for that," Nick said, clenching his fists in frustration.

"What?"

"As soon as you opened that door, it pulled a tripwire that set off a timer rigged to blow. Hunter was counting on anyone being so surprised by what they found in that room that they wouldn't notice the booby trap."

Moving stiffly, he rose to his feet and walked a little farther away from the inferno.

"I think almost being burned alive twice in one night is enough for me," he said flatly. "Let's get the hell out of here."

McCullough's eyes reflected the flames, glistening in the night. Beneath the mask of soot and grime on his face, his teeth shone white and bright as he smiled.

"Right on, man," he said with a tight, humorless laugh. "I think it's time we found that murdering son of a bitch and gave him a little payback."

Nick nodded, unable for a moment to tear his gaze away from the burning building.

"Yeah," he finally said, "but before you put the key in the ignition of your truck, let's check it out and make sure it's not wired to blow, too. Okay?"

McCullough smiled and, nodding curtly, said, "Sounds like a damned good idea to me."

"Wait right here," the faint, high-pitched voice said softly, just at the edge of hearing.

Without any hesitation, Holly pulled to a stop in the middle of the narrow dirt road and left the car running. It idled smoothly, purring like a contented beast.

"Leave the lights on," the voice said close to her ear.

Holly closed her eyes for a moment and tried to imagine that she could feel a wash of warm, living breath against her neck, but all she felt was a slight chilled ripple that ran like teasing fingertips across her scalp.

Gripping the steering wheel tightly, she opened her eyes and stared straight ahead down the road. It was like looking into a deep, bottomless tunnel with a thick wall of pine trees lining both sides of the road. She was reminded of the endless hospital corridor she had been in with Evan and got that same dizzy feeling. Off to her left, down a short embankment, she caught a glimpse of a fast-flowing river, its rocky banks glowing like dull silver in the moonless night.

She shivered as she looked around.

The tops of the pine trees swayed gently in the wind. Very faintly, she could hear their branches creaking and snapping from the cold.

She sighed, feeling so isolated . . . so alone . . . Tears filled her eyes, making her vision swim.

She couldn't help but question what she was doing out there in the middle of the forest, but she told herself that she could trust the voice that whispered to her.

She felt compelled to do whatever the voice said, as if she had little if any choice in the matter.

The voice sounded so much like Evan's that she had come to believe that it truly *was* her dead son, talking to her, giving her directions and orders that she was going to carry out, no matter what.

A small corner of her rational mind told her that this was impossible, that Evan was dead, and that she was being delusional, but she tried her best to ignore it.

She didn't want to believe that Evan was gone forever. She couldn't accept that.

Besides, what was wrong with wanting to hear and see her dead son again?

Even if she was imagining all of it, what harm was there in not wanting to let go?

It was natural to grieve.

It was normal to miss her son.

Even as she thought this, the voice whispered something else to her.

Without hesitation, she did what it told her to do.

She reached out and touched the stock of the stolen twelve-gauge shotgun that rested on the seat beside her. A hot, stinging sensation filled her eyes, and she realized that she was crying. The warm, slick tracks of her tears ran down her face and into the corners of her mouth. She tasted their saltiness and sniffed loudly. Withdrawing her hand from the shotgun, she wiped her eyes.

"Go ahead," the faint voice whispered insistently.

It came out of the darkness like the powdery flutter of a moth's wings.

"Pick it up. You're going to have to use it soon."

"But I-I don't know how to shoot a gun," Holly said.

She could hear the tortured strain in her voice, but she listened to it as though someone else was speaking. She had an odd feeling of disassociation, as though she was watching someone else's hand stretch out and touch the shotgun again.

A jab of ice ran up her arm as her fingers brushed against the cold wood of the shotgun stock.

It was electrifying.

Frightening.

No, this is wrong, a faint voice whispered deep within her mind.

Her view of the road up ahead melted into a watery blur that smeared the yellow glow of the headlights. The dark wall of trees on both sides of the road seemed to squeeze in on her, making it impossible for her to take a deep enough breath.

She felt like she was drowning.

"Get ready," the voice said, wavering in and out like a radio signal that was gaining and losing strength. "They're coming . . . They're almost here."

Against her will, Holly picked up the shotgun. It was heavy in her hand, but she pulled back the pump and then rammed it forward, hearing the satisfying sound as a shell entered the chamber.

"See how easy it is?" the voice said. "You know what you're doing . . . You know what you have to do."

Holly gritted her teeth so hard they made loud grinding sounds inside her head. She nodded her agreement and, sniffing loudly, wiped her eyes again with the back of her hand. It didn't help much. Her vision was still blurred. She was struggling to gain a measure of control over herself as wave after wave of dizziness swept over her like a powerful ocean tide pulling her far out into the darkness . . . into a darkness from which she knew she would never return.

But that's where Evan is, she told herself. *He's out there in the darkness . . . waiting for me. . . .*

If she went out there, then at least she'd be reunited with him. He was, after all, her only child and the one person she loved more than anyone else in the world . . . more than her long-dead husband . . . more than her parents . . . more than anyone.

A frightening realization hit her.

Everything she had done in her life, even her work with Roots and Branches, advocating children's rights, was a front, a cover for who—or what—she really was.

Deep inside, she was seething with hatred . . . hatred and an irresistible drive to avenge her son's death.

Nothing else mattered.

Nothing!

"Get out of the car," the voice suddenly said with a harshness that startled Holly.

She snapped to attention. Looking ahead, she saw twin pools of headlights coming toward her from out of the night. They materialized slowly, like some great and terrible beast, emerging from the fog.

Her hands were shaking, and she felt like she was going to vomit or pass out as she grabbed the door latch and yanked it.

The door clicked and swung open.

A sudden blast of cold air made her shiver. Her legs felt as thin and as pliable as rope. She wasn't sure they would support her as she stepped out into the night. Her shoes scuffed on the dirt road, setting her teeth on edge.

With one hand, she shielded her eyes from the approaching headlights. She kept the other hand—the one holding the shotgun—down below the edge of the car window so the driver wouldn't see it.

Not yet.

Not until she was ready to use it.

She jumped when the driver in the approaching vehicle tapped on his horn once as he slowed to a stop.

Holly waved a friendly greeting with her left hand and smiled as though meeting someone out here in the middle of nowhere at this ungodly hour was a perfectly normal thing to do.

The high-pitched squeal of brakes and the sound of tires skidding on the dirt road filled the night. Behind the vehicle, the cloud of dust it had raised glowed a baleful red in the glare of the brake lights.

The headlights were shining right into her eyes, making it difficult for Holly to see. She thought the vehicle was a dark pickup truck, but she couldn't be sure. She caught only a brief glimpse of motion as the driver and passenger doors opened and someone—two men, it looked like—got out on

161

either side. They slammed the doors shut and started toward her.

"Holly . . . ? Holly Brown?"

The voice came from out of the darkness, but it wasn't the voice that had been speaking to her before. It took her a moment or two to realize that one of the men from the truck had called out her name.

"Holly—" he said again. "What the hell are you doing out here?"

She thought she almost recognized the voice, but then the other voice—the one that spoke so frighteningly close to her ear, low and frantic with command—said, "That's him! That's Hunter."

Holly froze. Her mind was overloaded with a sudden rush of confusing input.

"You have to kill him!" Evan's voice said, now so close it sounded like it was inside her head.

With the headlights shining behind them, the men from the truck cast long, dark shadows that stretched out across the road toward her as they approached her.

Holly was still holding the shotgun inside the car, out of sight, but she knew that she had only a few seconds to act before it would be too late.

"I've spoken to Alex," the almost-familiar man's voice said. "She's really worried about you."

"*Do it! Now! Kill him!*" the voice inside her head shouted. It no longer sounded like Evan's voice.

"Alex . . . ?" Holly said, suddenly confused. "How . . . how do you know Alex?"

"What do you mean, how do I know her?" the man said. "It's me . . . Nick."

The man was still making his way toward her. With every step, the crunching sound of his boots on the dirt road got louder, setting Holly's teeth on edge. A high, whining noise like a chorus of cicadas rose in her mind.

"Alex is one of my closest friends," the man who

162

claimed he was Nick said. "I've worked with her for years."

"You have . . . ?" Holly said.

She was trying desperately to process all of this, but her mind was lost in a whirling chaos.

Nothing made any sense.

How had she come to be out here in the middle of the night with a shotgun, intending to kill a man in cold blood?

With the light behind them, it was impossible for her to see either man's face clearly. They loomed in front of her, looking impossibly huge.

Threatening.

Terrifying.

"*You have to shoot them now!*" the voice that no longer sounded like Evan said. "*That's Hunter! He killed me! Now you have to kill him! Kill both of them!*"

What happened next happened in such agonizing slow motion that Holly found herself watching it all like a clinically detached observer, instead of an active participant.

Clenching her teeth and muttering something under her breath that she didn't even understand, she stepped away from the car so she would have room to move. She raised the shotgun, but didn't bring it up to her shoulder. It weighed too heavily in her hand.

"Look out! She's got a gun," one of the men shouted.

Holly saw the men dart to opposite sides of the road as her hand, still holding the shotgun at her side, flexed involuntarily and squeezed the trigger.

The blast sounded like a firecracker going off much too close to her. The shotgun kicked back hard in her hand, almost tearing from her grip as the butt slammed painfully against her thigh.

A bright spike of orange flame flashed from the shotgun's barrel, and a cloud of yellow dust kicked up from the road inches from where the man who'd said he was Nick had been standing.

But he was no longer there.

Holly's eyes were still dazzled by the sudden muzzle flash, but in an instant she saw a dark silhouette bearing down on her like a runaway freight train that hit her, hard. The impact knocked her back against the car, punching the wind out of her.

Holly let out a shrill squeal as she fell backward. For a dizzying instant, she felt like she was tumbling head over heels in a freefall until she hit the ground. There was a sharp wrenching pain in her hand as the man yanked the shotgun from her grip and tossed it away. It clattered when it landed a short distance away in the brush.

"What the hell are you doing?" the man shouted.

He was on top of her, pressing down on her with his full weight, making it almost impossible for her even to take a breath, much less move.

Surprised and stunned with pain, Holly looked up at him.

It took her a moment or two, but eventually she recognized the face of the man who was leaning over her. He had been at the hospital with Alex.

"Oh, my God, Nick!" she whispered, gasping raggedly for breath.

A hot, choking bubble of acid filled her throat. "I thought . . . He told me that you were . . . Hunter. Oh, my God! I-I almost killed you!"

SIXTEEN

McCullough settled down in the backseat of the car and let Nick do the driving. They were on the road that led back to Trafton, moving a bit too fast for the narrow, winding road, McCullough thought. The first thing Nick did was call his friend Alex and reassure her that Holly was with them, and that she was doing just fine.

But maybe she wasn't so fine, McCullough thought. Holly was slumped in the passenger's seat with her head pressed against the side window. He couldn't tell if she was awake, asleep, or in a coma, but frankly, right now he didn't care.

He was exhausted and trying his best to relax, but—so far, anyway—he hadn't been able to. By any measure, it had been one hell of a night, and it didn't look like it was going to get better any time soon, either.

McCullough groaned softly as he rotated his head and massaged the back of his neck, trying to relieve the stiffness that had accumulated there. He wasn't very successful. Spikes of pain shot up his shoulders and behind his ears.

Sighing deeply, he closed his eyes and rubbed them gently as he ran through a quick checklist of everything that had happened so far.

For starters, he was a passenger in a stolen car.

True, the cops probably weren't looking for this car, at least not yet. The woman had told Nick that it belonged to some friends of hers who were away on vacation. If they could believe her, they'd probably be okay. Still, it was a damned nice automobile, and McCullough wasn't at all confident that he or Nick would be able to explain their physical condition if they were pulled over for speeding. Their faces were smudged with dirt and soot, and their clothes reeked of cordite from the explosives.

The plan was to get back to Mrs. Parker's Bed 'N Breakfast, wash up and get a change of clothing, and then drive down to Pembroke, Massachusetts, where Nick's friend Alex was staying at this woman Holly Brown's house.

McCullough thought Holly seemed like a first-class nutcase until Nick informed him that she had lost her ten-year-old son in the bomb blast that Hunter's militia had detonated at Plymouth Rock.

After learning that, McCullough decided to let it drop. In fact, his stomach twisted with guilt whenever he glanced at the woman and saw her tortured, haunted expression. He couldn't stop thinking that, while he hadn't done anything directly to manufacture, place, or detonate the bomb, he could have stopped it at any time . . . if only he'd had the courage to stand up to Hunter sooner.

Then again, if he had tried to stand up to Hunter sooner, he would have ended up in the stockade sooner.

—Or else dead!

But even without this load of guilt to deal with, it had been a hell of a night.

He'd been trapped in a burning building from which he'd escaped by just the narrowest of margins. If Nick hadn't been there to pick the lock of his handcuffs and knock down the burning door, he would have been fried to a crisp by now.

Then, while still weak with exhaustion, his throat and lungs stinging from smoke inhalation, he had entered the common building only to find that all his comrades had been systematically executed, and that the room had been wired to blow up. Again, if Nick hadn't been on top of things and seen the fuse burning, they both would have died in the blast.

And finally, while driving away from the compound, he had stopped on the road to assist what he took to be a stranded motorist, a woman who, he assumed, had broken down out in the middle of nowhere.

And—surprise!

She'd come up with a shotgun that had gone off in her hands and come a little too close for *his* comfort before Nick—once again—saved his ass and disarmed the crazy woman.

So all in all, McCullough thought, it looked like this Nick Boyle was one hell of a stand-up guy and someone he didn't mind hanging out with.

But now it turns out that Nick knows this woman who mistook him for Hunter, so she says, and tried to kill him.

Although Nick tried to fill McCullough in on some of the details, it sure as hell sounded like he and this woman were hooked up with some other people as well as with some organization called the Legacy, whatever the hell that was.

McCullough had never heard of it.

He suspected it might be another militia group, but when he asked Nick if that's what it was, Nick just chuckled and shook his head.

What they were up to was anybody's guess, McCullough thought, but he decided not to stick his nose too far into their business.

It was safer that way.

Back at Mrs. Parker's Bed 'N Breakfast, McCullough

and Nick showered and changed. Fortunately, Nick's clothes were a close enough fit for McCullough. Mrs. Parker seemed ready to burst with questions, but neither Nick nor McCullough told her anything about what had happened. They figured the less she knew, the better for her.

Before long they were back on the road, heading south on Route 16. What was uppermost in McCullough's mind was finding Hunter as soon as possible and taking him out . . . permanently. He was eager to accomplish this goal or die trying.

"There's a gas station up ahead," Nick said. "They probably have a pay phone."

"You thinking of calling the feds?" McCullough asked, making eye contact with Nick's reflection in the rearview mirror.

"Yeah," Nick said dryly. "I should have done it before now, but I didn't want to call from Mrs. Parker's or use my cell phone. It'd be too easy for them to trace it back to me. I'd think the forestry service would have seen the fire and smoke from the compound by now, but I want to let them know what to expect out there. I don't want them walking in unawares if the whole place is booby-trapped."

"Umm, good point," McCullough said, nodding. "But if you tip off the feds, they might get to Hunter before we do."

McCullough didn't like the edge he heard in his own voice.

"True. They might find him before we do," Nick said, glancing at him, his mouth a tight, thin line. "But personal revenge isn't the issue here. The important thing is to make sure Hunter is stopped before he follows through with any more bombing attacks."

"We have plenty of time before he does that," McCullough said. "Like I told you, he wasn't planning on making another move until New Year's Day in Times Square."

"Right, and after that Memorial Day at the Washington

Monument, and the Liberty Bell in Philadelphia on the Fourth of July,'' Nick said.

"At least that was the plan,'' McCullough said with a shrug. "But now, with most of his militia dead, I'd think he'd have a bit of trouble doing it alone.''

"He's still got Williams and Morgan,'' Nick said. "What's worrying me is, now that we know what he's up to, and he knows that we know, he'll most likely adapt his plan. Especially now that, as far as we know, you're the only material witness against him who's still alive.''

"Not a very comforting thought, is it?'' McCullough said softly.

He shivered and shifted forward in the seat as Nick slowed for the turn into the gas station parking lot. McCullough's hand slid across the seat and touched the outline of the spare hunting knife in Nick's travel bag beside him. For a moment, he considered drawing the knife and doing whatever he had to do to make sure Nick didn't call the authorities . . . at least not until he had his shot at Hunter.

But McCullough knew that Nick was fast, and he was a good fighter even when caught off-guard. The bottom line was, in the short time they'd been together, McCullough had grown to like and respect the man. He tended to feel that way about someone who'd saved his life three times in one night.

McCullough cleared his throat and, bringing his hands together, folded them tightly in his lap.

"I think he'll still probably try to bomb those places,'' he said. "But if anything—''

"If anything, he's going to come looking for us, first,'' Nick said, finishing McCullough's thought for him.

"Yeah, I think so.''

The car rolled to a stop beside the phone booth at the far corner of the store. The ambient light from the street-lights cast thin shadows over the area. Nick dug some change out of his pocket but hesitated before opening the car door.

"So what do you think?" he said, turning in the seat to face McCullough directly. "Do we call now or not?"

McCullough considered for another second or two, then nodded grimly.

"The feds are gonna be able to trace a call from here, too, you know."

"Sure," Nick replied, "but as long as we don't do anything to draw attention to ourselves, as long as we just make the call and leave, we'll be out of here before they can get anyone on the scene. When we leave, I'll even head back north for a while, just so if anyone notices us they'll report that we were driving in the wrong direction."

"Good thinking," McCullough said as he let his gaze drift out the window.

There was a solitary car parked at the pump. A skinny kid with long, greasy black hair and wearing jeans and a thin denim jacket was pumping gas into a black Trans Am. He looked cold and in a hurry to get back into his car. He wasn't going to notice anything. The solitary clerk inside the store had his back to the window and was busy reading a newspaper.

"Yeah," McCullough finally said. "Make the call."

The drive south was pure hell for Holly.

She couldn't stop dwelling on the terrible tragedy that had almost happened. What would have happened if Nick had been killed when the shotgun went off? She hadn't meant to squeeze the trigger. It had been mere reflex, but for a while she had been absolutely convinced that Nick was Hunter. At the urgings of her dead son, she wanted nothing more than to see Hunter pay for what he had done to her and Evan.

But how could she have been so wrong?

How could the voice-- Evan's voice—have been so wrong as to mistake Nick for Hunter?

It had to have been a simple case of mistaken identity, but Holly couldn't help but think that maybe it hadn't been.

Maybe Evan had been trying to trick her so she would kill Nick.

She had no idea why that would be.

As far as she was concerned, there was no reason to doubt Nick's friendship or loyalty, if only because he was such a good friend of Alex's.

So why in the name of God would Evan lie to her about it?

If she truly was in communication with her dead son's spirit, then he wouldn't have—he *couldn't* have made a simple mistake of identity.

Could he?

Souls on the spiritual plain must have clearer sight, she thought, and the voice had clearly told her that Nick was Hunter, and that she was supposed to kill both him and the other man.

And she almost had!

She had been trying to steel her nerves to raise the shotgun, aim, and shoot at two innocent men. If it hadn't been a mistake, then Evan had deliberately tried to deceive her.

If that was the case, then Evan—her sweet, loving little boy—had changed, somehow, into something vindictive and evil.

What in the name of heaven could have happened to turn Evan into a being of evil?

Could it be something as simple as the shock and terror of experiencing death?

Or was there something else, some other force at work here that she didn't understand?

Such thoughts made Holly shudder. They filled her with a cold, twisting sadness. Moaning softly to herself, she stared, unblinking, out at the night-cloaked landscape as it zipped past the car. Holding her breath, she waited and listened for Evan's voice, but he was silent.

For now, at least, he was gone.

She could no longer sense his presence as she had before, and his absence left a deep vacuum inside her. The thought that her son might truly be lost forever to her, lost and alone somewhere in a cold, dark, eternal void, searching in vain for solace and peace, filled her with heart-squeezing misery.

Maybe it was true, she thought.

Maybe Evan would never rest in peace until the man who had killed him was also dead.

And it's all my fault, she thought. Her insides twisted with agony. The grief of her loss welled up inside her like dark, fetid water. It was impossible to think that it had been mere fate or simple bad luck that Evan was where he was at the time the bomb was detonated.

It had to be more than that!

Holly realized that she was crying. In the dim glow of the dashboard lights, she could see her reflection in the car window beside her, distorted by the concave curve of the glass. The pale, sallow skin of her face looked like it was stretched too thin. It gave her a horrifying, skeletal look. Her eyes were dark, sunken pits that showed not the slightest spark of life. Her tears blurred her sight, making her vision double.

Suddenly the terrifying thought hit her that maybe she was already dead . . . that maybe she had really died in the explosion, and everything that had happened since then was simply part of the torment, the hell she imagined for herself in the afterlife.

Clutching fear gripped her heart, and she felt no reassurance when she detected the high, rapid throb of her pulse in her chest.

All she could think was *That's it! I'm already dead . . . I'm already dead. . . .*

The hollowness of loss at the core of her being only further confirmed it.

When she moaned softly, it sounded like someone else was making the noise. She was distantly aware that her face was slick with tears, but she didn't wipe them away.

What did it matter?

She just sat there, staring at her reflection in the car window and thinking that she was gazing into the eyes of a dead person.

"Hey . . . Are you all right?"

Holly jumped when the voice spoke so suddenly beside her. For a shattering instant, she thought that it might be Evan, but then she realized that it was Nick. He reached out and touched her gently on the shoulder.

She tried to say something in response, but her throat was closed off as surely as if someone were choking her. Not even the tiniest sound would escape her, and she thought that, if she had spoken at all, she would have only been able to say, *It doesn't matter . . . I'm already dead.*

The darkness of the countryside flashing by outside the car was broken intermittently by streetlights and the soft glow of lights inside farmhouses and homes.

But the darkness inside Holly swelled even stronger— deep, eternal, and hungry.

A surge of panic filled her when she realized that the dark void inside her was expanding, spreading out and eager to engulf her. She knew that she was being drawn irresistibly into it, and that as soon as she gave herself over to it, it would swallow her, body, mind, and soul.

". . . no . . ." she said, no more than a whimper that she didn't think was even audible.

She jumped again when Nick squeezed her shoulder, his grip tightening, but it was reassuring, not painful.

"Do you want to call Alex?" he said.

Out of the corner of her eye, she saw that he was holding the cell phone out to her.

"Maybe it'd help if you talked to her."

Holly considered the offer but said nothing. She didn't reach for the phone. Even someone as dear to her as Alex wouldn't understand what she was feeling. No one who hadn't suffered a loss identical to hers could understand.

Holly's shoulders shook as a deep shudder rippled through her. She closed her eyes and stared into the darkness that swelled behind her eyelids. She tried not to imagine that somewhere deep within that darkness was Evan.

I'd give anything to be with you right now, she thought, and the desperate emotions that thought raised rushed through her with a hot, salty surge. More tears gushed from her eyes, and her throat made a strange gagging sound that almost cut off her air.

Holly shook her head, hoping that Nick would understand that she didn't want to call Alex . . . that talking to Alex or anybody else right now wasn't going to stop the pain or assuage even a fraction of the misery she was feeling.

She opened her eyes to slits and looked down at her hands.

They were folded tightly in her lap, looking thin and pale, almost like a skeleton's lifeless hands.

But these hands move, she thought. *I'm still alive!*

Although she couldn't hear Evan's voice anymore, she suddenly sensed his presence, and it filled her with an unnameable dread.

"No," she whispered, trying to focus her mind and pierce the darkness inside her.

"Go away! Leave me alone!"

She pressed her forehead against the car window, telling herself that she couldn't allow herself to be swept away by the darkness. She couldn't give herself over to grief and despair.

"You lied to me," she whispered, watching her breath— the breath of life!—fog the cold glass.

She looked down at her hands again and slowly flexed her fingers. Even the slightest motion sent waves of pain shooting up her wrists. It was like watching a movie as her right hand rose from her lap and touched the cold metal of the door latch. She imagined that she could see thin, trailing forks of blue energy pass like lightning between her fingertips and the door latch.

She let her gaze shift once again out at the night. Beyond

the black lace of the treetops that whizzed by, she could see the flat, gray, starless sky. The lowering clouds looked cold and dense. Closer to the car, the roadside was moving past them with near blinding speed. Even closer, she saw—or thought she saw—a blur of motion . . . something that was just outside the car and keeping pace with it.

She sniffed and wiped her eyes, trying to see if it was the shadow of the car or something else. With a sudden flutter of fear, she saw a face resolve in the window beside her. For an instant, she thought it might be Nick's reflection from the dashboard lights, but then she saw that it was Evan.

He appeared to be outside the speeding car, drifting along beside it and staring at her, his cold, dark gaze boring into her.

Before she knew what was happening, Holly heard a loud *click*, and the passenger's door swung wide open.

The sudden blast of frigid night air slammed into her hard, taking her breath away as it ripped like a chain saw into her lungs.

She let out a sharp, piercing scream, but the sudden rush of wind forced it back inside her as she felt something grab her wrist and start pulling her out the open door. Stark terror filled her when she looked down at the blur of the road beside her and imagined herself falling out. She knew she would die instantly if she hit the road at this speed.

The force that was holding her dragged her inexorably forward, out into the darkness. Holly knew that she was still screaming—or at least trying to—but the blasting wind made it impossible for her to breathe. She felt like she was suffocating.

Within seconds, she knew that she was going to be dragged out onto the highway. The force was too strong to resist. When she caught a brief glimpse of Evan's face, he was smiling wickedly at her as he gripped her wrist and tried to pull her out into the night.

But then, something caught Holly by the left shoulder,

and she felt herself being pinned against the car seat.

Something was holding her back.

Her mind was a screaming chaos of confusion. She had no idea what was holding onto her, but no matter how hard the force outside the car tugged at her, it couldn't yank her out of the seat and dash her against the road.

The whining sound of the car's engine and the steady hiss of the tires on the pavement suddenly dropped, and Holly felt the car slowing down. She heard the loud ripping sound of the tires skidding on the asphalt as Nick applied the brakes. The force was still trying to pull her from the car, but she could feel it lessening. Within seconds, the car was moving slow enough so she knew, even if she fell out now, she probably would only be hurt and not killed. A desperate sense of relief filled her.

"What the hell are you doing?" Nick shouted, close beside her.

"I . . . I don't know," Holly said as her confusion began to clear, and she realized that Nick was steering with one hand and hanging onto her with the other. The man in the backseat—right now she couldn't even remember his name—was leaning forward and pinning her shoulders so tightly against the car seat that it was painful.

At last the car coasted to a stop in the breakdown lane on the side of the road. Exhausted, Holly sagged back against the car seat and let out a deep, tortured moan. The door was still hanging open, and the frigid night air circulated around her like a polar whirlpool, making her teeth chatter wildly.

She looked down at the road just outside her open door. It was illuminated by the car's dome light, and she could see the textured pebbled surface of the asphalt in amazing detail. She couldn't help but imagine how the jagged edges of all those tiny stones would have flayed her skin off if she had fallen out. The image filled her with deep, trembling fear.

She let out a long, dry sob that started somewhere deep

in her bowels. Leaning forward, she covered her face with both hands and started to cry.

I'm already dead . . . she thought as black misery embraced her like a dead lover. She wished she could say it out loud so Nick would understand.

. . . I'm already dead. . . .

SEVENTEEN

A lex was worried.
Even though Nick had called a little past two o'clock in the morning and had reassured her that they were on their way back to Holly's house, and that Holly was with him and doing at least as well as could be expected, she couldn't dispel the gnawing worry that something was terribly wrong.

Maybe it had been something in the tone of Nick's voice.

Nick tried hard never to allow worry or fear to show in his voice; but when they had talked, his voice had broken once or twice.

Not much.

Anyone who didn't know him as well as Alex did wouldn't have detected it, but she'd heard it.

It was there.

He had tried to pass it off as a bad connection with the cell phone, but she sensed that he was really worried about something. He just wasn't going to tell her what it was.

Not yet, anyway.

Alex tried not to think the worst. She told herself that if it was something bad about Holly, and Holly was there with him, he would be reluctant to mention it within her hearing.

Whatever it was, she tried to reassure herself that she'd find out about it as soon as he got to the house.

Waiting was the hard part.

After talking to Nick, she called Derek at Legacy House. Rachel answered the phone and told her that Derek had gotten back from San Diego that evening and gone straight to bed. He'd been without sleep for more than forty-eight hours straight and really needed to rest.

Rachel was still awake, though. She had to finish packing for her flight back East at seven o'clock in the morning, but she was willing to talk. Alex apologized for disturbing her and, even though Rachel insisted that she could catch up on her sleep during the flight, Alex thanked her and hung up.

So now she was alone in the house.

The silence of the cold night was broken every now and then by the low rumble of the furnace in the basement and the sudden snaps and bangs of the hot-water pipes throughout the house. When the wind gusted outside, it rattled the windows, sounding like someone trying to get inside. The streetlight in front of Holly's house cast tangled shadows of bare tree branches across the window shades. Alex tried to tell herself that they didn't look like claws, scratching at the windows.

Her nerves were on edge. She knew she should get some sleep, too. She wasn't going to be any use to Holly or Nick or herself if she pushed herself past the point of exhaustion, so after making sure the doors and windows were locked, she settled down in her bed.

It wasn't long before she was downstairs again, sitting in the kitchen, waiting for the water to heat up so she could brew a cup of herbal tea.

To relax, she told herself, but when she sat down on the living room couch and sipped it, even the tea's soothing warmth couldn't begin to erase the chill deep inside her.

She considered turning on the TV but decided against that. All of the channels would still be broadcasting their coverage of the bombing at Plymouth Rock.

She didn't need that.

She'd had her fill of reporters and investigators trying to get statements from her because of her association with Holly and Holly's tragic loss, and she didn't want to see or hear any more about it.

She was worried that, if the media learned Holly was missing from the hospital, they'd be at her front door first thing in the morning, shoving microphones into her face for a comment.

She'd be interested in the news only when—and if— they arrested the people responsible for the bombing; but after what Nick had told her about Hunter, she wasn't so sure that would ever happen. What bothered her most was the feeling deep in her gut that this was something the Legacy was going to have to resolve.

The minutes dragged by slowly.

She took another sip of tea, then placed it on the end table beside the couch.

She tried listening to some of Holly's CDs, but nothing held her interest for long. She collected a handful of books and magazines and started thumbing through them, but nothing caught her interest there, either.

Earlier that day, Rachel had faxed her some of the information Derek had uncovered about the Jewish tradition of the "Hidden Saints," but she had already read it over more than a dozen times. After reading it one more time, she had gleaned nothing new. She wasn't entirely convinced that Holly could be one of the *lamedvovniks,* but she guessed it was possible.

Anything was possible, and over the years in her work with the Legacy, she had encountered much stranger things.

Alex stood up and walked over to the living room window. Holding the lacy curtain aside, she looked outside. The street was well lit, but it still looked desolate. Bleak. She considered going out for a walk, but the idea of being outside—alone—on such a cold night made her uneasy.

After making sure that all the lights were on throughout the house, she sat back down on the couch, leaned her head back, and just waited for the phone to ring or—better yet—to hear the sound of Nick and Holly's footsteps at the front door.

At some point she began to drift into a light sleep.

As she skimmed the surface of sleep, never really dropping down all the way into it, she began to hear voices.

She couldn't make out anything they were saying, but the gentle buzzing sounds they made were pleasant and reassuring. It reminded her of the sounds in a summer field, humming with insect life.

Alex didn't even try to make out anything that was being said. She allowed the voices to rise and fall around her, wafting over her like the wind that was carrying her deeper and deeper into sleep.

But then one voice in particular rose up louder than the others, and Alex began to register brief snatches of what it was saying.

". . . think you could . . . away from me . . . watching her . . . wasn't even him . . ."

Groaning softly, she stirred on the couch.

Then the voice spoke again, louder.

"It won't be long now," the voice said in a low, gravelly tone. It was a man's voice. That was all Alex could determine.

Caught halfway between wakefulness and sleep, she muttered something unintelligible in reply. She shivered as a subtle chill raced through her, but it still wasn't enough to bring her fully back to consciousness.

She had done some work with lucid dreaming and was distantly aware that she must be dreaming, or at least letting

181

her mind roam freely enough so her subconsciousness was stirred.

But there was something immediate about the voice that alarmed her. She tossed around fitfully on the couch, waving her hands as if trying to fend something off.

"Did you really think that you—that *any* of you could get away from me?" the voice asked.

It ended in an animal-like growl that raised goose bumps on Alex's arms.

"I . . . I don't know," Alex muttered dreamily. "But we . . . we do have to try."

The only response she got was a soft, dry chuckle that immediately woke her up. She inhaled sharply enough to hurt her chest as she sat bolt-upright on the couch and looked around.

The living room was deserted except for her, but she couldn't shake the sensation that she wasn't alone.

She glanced over to the windows, braced and ready to see the dark silhouette of someone outside, gazing in at her, but there was no one there. The streetlight cast only the shadows of the tree branches against the curtains.

Alex noticed her cup of tea on the end table where she had left it. She grasped it and took a sip, surprised to find that it was cold. She glanced at her wristwatch, amazed to see that she had been dozing for more than an hour.

When she stood up, something low in her back popped. Her arms and legs throbbed with a deep ache. Still poised and ready for danger, she looked around the room, unable to dispel the eerie feeling that—somewhere—unseen eyes were watching her and silently enjoying her rising apprehension.

"Evan?" Alex called out in a shattered whisper. "Is that you, Evan? Are you here?"

But the house remained silent except for a single, loud snapping sound that seemed to be coming from the kitchen.

Moving slowly, Alex tiptoed from the living room into the kitchen.

The room was empty.

The ceiling light was on, casting a bright glow into every corner.

Still, Alex felt on edge.

She glanced over at the wide patio doors that led out into the backyard. The blinds were drawn shut, and Alex wasn't sure she would dare raise them to have a look outside.

"It's just my imagination," she whispered, irritated with herself, but even that didn't give her much courage. The voice had been as clear as if someone had been right there in the room with her.

Ever since she was a little girl growing up in Haiti, Alex had experienced psychic episodes, but none of them had ever felt quite like this.

The contact had been direct and immediate, but it hadn't been accompanied by the flashes of insight and vision which she typically got. She didn't like the way the lingering memory of the voice made her feel.

It was cold and hollow . . . dead-sounding.

Alex told herself, even if she had made a psychic connection with someone or some entity, it was just a voice, making a casual comment.

It didn't have to be negative.

But the voice had been laced with such menace that Alex felt increasingly disoriented the more fully awake she became.

"Evan, if you're here, I'm willing to talk to you," she called out, trying to sound braver than she felt. Her memory of the voice, which was already starting to fade away, was that it had been a man's voice.

"Come on out where I can see you."

In response, she heard a faint sniffing sound that could have been repressed laughter or someone crying. It was too fleeting, and it disappeared before she could be sure that she'd even heard it.

"I'll be seeing your mother soon," Alex said. "If

there's anything you want me to tell her, you can tell me.''

Every muscle in Alex's body was tensed as she waited for a reply, but none came. She walked cautiously over to the patio door and grasped the pull cord for the blinds.

Did she dare raise them and look outside?

She wanted to, desperately, but she was unable to ignore the terrifying images that suddenly flooded her mind.

What horrible creature might be lurking out there in the darkness . . . right out the door . . . coiled and ready to pounce on her?

Slowly, her hands trembling out of control, Alex twined the pull rope around her hand. The motion made the blinds shift. They scraped gently against the wood frame of the door, making a harsh scraping sound that set her teeth on edge.

''There's nothing out there,'' she said softly to herself, and then, after counting to three, she let out a soft grunt and yanked the cord down.

The blinds clattered as they went up like a collapsing accordion. Alex let out a squeal when she found herself staring in amazement at her own reflection in the glass that, with the night sky behind it, looked like polished black marble.

Realizing that she'd been holding her breath, she let it out in a long, slow sigh before lowering the shades again.

This is absolutely foolish, she chided herself as she wiped a hand across her sweat-soaked forehead.

She was worried about Nick and Holly, and she was letting her imagination get the better of her.

That's all it was.

Forcing herself to relax a little, she had turned and was heading back into the living room when she heard a car outside.

They're here! she thought as she ran to the front window and looked outside.

A dark car had pulled up to the curb a few houses down from the house. Alex didn't recognize it, but Nick had told her that Holly had borrowed a car from some friends in Duxbury who were away for the weekend.

The passenger's door opened and slammed shut. The sound carried clearly in the night air. Alex saw a dark figure get out and start across the lawn to the front door. Her body was flooded with relief when she saw that it was Nick.

She raced to the front door and snapped on the outside light, then reached to undo the dead bolt lock. Her hands were trembling with excitement, but suddenly she hesitated.

Where was Holly? she wondered.

Why isn't Holly with Nick?

Cautious, now, Alex hesitated when she heard the heavy clump of footsteps on the front steps.

Standing on tiptoes, she looked out through the small square window at the top of the door.

In the soft glow of the outside light, she clearly saw Nick's face. He seemed curiously expressionless as he mounted the front steps.

Alex was filled with a sudden panic that something terrible had happened to Holly. She couldn't control the shaking in her hands as she unlocked the door, turned the doorknob, and threw the door open.

A gust of cold air slapped her in the face, and she found herself face-to-face with a man that she didn't recognize.

''Where's Nick—?'' she started to say, and then her voice choked off as the man smiled wickedly back at her.

''Good evening,'' he said, bowing his head slightly.

There was something frighteningly familiar about his deep-toned voice that sent a chill through Alex. She took a single step back, but before she could think about slamming the door shut in his face and locking it, the man reached out and braced the door open.

''Or perhaps I should say good morning . . . After all, it is morning.''

Alex looked past the man and saw that the driver's door was open, and another man—thickset and dangerous looking—was standing beside the car, watching impassively.

The man barely glanced over his shoulder as he snapped his fingers. The driver obediently got back into the car, started it up, and drove away.

"My name is Adam Hunter," the man said, turning to face Alex and making no attempt to mask the sinister tone of his voice. "I believe you and your friends have been looking for me. And now—imagine that—I've found you."

"I think I understand it completely now."

Derek's voice, speaking so suddenly behind Rachel, made her squeal and drop the sweater she had folded to pack. She spun around to face him.

"You startled me," she said, after catching her breath.

Derek was standing in the doorway to Rachel's bedroom. The only light in the room came from the lamp on the end table beside her bed. Its pale lemon glow made Derek's face look drawn and sallow. There were dark shadows under his eyes.

"I thought you were asleep," Rachel said. "I hope I didn't disturb you."

"No . . . no," Derek replied, shaking his head as he rubbed his forehead with one hand. "I wasn't able to sleep. I can't stop thinking about what's happening to Alex and her friend, and I think I've finally figured it out."

Rachel pushed her suitcase aside and sat down on the edge of her bed. The bedsprings creaked beneath her weight.

Derek remained where he was, standing in the doorway and leaning against the doorjamb as if he needed it for support.

"I think there's a connection between what happened at Plymouth Rock and the murder of Fra Felipe," Derek said. "And I think that's only the tip of the iceberg."

"I . . . I don't understand," Rachel said, shaking her head.

Derek heaved a heavy sigh and closed his eyes for a

moment. Rachel could see that he was so far past the point of exhaustion he was close to collapse. But she acknowledged that Derek was driven in an almost inhuman way by his work with the Legacy, and that he wouldn't stop until he had done everything in his power to stop the forces of Evil in the world.

"These Hidden Saints," he said, his voice heavy with weariness, "the *lamedvovniks*. According to Hebrew legend, they're saintly people who are quietly working for the forces of good in the world. It's only through their good deeds that God withholds His hand and doesn't bring on the Apocalypse."

Once again, Derek heaved a deep sigh. His head started to nod, and he looked like he was about to fall asleep on his feet, but then he caught himself.

"You're driving yourself too hard, Derek," Rachel said softly. "You need to get some sleep."

"I know, I know," he said, "but it just . . . I was lying in bed trying to sleep when the thought occurred to me that perhaps the forces of evil have a plan."

"A plan . . . ? I'm not sure I understand."

"If the only thing holding back the Apocalypse are these thirty-six Hidden Saints, then why not identify them and eliminate them?"

Rachel was dumbfounded.

The idea appeared so simple she was amazed they hadn't thought of it before now. And—worse—it made perfect and terrifying sense.

"Yes, I suppose that would work," she said, "but the problem would be identifying who these thirty-six Hidden Saints are."

"True. According to the tradition, if any of the thirty-six saints dies, another one replaces him or her . . . But I wonder . . . How long does it take to replace them?"

"I . . . we have no way of knowing," Rachel said, shaking her head as a tremor of nervousness ran through her.

"Exactly," Derek said, "so if a demonic force knows

how to identify them—and has—now they can send out a legion of demons to destroy as many of the *lamedvovniks* as they can find—''

''—and bring on Armageddon,'' Rachel said, completing his thought.

''Eternal night,'' Derek said grimly.

He looked at her, the exhaustion and worry etched deeply in the lines of his face.

''But even if Fra Felipe is—or was—one of the Hidden Saints,'' Rachel said, ''they didn't succeed in killing Holly . . . if she is, in fact, one of them.''

''True, but we have to consider that maybe it wasn't Holly they were after.'' Derek stifled a yawn behind his hand. ''Maybe they wanted her son, Evan, destroyed. As you said, we have no way of knowing who the Hidden Saints are.'' He paused and shuddered as he took a deep breath. ''But maybe they've found a way of identifying them. Maybe the forces of evil *do* know.''

He exhaled noisily and sagged back against the door-jamb, his head slumped down. When he spoke again, his voice was distant and dreamy, as if he were mumbling in his sleep.

''I want you to call Alex immediately and warn her,'' he said tiredly. ''Get in touch with Nick, too.''

''I've tried earlier and didn't get through to him,'' Rachel said. ''Either his cell phone's not working, or something's blocking him from receiving it. But I'll try again.''

''Good,'' Derek said, ''but in any case, make sure you contact Alex. She'll have to be on her guard at all times. It may be that her intervention was the only thing that saved Holly the first time. If that's the case, and they're on their way to Holly's house, I'm sure the forces of evil will try again to harm her.''

EIGHTEEN

Alex was tense and coiled for action as she backed away from the door. Moving quickly, she tried to slam the door shut, but Hunter had his hand on it, stopping it easily and blocking it open with his foot. The impact sent a shock up Alex's hand, making it feel like she had just punched a stone wall.

"You're not being very hospitable, Ms. Moreau," Hunter said with a wicked smile as he casually pushed the door wide open and stepped inside. A swirling draft of cold wind ushered him into the house.

"H—how do you know my name?" Alex asked.

Hunter's feral smile widened, and his eyes seemed to glow with a deep, red fire.

"Oh, there's not much that I don't know . . . or can't find out," he said. His words were followed by a trace of hollow laughter that chilled Alex all the more.

She could sense Hunter's power, and she knew that it would be futile to try to fight or run away from him. Backing up slowly, she moved into the living room, hoping at least to put some distance between them.

She found it difficult to look directly at Hunter. There was something about his face . . . something in his eyes that was extremely disconcerting. It may have been her imagination, but she thought she caught flashes of rippling red light, shifting like distant forks of lightning in the depths of his eyes. There was no doubt that there was something uncanny . . . something supernatural about him.

After slamming the door shut behind him, Hunter followed her into the living room. Making like a boorish guest, he sat down heavily in one of the stuffed chairs and stretched his legs out. He was still smiling as he leaned back and clasped his hands behind his head, but there wasn't a trace of genuine warmth or friendliness in his smile.

"Your friends should be along any minute now," he said after glancing at his wristwatch. "Why not make yourself comfortable until they arrive?"

"And then what?" Alex asked.

She had no intention of acceding to his request—if, indeed, it was a request and not a command. If he was going to insist that she sit down, then he was going to have to be a little more emphatic.

"What then . . . ? Ahh, yes, what then indeed?" Hunter let his voice drift off as he gazed up at the ceiling for a moment, apparently lost in thought.

"Then," he said, "I suspect what will happen is you and your friends will all die . . . that is, after Holly Brown kills me."

"What the hell are you talking—" Alex started to say, but her voice cut off, and she jumped with a start when her cell phone suddenly beeped.

"Don't answer that!" Hunter shouted, leaning forward in the chair, his fists clenched so hard his knuckles showed white.

Alex glanced at her phone on the end table beside the couch where she had left it. The electronic beeping continued for almost a full minute, drilling her nerves until—finally—it cut off in mid-beep.

"Now, who do you suppose would be calling you at this late hour?" Hunter asked.

His expression darkened as he slowly got up from the chair and walked over to the couch, scowling as he picked up the now silent phone. He turned it over in his hand a few times as though studying it carefully.

"I haven't a clue," Alex said, shaking her head.

She was racking her brain, trying to think of what she could do, but—so far—she didn't see any opportunities.

She knew it had to have been either Derek or Rachel calling from San Francisco, or else Nick, calling en route to the house. She seethed with frustration, wishing there was some way she could get word to Nick and Holly to avoid coming back to the house.

"It won't do you or him any good," Hunter said as though reading her mind. This time when he smiled, Alex saw that his teeth looked . . . different, as if they had extended, like a vampire's, preparing to bite. His features looked like they were transforming into a wolf's.

Alex stared at Hunter, her mind a complete blank. Before she could think of anything more to say, the cell phone started beeping again.

The sound grated on her nerves, and she wished to God that she had the strength to wrestle the phone away from Hunter.

Regarding her steadily, Hunter kept his thumb poised over the answer button as if he were considering answering the call. Then he bent down and placed the phone on the floor by his feet. Keeping his gaze locked on Alex, he slowly, very deliberately placed his foot on top of the phone and then stepped down hard, applying a steady pressure until the plastic housing cracked.

The beeping sound cut off with a funny little *chirp* and was replaced by the sound of crunching plastic and electronic components as Hunter ground the phone into the carpet.

"There," he said, brushing his hands together and smiling with satisfaction as he kicked the wreckage away. "I guess he won't try calling again tonight."

"Do you know who that was?" Alex asked.

There was a low trembling quality to her voice that she wished she could mask but wasn't able to.

Hunter regarded her with a steady gaze that unnerved her.

It took her a moment to figure out why, but finally she realized one thing about Hunter that bothered her was that he never seemed to blink. He held his eyes open, regarding her with the cold, steady stare of a reptile.

"Please," he said, indicating the couch with a courteous sweep of his hand. "Sit down. The others will be arriving soon."

Alex was frozen where she stood but then she moved over to the couch and sat down stiffly.

"What do you want from us?" she asked, her voice catching in her throat.

Hunter stared at her for a moment. The corners of his mouth twitched, making him look like a hungry animal that was eager to feed.

"Why, as I said, I want you to die, Ms. Moreau," he said.

His voice seemed to come from far away, and it had a hypnotic effect . . . like his steady, unblinking stare.

"I want you and your friend Nick to die. As for your friend Holly Brown . . . I expect a little more from her."

"You said she was supposed to kill—"

"Ut-ut," Hunter said, cutting her off with a wag of his forefinger. "Let's not discuss that right now. They'll all be here soon, and then you'll see what I mean."

Alex closed her eyes and shook her head, grateful—for a moment—to break the spell of his gaze. But even with her eyes closed, she could feel the cruel, hungry look in

Hunter's eyes boring into her. The feeling was the same as the one she'd had earlier, and she knew that—somehow—he had been watching her even before he'd arrived at the house.

"You've spent your entire adult life investigating the supernatural . . . the paranormal, Ms. Moreau. So you should be happy."

He clapped his hands together sharply, making Alex jump.

"Within one short hour," Hunter continued, "probably much less, you will have all of the answers to every question you ever had about the existence and condition of the soul after death."

Every word he spoke echoed in Alex's ears like the heavy blows of a hammer against an anvil. Inside, she was feeling numb . . . absolutely lifeless . . . unable to respond even with a scream.

Opening her eyes, she stared blankly at the wall in front of her as she waited . . . waited for Nick to arrive. . . .

"I don't like this at all," Nick said as he pulled to a stop by the curb in front of Holly's house. He heard the upholstery in the backseat creak as McCullough shifted forward and stared up at the house with him.

The drive south from New Hampshire to Pembroke had been relatively uneventful following Holly's nearly fatal accident—if, in fact, it had been an accident. Nick wasn't sure he believed her when she said the door had opened on its own and something had tried to pull her out of the car.

For a while Holly had been hysterical, but before long she had calmed down. For the last hour of the drive, she had been so quiet that Nick wondered if she had fallen asleep or passed out. As a precaution, he had insisted that she sit in the backseat with her seat belt on beside McCullough. After locking the door on her side, he unscrewed the lock tab so she wouldn't be able to open the door from the inside.

"I think it's all right," Holly said, speaking in a flat, lifeless monotone. "I'm exhausted. I just want to go to bed and get some sleep."

Nick glanced at her over his shoulder and said, "After we check out the house and make sure Alex is okay, don't you think it'd be best if you got readmitted back into the hospital?"

Biting her lower lip, Holly shook her head firmly. Her eyes glistened like wet marbles in the dark. It was obvious that for much of the ride home she had been crying.

"No," she said, her voice barely above a whisper. "I'll be fine. Honest. I just need to sleep in my own home."

Nick regarded her in silence for a moment.

He wanted to ask her why or how she could have mistaken him for Hunter.

Maybe her nerves had been so jangled that she'd made a legitimate mistake, but Nick couldn't shake his concern.

Although he didn't know her very well, when they had been out there on the dirt road, Holly had acted strangely . . . not herself, at least as he knew her. It had seemed almost as if she was hypnotized or acting under the control of someone else.

Leaning across the front seat, Nick stared up at the house, studying it while he dug into his travel bag until he withdrew his .22 pistol.

It wasn't much, but it was all he had. The shotgun Holly had taken from her friends was useless because she'd loaded only one shell into it, and that one was expended.

The house looked safe enough. All of the windows glowed with bright lights that pushed aside the night shadows. The front porch light was on. It cast a yellow wash of light over the doorstep and walkway that led up to the door. The neatly trimmed lawn was now seared yellow with oncoming winter, and the flowers had been cut back and covered with piles of raked leaves to protect them from the snow. A high night wind was blowing, tossing the trees and shrubbery gently back and forth.

The house certainly looked like an island of safety and tranquility in the cold, autumn night.

And that's exactly what bothered Nick.

Where was Alex? he wondered.

Why hadn't she come to the door?

Even if she'd been asleep, she must have heard the car pull up.

But she hadn't come to the door.

And before that, she hadn't answered her cell phone even though he had called several times. He had thought the mountains were blocking his signal, but even further south he hadn't been able to get through. Unless the battery had run down or she was an extremely sound sleeper—which Nick knew she wasn't—then no matter how secure the house might appear, there definitely *seemed* to be *something* wrong.

"I want to have a look around first," he said.

He switched off the ignition and, grasping the pistol tightly in his right hand, opened the car door.

Cold air blasted into his face, making him catch his breath as he got out. A subtle shiver raced up his back as he straightened up and looked around.

Although he rarely had distinct, intense psychic flashes the way Alex did, Nick had learned over the years to trust his intuition, and right now his intuition was telling him that something was definitely wrong with this picture.

He scanned the house and adjacent yards, but here in suburbia, everything was so well-trimmed and manicured that there wasn't much he could use for cover.

Of course, he could walk up to the front door and ring the doorbell.

That's what he should do. Nothing was stopping him.

Except, he thought, he could very easily be walking into another trap.

"You want to go to the left? I can swing around the right?" McCullough asked from the backseat.

Nick considered the option, weighing how much he

needed backup and how important it was that someone stay with Holly. She seemed docile enough now, but—given her physical and emotional state—she could be fairly unpredictable. Her attempt to kill herself by jumping out of the moving car was proof of that.

"No," he finally said. "Wait here with Holly. I want to make sure we're not walking into anything."

"What could we be walking into?" Holly asked. Her voice still sounded flat and empty, drained of emotion. "Look, Nick, I appreciate everything you and Alex have done for me. I really do. But I've been through hell and back these past few days, and right now, all I want to do is go to sleep in my own bed."

"I can appreciate that," Nick said, bending down and looking her straight in the eyes. "But not until I know that everything's safe."

Gun in hand, he moved away from the car. Keeping to the shadows as best he could, he cut across the lawn, heading toward the right side of the house where the garage was. He was about halfway there when he heard a loud click, and the door swung open.

Nick froze in midstep, knowing that he'd been seen.

He felt only a slight measure of relief when he saw Alex standing in the doorway. He couldn't see her face clearly because of the light coming from behind her inside the house.

"Hey," Alex called out, waving a lethargic greeting with one hand. The other hand was behind the door, holding it open. "You finally made it."

Nick nodded, saying nothing.

"Everything's okay," Alex said. "Come on. All of you. Come on up."

Glancing back at the car, Nick saw that it would have been impossible for Alex to see either Holly or McCullough in the backseat. The car's tinted windows reflected the house lights like polished mirrors. And Nick couldn't help but notice that Alex had said "*all* of you" . . . not "*both*" of you.

How did she know that there was anyone with him besides Holly?

Maybe he was overreacting, but he also thought that he detected something in Alex's tone of voice that didn't sound quite right. He knew that she would have been worried about him, and he realized that he'd been expecting her to come rushing out of the house to greet him, happy that both he and Holly were safely back home.

But Alex just stood there stiffly in the doorway, her hand lowered now, and clenched into a fist at her side.

"Yeah . . . All right," Nick said, but for several long seconds, he didn't take a step from where he stood. He stared up at Alex, tensed and waiting for her to make the next move.

When she did, he wasn't ready for it.

Ducking to one side, Alex suddenly threw the front door wide open. Nick heard a loud *thump* sound and saw that there was someone standing beside her, hidden—until now—by the door.

It was a man, and Nick immediately recognized who it was.

"Hunter," he whispered, watching helplessly as Hunter grabbed Alex by the arm and wrenched her backward so hard she almost fell down.

"Go on! Run! Get out of here!" Alex shouted, but then he clamped his hand over her mouth to shut her up. She thrashed about wildly, trying to break the grip Hunter had on her upper arm, but he was too strong, and he easily overpowered her.

Rather than running for the car, though, Nick started running across the lawn toward Hunter and Alex. He raised his .22 pistol to fire, but Hunter was using Alex as a shield. Nick knew that he couldn't get off a clean shot without risking hitting Alex.

"It's all a matter of who wants to die first and when," Hunter said.

His voice was steady and calm. It echoed in the darkness, so loud Nick couldn't help but feel goose bumps spread across his arms.

"Let her go, Hunter," Nick called out, stopping about twenty feet from the front door. He braced his right arm with his left, all the while keeping a steady bead on the two of them.

"Go ahead," Hunter shouted, his face split by a wide smirk. "Shoot her to get me if you want to. I honestly don't care."

He started to laugh and had to gain a measure of control over himself before he could finish.

"You're just the pawns in this little game, anyway."

Nick watched as Hunter took Alex's left arm and, holding her right shoulder, cocked her arm around up behind her back. He stared straight at Nick, his mouth a thin, cruel line as he jerked Alex's arm up hard.

Alex let out a small whimper of pain, but that was all. Her eyes fluttered and glazed over, but she didn't cry out.

"Forget about me, Nick!" she said, struggling against the pain as Hunter applied more pressure to her bent arm. Her legs buckled and almost collapsed. "It's Holly that he's after! Get her out of here!"

Nick cringed when Hunter laughed again, a dry, hollow laugh that reached deep into his soul.

"You know he won't leave you behind," Hunter said, practically spitting out each word. "You must know by now that your friend Nick, here, is a natural born hero. He's not going to leave until he saves you and Holly . . . or dies trying. So come on, Nick! Come up here and save her!"

He gave Alex's arm another, even harder twist that made a loud *popping* sound. Alex cried out.

"Why don't you and your friends come up to the house so we can have a little chat about this . . . like civilized people," Hunter said.

Slumped on the floor, Alex glared at Nick. Pain flared like wildfire in her eyes as she called out to him, "Don't do it, Nick! Please! Don't!" She gasped in pain. "You'll just be giving him what he wants!"

"You know I can do a lot worse to her, Nick," Hunter said with a sinister smile. "So put the gun down. *Now!*"

Knowing that he was beat, Nick lowered his pistol and dropped it to the frozen ground. He glanced over his shoulder when he heard the car door open and slam shut, and saw McCullough and Holly getting out. Holly looked pale and ghostly in the dim light, but even at this distance, Nick could see that she was trembling violently.

He couldn't help but wonder once again if he'd been set up all along for this, if McCullough was still working for Hunter and had been stringing him along the whole time. Simmering with anger, he watched as McCullough took Holly by the arm and directed her toward the front steps.

"See?" Hunter said. "I'm glad some of you can be reasonable."

As they walked past Nick, McCullough hesitated and made direct eye contact with him. Smiling slightly, he nodded as he patted a small bulge in his jacket pocket.

"Don't worry," McCullough whispered under his breath. "It ain't over yet."

NINETEEN

When the car pulled to a stop in front of her house, it seemed to Holly as though she was dreaming.

In fact, it seemed like ever since Evan had died *everything* had been a dream . . . or a nightmare.

Something as basic as her visual perception seemed to have been changed—sometimes subtly, sometimes not so subtly. People and objects often moved around her in excruciatingly slow motion; and sometimes, especially at night, things she looked at would appear distorted with a hallucinatory intensity.

Her sense of hearing seemed altered, as well. Sounds of such everyday things as people talking or cars passing by created weird Doppler effects that reverberated with curious echoes. Worse than that, there were other sounds she heard on occasion—sounds she couldn't begin to identify—that seemed to come out of nowhere and vanish like windblown smoke. Sometimes these almost sounded like distant voices, and faint, chattering laughter.

Even her sense of balance seemed oddly different, as

though—somehow—her center of gravity had shifted. Whenever she did simple, physical acts—things she used to do every day without thinking, such as walking or turning her head—a powerful feeling of vertigo would sweep through her.

It was terrifying.

She couldn't help but wonder if these sensations were due to stress and grief, and would eventually subside, or if they were now an essential, permanent part of her.

"Come on. Let's go," said the man whose name she couldn't recall. He was sitting beside her in the darkness. His voice sounded unusually loud in the muffled silence of the car.

Holly regarded him with a long, blank stare until what he'd said finally registered.

When she nodded, she heard something in her neck or the back of her head crackle like someone was crumpling paper. Her legs felt as thin and inflexible as stilts, and she moved with a maddening, sludgy slowness as she opened the door and stepped out of the car. The man followed close behind her and took hold of her arm with a tight grip. Side by side, they started toward her house.

She shivered wildly, not so much from the frosty night air as from the clutching cold that gripped the core of her heart. Her throat and lungs felt like they were on fire whenever she tried to take a deep breath. Waves of dizziness washed through her, threatening to pull her under.

She couldn't believe this was *her* house.

It seemed like a lifetime ago that she had lived here with Evan . . . a lifetime or more.

Light spilled from the open front door, casting a thick, surreal yellow glow over everything. Shadows—even the smallest shadows of dried flowers and dead grass—stood out in stark relief, like splashes of black ink against a brilliance so intense it hurt her eyes.

All around her the darkness swelled, pulsating with a terrible energy. Holly tried to resist the thought that the night was a monster eager to devour her and her friends whole.

She glanced over at the man holding her by the arm, leading her toward the front steps.

She didn't like him.

There was something dark and dangerous in his eyes. Something vacant.

She had no idea what he meant when he paused in front of Nick and, leaning close, whispered to him: "Don't worry . . . It ain't over yet."

She studied Nick for a moment, still not exactly sure what she thought about him, either. Alex had told her that he was one of her closest friends, someone she could trust with her life, and that should be enough; but he—like the man walking beside her—had an edge that Holly found threatening.

And what about Alex . . . ?

She was standing in the doorway, and a man—a man Nick had called "Hunter"—had her arm twisted up behind her back. When she got closer, Holly could see that Alex was wincing with pain but trying hard not to let it show.

Fear and confusion surged like hot metal through Holly.

If this really was Hunter, the man she was looking for, what the hell was he doing here?

How had he found her?

Did he know somehow that she was looking for him and had come after her instead?

Or was there something else going on . . . something that she didn't fully understand?

. . . you will . . .

The voice, so faint it was barely audible and almost lost in the whooshing sound in Holly's ears, carried to her like a gentle puff of wind . . . like a cold breath on the back of her neck. It filled her with a deep sense of dread.

Right now, all she knew for sure was, if this really was Adam Hunter—the man who had killed her child—then all of them were in serious danger. A man who could detonate a bomb in a crowd, killing and maiming scores of innocent men, women, and children, would certainly have no qualms about killing any or all of them.

When she thought this, Holly seethed with anger at herself for letting this happen . . . for *allowing* it to happen.

Yes, it was all her fault.

None of this would be happening right now if not for her.

Perhaps it had started as long ago as last spring, when she had first invited Alex back East for the Thanksgiving holiday . . . maybe it had started much earlier than that.

Or maybe it was simply unavoidable fate, something none of them could have done anything to prevent.

There was no way of knowing.

But Holly was positive that none of these people would be in jeopardy right now if it hadn't been for her.

The problem was, she couldn't see any way of getting them out of danger. She was so numb with fear and grief and anger that she couldn't even think straight. Her vision got blurry and started to spin, and she realized she'd be lucky not to pass out.

No! she commanded herself, gritting her teeth as she clung to the man supporting her.

Hang in there! . . . Don't let go! . . . Don't give up! . . . Alex is in danger!

She couldn't give up.

Not yet.

No matter what else, she had to try to get her best friend out of this horrible situation. After that, Holly genuinely didn't care what happened to her. If she died, then at least she'd be at peace . . . and there was always the possibility that she would be reunited in death with Evan.

Holly was so lost in her worries that she wasn't looking where she was going. She stumbled and almost fell as she started up the stairs, but the man holding her caught her in his strong grasp and held her.

For just an instant, their eyes locked. The fact that he

didn't let her fall gave Holly a glimmer of hope that—maybe—he really was a good person who would look out for her . . . and maybe help her.

Still holding Alex in an arm-lock, Hunter backed away so they could enter the house. As Holly passed by Hunter, he smiled at her with a wicked grin that made her think of an animal, sick with rabies.

Nick followed them in and was the last one inside the house. Hunter nodded once, sharply, in the direction of the door, and Holly heard Nick slam the door shut behind her.

"Lock it," Hunter commanded.

The sound of the dead bolt snapping in place reminded Holly of the solid click a coffin lid made when it shut down.

The short walk from the foyer into the living room seemed to take forever. The walls on both sides of her appeared to lengthen and stretch upwards until they were lost in the swimming brightness of the lights. Holly had the distinct feeling that she wasn't even walking.

No.

She was gliding . . . drifting like a dandelion puff, carried on the wind.

The short corridor leading into the living room telescoped sickeningly outward. The walls rippled and shifted as though made of putty. Holly looked down at her feet, amazed to see how far away they appeared.

She swallowed with difficulty and heard her breath hitch in her throat, the sound seeming to keep time with her accelerating heartbeat.

You're dreaming this, she told herself. *Wake up.*

Her eyelids fluttered as she shook her head, trying to clear it. She was almost overwhelmed by the thought that she might be back in the hospital, lying in bed, dreaming or hallucinating all of this.

Yes . . . Please let me be imagining all of this! she wished desperately as she walked into the brightly lit living room, but there was nothing imaginary about the sharp pain she felt when she banged her knee against the end table before flopping down onto the couch. Looking down at the floor, she saw the crushed housing of a cell phone on the carpet but barely registered what it was.

"Well, well, well," Hunter said.

His voice had a deep vibrancy that sounded to Holly like a distant rockslide.

"We're all here. And isn't this just the coziest little get-together?"

Tilting her head back slowly, Holly looked up at the man. For a shattering instant, she saw—not a man at all, but a huge, dark, amorphous shape that towered above her, leering at her with hungry, glowing red eyes.

Behind the man—or monster—she saw the doorway that led into the dining room. Dense darkness swirled behind the figure, deepening and expanding like an evil, living thing that oozed from him and threatened to swallow her whole.

Holly blinked her eyes rapidly, trying to see more clearly, but her vision was cloudy and kept drifting in and out of focus. Whimpering softly, she sagged back against the couch cushion and let her breath out with a long, stuttering sigh. It was only when she was taking another breath that she heard a sound . . . a faint, whispering voice, teasing at the edge of hearing.

. . . this is your last chance . . . you have to do it now . . .

Holly immediately recognized Evan's voice, faint with distance. She narrowed her eyes, concentrating hard, but wasn't at all sure that she had heard the voice correctly.

He sounded so far away . . . so lost.

Hot tears filled her eyes, and the light in the living room shattered into thousands of brilliant shards that stung her like wasps.

She was positive it was Evan, but she was no longer sure that she could trust him. He had been wrong—or had lied to her—before and almost caused her to shoot Nick.

How could she trust him now?

She had no sense of moving her head. It felt more like the entire room rotated around her as she looked first at Alex, then at Nick, then at the man who's name she didn't remember, and—finally—at Hunter.

They all appeared to be frozen in place.

Motionless.

Their eyes were wide open and staring. All of their mouths were closed except for Hunter's, whose mouth was hanging open in the middle of forming a word.

The room was filled with dense silence. A panicky, suffocating feeling gripped Holly when she realized that she hadn't taken a breath.

She couldn't breathe!

...I know you can hear me, Mom...

The voice was low and teasing ... like a lover, tempting her in the darkness.

No...I can't...You can't ask me to...to do something like that, Holly thought, unable to speak aloud.

Her eyes darted frantically back and forth as she searched for something on which to anchor her gaze. She tried to inhale but found that she couldn't. Tiny trailing white spots of light danced and weaved like fireflies in front of her, but she could still see Hunter standing motionlessly in front of her. His huge bulk blocked her view of the doorway that led into the dining room, but behind him, she caught a hint of motion.

...you have to kill him now... you know that...

You know I'd do anything... anything *for you,* she thought with a sudden desperate sense of acceptance of what the voice was urging her to do.

She struggled to get up from the couch and suddenly had the peculiar feeling that—somehow—she was floating outside of her body. She rose into the air like a feather, caught in an upward draft of wind and sailed past Hunter, who remained frozen in place. She felt herself being pulled toward the dense darkness that was framed by the doorway.

Beyond the doorway, she saw a long, dark corridor that

stretched back . . . back . . . narrowing until it was lost in an impossibly distant vanishing point.

Holly tried desperately to speak, but she had no breath, no voice. The muffled denseness of the silence that surrounded her was terrifying. Although she had no sensation of physically doing anything, she found herself being drawn further and further into the gaping maw of darkness.

And the further she went into it, the clearer Evan's voice became. She grew dizzy from a lack of air and struggled to take even a tiny sip of breath.

This is it. . . . This is your only chance. . . . Evan's voice said. *Your last chance . . . You have to kill him! Now!*

"No . . . Honey . . ." she gasped.

The air in her lungs felt like fire. Holly wasn't sure if she said the words out loud or simply thought them. The darkness pulsated around her like grasping hands, but far off, in the center of it all, she saw something else. . . .

A face, resolving like a slowly developing photograph.

Holly's heart lurched coldly in her chest and sent a stabbing pain through her when she saw that it was her son. . . .

Her dead son . . .

"Oh, honey . . ." she whispered, nearly overwhelmed with grief and despair.

Evan's features continued to resolve more clearly. Holly could see that he was staring back at her . . . and smiling a wide, wicked smile that exposed his teeth in a feral grin. His eyes never blinked, and his steady gaze sliced through her with chilling intensity.

"No, I . . . I can't," she said, fighting against the rapidly mounting fear that welled up inside her like poison. "I can't and I won't!"

But you have to. . . . Don't you understand that, Mom? I can't rest. . . . My soul won't be at peace until you kill him!

Holly shook her head and struggled to pull back, but she felt herself being dragged relentlessly toward Evan and the solid wall of darkness that surrounded him.

"You're not my son!" she shouted as every fiber in her being rebelled against what Evan or the thing masquerading as Evan was telling her to do. "You never were. My son would never give in to such hatred . . . to such evil!"

As soon as she said this, she felt a sudden powerful tug, an almost overwhelming sensation of weight returning to her body.

Panic filled her, but the more she resisted going to Evan, the more intense the feeling of weight returning to her body became.

She was no longer a feather.

She was a stone, falling . . . plummeting . . . sinking down . . . down into the darkest depths of the ocean.

A terrible howling sound filled her ears until it sounded like a chorus of voices, screaming. The sound rose louder, becoming increasingly shrill until it gradually blended into Evan's voice.

Only now it wasn't Evan's voice.

It was the bellowing roar of a monster.

Then if you won't do it . . . you'll have to kill yourself!

Holly closed her eyes and shook her head, resisting, but that only intensified the falling sensation. She was spinning head over heels, and all the while the voice thundered in the darkness and inside her head.

YOU'LL HAVE TO KILL YOURSELF!
YOU'LL HAVE TO KILL YOURSELF!

She screamed when she opened her eyes and saw—not Hunter, but Evan, standing in front of her, inches away. He was still smiling at her, his lips pulled back in a cruel grin. His eyes glowed with an intense red light that bathed the darkness around him like a wash of blood.

Transfixed with terror, Holly watched as Evan slowly raised his arms and extended both hands to her. For an instant, it looked like he was reaching out to her for a loving embrace.

Then, in agonizing slow motion, Evan's body split open,

and a huge, black-winged beast slowly unfolded from inside the husk that had been his body.

The creature howled as it expanded, its dark wings flapping with a sickening wet sound as they reached out until they scraped the opposite walls. Its head touched the ceiling, yet it continued to expand until it was hunched over. Twisting threads of blue light engulfed the beast, charging it with a terrible energy as it reached for Holly with grasping hands tipped with thick, wicked-looking claws.

In the grips of terror, Holly cringed away from the monster as its cold, foul breath washed over her with the stench of fetid swamp water. She scrambled over the side of the couch in an attempt to get away from it, but she knew that escape was hopeless. The only thought that filled her mind was that this demon was going to destroy her and everyone in the room.

In her panic to get away, Holly almost didn't notice the set of fireplace tools beside the hearth, but her gaze fastened on the poker, and she lunged forward to grab it.

She was filled with an amazing surge of energy as she gripped the implement and wheeled around to face the creature.

She knew that it was insane and futile, but she raised the cast-iron poker above her head and charged the monster in front of her.

Everything happened too fast.

Nick was desperate to do something, but as long as Hunter had Alex pinioned, he couldn't do anything. He followed them into the living room and was just about to sit down when Holly collapsed onto the couch and let out a frightful moan.

Still holding Alex as a shield, Hunter moved closer to Holly. It filled Nick with fury to see the way the man was grinning.

He had won, and he knew it.

And now—before he killed them all—he was going to torment them with his victory.

But then in a move so fast it caught Nick off guard, Holly let out a wild scream and was off the couch, scrambling to reach the fireplace implements. She knocked over the set, but her hand caught the cast-iron poker, and she spun around with the hooked iron rod raised above her head.

"No!" Nick shouted, seeing that, in her panic, Holly was about to bring the implement down onto Alex's head.

He reacted without thinking and propelled himself forward, tackling her at the waist and wrestling her to the floor. Holly's body seemed charged with energy, and it was harder than Nick thought it should be to disarm her. He wrenched the poker from her grip and tossed it aside. Behind him, he heard the menacing baritone of Hunter's laughter.

Fists clenched, he rose to his feet and wheeled around to face Hunter. A jolting shock ran through him when he saw the huge, gnarled figure of a demon instead of a man standing before him.

The creature's eyes glowed with a baleful red as it stared at him. A whirlwind filled the room as the demon flapped its thick, leathery wings. Bright bolts of lightning flashed, exploding the windows outward.

"You meddling fool!" the demon shouted.

Its voice rose above the sounds of shattering glass and the high-pitched screaming of the wind.

"She was supposed to kill Hunter first!"

The creature lashed out at Nick, its thick, yellow claws raking down the side of his face. Intense, burning pain shot through him as the claws dug into his shoulder and then pulled away.

A hot wash of blood flowed down Nick's side. He staggered backward, trying to keep his balance, but his legs went all goofy on him, and he pitched backward onto the floor. He hit hard enough to knock the wind out of him. He looked up at the beast in utter disbelief.

"First she'll die," the demon shrieked, "and then each one of you will die! I'll take you all with me down into the burning center of hell!"

Nick struggled to rise. It was in his nature to fight, but he couldn't move. The wounds on his face stung with a curious numbing tingle. The gash in his shoulder made his arm and chest feel like they were on fire.

And then, on the edge of his vision, he saw McCullough move. Screaming at the top of his lungs, the man charged at the demon with both hands clenched into fists and raised above his head.

Nick's vision began to dim as clouds of pain billowed in his brain. He didn't see that McCullough was even holding a weapon, but then, fighting to stay conscious in spite of the pain, he thought that maybe McCullough wasn't so foolish after all.

Maybe he simply wanted to get it over with quickly and make sure he was the first of them to die.

TWENTY

McCullough was struggling to maintain control of himself as he watched events unfold, but it was difficult.

The seething hatred he felt for Hunter almost overwhelmed any clear thinking. It was bad enough that earlier that night the man had deliberately tried to burn him alive. Worse than that, though, McCullough couldn't believe that he had been so caught up in his political cause that he had willingly contributed support to a man who was willing, almost eager, to carry out a plan to kill and maim innocent civilians, all in the name of his struggle against the U.S. government.

Several times, even while they were still outside the house, McCullough considered rushing the man and trying to overpower him, but something deep inside him told him that it would be futile.

He sensed something inside Hunter, a terrible power that frightened him.

It wasn't just that for several years the man had been his commander in the militia, and that he was conditioned to obey and respect him.

It went way beyond that.

There was something else about Hunter . . . something that told McCullough on a deep, subconscious level that this was the most dangerous man he knew.

If he even was a man.

From listening to the way Nick talked, especially when he was on the phone to his friend Alex, McCullough had begun to have doubts even about that. In fact, by the time they arrived in Pembroke, he was convinced that Hunter wasn't a man at all . . . that he was, in fact, a devil incarnate, like Hitler or Mussolini.

During the drive south, McCullough had surreptitiously searched Nick's travel bag. He had found nothing of interest except for one thing—a small vial of clear liquid.

While leaning against the door and pretending to be asleep, McCullough had quietly taken off the top of the vial and inspected the liquid it contained.

It was odorless and colorless.

When he put a drop of it on the tip of his tongue and tasted it, it had been tasteless, too.

As far as he could tell, it was nothing but pure, plain water.

So why would Nick be carrying around a vial of clear water?

That question had occupied McCullough for much of the drive south to Massachusetts. And—finally—he had come up with what seemed like the only possible answer.

It was a vial of holy water.

It was a crazy notion, but if that was true, then McCullough figured Nick and his friend Alex weren't just mercenaries. They were members of an organization that fought against something a lot more powerful than mere militias.

It was bad enough to be involved with political crazies, he thought; it could be a lot worse to be hooked up with religious fanatics on a holy crusade.

Maybe this organization Nick had mentioned, the Legacy, was a group of religious fanatics who were fighting—

or thought they were fighting—a war against demons and evil spirits.

McCullough didn't know much about logic, but it made a crazy kind of sense, and before long he became convinced that's exactly what was going on.

By the time they reached Holly's house in Pembroke, he was positive that Hunter was an evil spirit or demon that had assumed the shape of a real man, but was, in fact, far from human.

As they were walking up to the house, McCullough paused in front of Nick and patted his jacket pocket where he had hidden the vial, which he was now convinced was holy water.

"Don't worry . . . It ain't over yet," he whispered.

Even as he said that, he realized how foolish he was to think that's really what they were up against here—a demon that had assumed the human form of Adam Hunter in order to wreak its vengeance and accomplish its goals.

But as they filed into the living room, he saw that he was going to have to act fast if any of them—other than Hunter—were going to survive the night.

He watched as Holly, looking pale and drawn, and on the verge of a nervous breakdown, collapsed onto the couch. She sat there for a moment, staring straight ahead at Hunter. But she looked like she had checked out, and her mind had snapped. Her eyes were glazed and looked like they were focused on something way off in the distance, and she was watching something that none of the rest of them could see.

Then, before either he or Nick could react, she had leaped off the couch and attacked Hunter with a fireplace poker. He saw Hunter push Alex forward, directly into Holly's attack, but before Holly finished her swing, Nick tackled her and wrestled the poker away. And then McCullough watched in stunned disbelief as Hunter's body began to . . .

Dissolve.

That was the only word he could think of as the shape that had been Hunter slowly metamorphosed into something else . . . something horrible.

Within seconds, Hunter transformed into a huge demon with widespread wings and claws in the place of his arms. The creature's body thickened with muscles covered by black scales. Its eyes flashed with wicked red fire as it roared, filling the living room with its unearthly, keening voice.

Almost overwhelmed by his terror, McCullough wished he could convince himself that he was imagining all of this, but it was too horrifyingly real. The demon continued to expand until its head pressed against the ceiling. A terrible rushing sound of wind tore through the room.

Reaching into his jacket pocket, McCullough felt for the vial of water. He felt suddenly foolish for thinking that something as pitifully small as a simple jar of water could have any effect on something this terrifying.

Amazed and almost immobilized with fear, McCullough watched Hunter's transformation into what he realized must be his true form. The brilliant flashes of light that flickered in the room dazzled his eyes. The strobe-light effect made it almost impossible for him to see clearly. Everything was flickering like the frames of an old-time movie gone out of control.

Suddenly the living room windows exploded outward with a deafening concussion. Glass and small objects flew everywhere. Something hit McCullough hard on the side of the head, almost knocking him out cold, but he shook it off and watched, transfixed by what was happening.

"You meddling fool!" the beast shouted. "She was supposed to kill Hunter first!"

When the creature slashed its clawed hand at Nick and ripped open the side of his face, McCullough finally reacted. In a dim corner of his mind he suspected that it was a feeble, foolish thing to do, and that he would be dead within seconds, but he raised both hands above his head and charged. His fingers were numb, useless. He struggled to open the vial of water but couldn't get the top off. Finally, in frustration, he flung the bottle at the beast.

"You son of a bitch!" he screamed in frustration when he saw the small bottle bounce harmlessly off the beast's chest. The vial hit the carpeted floor and rolled away out of sight, underneath the couch.

Tossing its head back and stretching its arms wide to either side, the beast let out a ferocious roar that practically shattered McCullough's eardrums. With one clenched fist, it swung around and nailed McCullough with a powerful backhand swat.

The concussion was like getting hit by a cannonball. McCullough heard something inside his head snap like a tree branch. He thought it must have been his neck or back as he was swept off his feet and flung backward through the air until he slammed against the living room wall and then fell into a heap on the floor.

Slumped against the wall, he watched in stunned silence as everything slowed down to a sludgy slow motion. Nick was on all fours, his face a mask of blood and pain as he scrambled across the floor. The beast's attention still seemed to be focused on McCullough, though. It seemed not to be aware of Nick as he leaned forward and fished around madly underneath the sofa.

The fringes of McCullough's vision began to fill with a dense, vibrating blackness as he struggled to comprehend what was happening. The only clear thought he had was that, in a very short time, they were all going to be dead— or worse than dead.

But then, cutting through the fog that threatened to pull him under, another thought arose in McCullough's mind. At first, as it began to form, he was almost afraid to think it, fearing that the beast would somehow read his mind and know what was happening.

But seeing Nick reaching under the couch for the vial

of water made McCullough remember just how much of a fighter Nick was.

The man wouldn't quit for anything. Even when they had been left locked inside a burning building, Nick hadn't lost hope or stopped trying.

And he still, obviously, hadn't lost hope, even against this beast or demon or whatever this thing was that the last small, rational corner of McCullough's mind told him was impossible.

But Nick was still fighting . . . still trying to find a way to vanquish the creature, no matter what it was.

McCullough moaned softly—that was the only sound he could make—when he saw Nick roll over onto his side, holding up the small, clear vial of water. Grimacing with pain, Nick tried to remove the top, but his hands kept slipping. Finally, in a sudden burst of fury, he smacked the top of the bottle against the edge of the coffee table, shattering the thin neck of glass.

Some of the liquid spilled out.

But not all.

McCullough struggled not to lose consciousness as he watched Nick's last, desperate effort. He shifted onto one side and then threw the bottle at the beast with what had to be his final burst of strength.

Water sprayed from the bottle as it flew through the air and then struck the colossal black figure square in the face. In an instant, Nick scrambled for cover behind one of the armchairs.

Cowering in fear and pain on the floor, McCullough could do nothing but sit and watch in stunned amazement at what happened next.

The air suddenly felt like it had been sucked out of the room as a whirlwind, howling with a shrill whistle, swept over McCullough, ripping at him like a million grasping hands. The flashing lights in the room almost blinded him, but he clearly saw places on the beast's face and chest where the water had hit.

Most of it had splashed across its arms and chest, but apparently some of it had also gotten into its eyes. A loud, sizzling sound, like overloading electrical circuits, filled the room. The creature staggered backward as it wiped frantically at its eyes. Thick, curling tendrils of gray smoke rose from its body.

The loud hissing noise sounded like a nest full of angry snakes as it rose louder and louder until that was all McCullough could hear above the shrieking of the wind. He glanced over at Alex and Holly, and saw that they— like Nick—were watching in amazement. Their mouths were open, and they appeared to be screaming, but he couldn't hear them above the terrible chaos that filled the room.

The creature howled as it fell down and thrashed wildly on the floor, clawing with one hand at its eyes as it lashed out wildly with the other. The smoke rising from its body thickened as it spread across the beast's scaly hide, consuming it. Patches of bright light rippled from beneath the creature's skin, and wicked tongues of flame quickly engulfed its entire body.

Thick black smoke and the noxious stench of burning flesh filled the room. The beast continued to bellow its rage and frustration until, finally, still writhing in agony, it began to dissolve. Its body slowly caved in upon itself until there was nothing left but thick, flaky chunks of seared flesh and charred bones. As these dissolved away into powder, the wind subsided gradually, and the flashing lights faded away.

Within seconds, all that remained on the floor was a dark smear of thick, greasy soot.

Exhausted and stunned by what he had just seen, McCullough tried to stand up but he wasn't able to and collapsed back against the wall. His face was slick with cold sweat. After a moment, he realized that he was squeezing his hands together tightly.

Slowly, painfully, he unclasped his hands and extended

his fingers. Looking at his hands, he saw that the palm of his right hand was marked by a bright red patch of skin that looked exactly like an imprint of the glass vial. Already, the wound was beginning to blister, and it was starting to itch terribly.

Turning his head slowly, painfully, and distantly aware that he was in shock, McCullough looked over at Nick, who was lying on the floor. The wounds on his face and shoulder were bleeding, but his eyes were open, and he looked alert and conscious.

"What the . . . what the hell just happened?" McCullough asked.

Nobody paid any attention to him.

Holly had collapsed onto the floor, both hands covering her face as she rocked back and forth. Her body was wracked by loud, wrenching sobs as she wept. Alex, her left arm hanging uselessly at her side, came over to Nick and, kneeling beside him, inspected his wounds. Then she grabbed the living room phone and dialed 911.

After giving the medics directions to Holly's house, she leaned over Nick again and, wincing with her own pain, smiled down at him.

"Hey," Nick said.

He sounded weak and dazed, but McCullough could tell that he wasn't hurt too seriously. He'd certainly survive.

Finally, Alex glanced over at McCullough and forced a smile.

"You want to know what just happened?" she asked.

Her voice was flat and barely audible above the ringing sound that filled McCullough's head. Her eyes narrowed as the initial shock wore off, and she started feeling the intense pain of her dislocated shoulder.

"What happened was . . . Nick just saved all four of us."

"Do you think we really destroyed the demon?" Alex asked.

Sighing deeply, she settled her head back against the crisp pillow and closed her eyes. The sheets were cool against her skin, like a soothing wash of water. Her left arm and shoulder were immobilized in a sling.

"You know, that's a damned good question."

She had the phone pressed tightly against her ear, but it was still difficult to hear Derek's voice. They either had a poor connection, or else she still had some hearing loss due to the bomb blast and everything else that had happened, especially the previous night at Holly's house.

"I don't know if we destroyed the demon or not," she finally said, licking her lips. "We killed . . . something . . . but I can't help but think that the body that we destroyed was Hunter's, and not the demon's."

"You mean the body which the demon possessed and used," Derek said.

Just hearing the inflections of Derek's voice filled Alex with relief.

"You could be right," Derek continued. "I suspect that Hunter—the human being named Adam Hunter, that is— died a long time ago, back when the demon first took possession of him. There is no way you could have saved him. My greater fear is that the demon may have survived . . . and will strike again when it thinks it's ready."

Alex nodded and swallowed with difficulty as she opened her eyes and looked around the hospital room. She was greatly reassured just to see Rachel seated in the chair beside her bed and Nick standing by her bedside. His shoulder and face were bandaged, but there was a bright gleam in his eyes as he smiled at her.

Alex didn't think she really needed to be there, but the doctor had insisted that she stay in the hospital overnight for observation.

Besides her dislocated shoulder, his diagnosis had been simple:

Exhaustion.

There was another bed beside Alex's, and Holly was

asleep in it. In spite of the bruises and small cuts on her face, Holly's features looked composed and relaxed. The doctor had given her a sedative to help her sleep.

Alex looked past her friend to the far side of the room and saw the thin, gauzy shadows over by the closet. A slight shiver ran up her back. She knew that it had to be just her imagination, but for just an instant, she was positive that she saw the shadows deepen and shift ever so slightly.

"That was good thinking on McCullough's part . . . to bring the bottle of holy water against the demon," Derek said. "I'm surprised that Nick didn't think to use it."

"As it turns out, he did," Alex said as she shot a quick smile in Nick's direction.

"Where is McCullough now?"

Alex shrugged. "He took off before the police arrived. I would guess, as a member of the First Step, that the F.B.I. will be looking for him."

"If they know enough to look for him," Derek said. "I suspect, in time, we'll hear from him, and we'll do what we can to help him if he's truly innocent. But you know— I'm still a bit puzzled about one thing."

"Oh? What's that?"

"Why would Nick be carrying something like a bottle of holy water around with him?"

Alex smiled weakly and glanced over at Nick.

"He told me it was a present from Philip before he left the Legacy," she said. "Philip always told him that a soldier is never fully armed unless he has the right weapons with him before he goes into the battle."

"Well, in this case, I guess he was right," Derek said with a dry chuckle.

"Yeah, I guess so, but I just . . . I can't help thinking that the demon got away . . . that somehow it survived," Alex said.

A shiver raced up her back, and she couldn't ignore the uneasy feeling that she was being watched.

"I understand your concern," Derek said, "but that's

something we can never really be sure about. And anyway, you know there will always be forces of darkness in the world. They're powerful and they're everywhere, and we must always be on our guard against them."

"I know," Alex said, suddenly feeling so tired she could barely manage a whisper. Maybe the doctor had also given her an injection to help her rest. Her mind was getting hazy, and right now, she couldn't remember and didn't seem to care.

Her throat was parched. She leaned forward and took a sip of ice water from the cup on her nightstand. The water felt indescribably good going down.

"We reported to the police that Hunter, knowing that Holly suspected him of the Plymouth Rock bombing, had tracked her down and tried to kill her by setting off another bomb at her house. His two goons are dead. Early this morning, I heard on the news that a motorist found Morgan's body on the roadside in New Hampshire. We also heard that Hunter's car was found parked a few houses down from Holly's house. Williams was slumped over the steering wheel, dead. His neck had been broken."

"Hunter didn't like leaving behind any loose ends, did he?" Derek said.

"No, he didn't," Alex said. "We told the authorities that Nick got cut from the glass when the explosion knocked him through the living room window, but the doctor who attended him seemed at least somewhat suspicious. He commented on how the wounds looked more like claw marks."

"Nick's lucky those cuts weren't more serious," Derek said.

"Absolutely. Although our explanation seemed to work for the local cops, I'm sure the feds will follow up on Nick's lead. With the evidence they'll collect at the compound in New Hampshire, it won't be hard for them to establish that Hunter and his group were responsible for the

222

Plymouth Rock bombing. Then they're going to go through everything here in detail."

"I think your cover story will hold up," Derek said. "Who's going to contradict it? As far as they know, all the members of the First Step Militia—including Hunter—are dead. There's clear evidence of a fire in Holly's living room and, as you told me, all of the windows in the downstairs were blown out. That certainly will suggest that a bomb was detonated there."

"I'm sure it will," Alex said, "but Nick pointed out that the investigators won't find any traces of the same explosive materials that Hunter used at the Plymouth Rock bombing."

"That may not be so bad," Derek replied. "It might make them close the case all the sooner. As far as we can determine, the situation is over. I'd rather not have the feds investigate too thoroughly . . . not if it might expose the Legacy any more than necessary."

"I agree," Alex said. "Still I'm really worried about Holly. She's been devastated by everything that's happened."

"I can't tell you how much sympathy I feel for her," Derek said "How is she doing?"

"She's asleep right now," Alex said, stifling a yawn as she glanced over at her friend.

"Well," Derek said, "from what you've told me, she's an incredibly strong person. And I'm glad she's accepted our offer to come out here to stay at Legacy House while she continues her recovery. If she does want some therapy, I'm sure Rachel will be more than willing to help her. I believe she'll recover much faster than you think."

"I hope so . . . I really do," Alex said wistfully.

Her gaze drifted out the window. A deep shudder quaked her body. The pain she felt for her friend was deep and unfathomable.

"I think it's imperative that we keep a very close watch on her for a while," Derek said. "If she truly is one of the *lamedvovniks*, as I suspect she is, then I'm sure the forces of evil will try once again to overcome her. While she's under our protection is one thing, but we have to give her the tools and knowledge to fight back on her own terms.''

"I just don't see why, if the demon wanted her to die, it didn't just kill her outright," Alex said.

"Because that wouldn't have accomplished its goal," Derek said. "From everything I've learned while investigating Fra Felipe's death, I concluded that he was murdered, but not by the altar boy. Something far more sinister is at work here."

A strong chill squeezed Alex's heart when she let it sink in that her friend Fra Felipe really was gone . . . forever. She choked up and almost couldn't breathe. Tears of grief streamed down her face. She wiped them away with her fingertips, but more followed.

"I . . . I just can't believe he's dead."

Her voice caught with a painful sob.

"He was such a good man."

"Yes, he was," Derek said, "but the forces of evil are strong, and they got to him . . . just as they tried to get a hold on Holly . . . and you. If they wanted to destroy her themselves, I'm sure they could have done so quite easily. But then, they would have lost."

"I don't see how," Alex said, almost choking on the words.

"Because she wouldn't have contributed to her own downfall," Derek said. "In order for her to counteract all of the good deeds she's done in the world, she has to be corrupted. She has to be responsible for her own destruction."

"You mean she has to commit suicide," Alex said. "What you're saying is, Hunter—or the thing that was possessing him—wanted to force her to kill herself."

"Or else damn herself by giving over to her rage and killing the being she thought was Hunter. Yes. If they destroyed her outright, then she would become a martyr, and according to the Jewish legends, when a *lamedvovniks* dies, either naturally or a martyr's death, then they are replaced—"

"—and the balance is maintained. But what about Fra Felipe? If he's dead, aren't all of the other Hidden Saints in jeopardy now?"

"My research indicates that all of the *lamedvovniks* are replaced when they die unless or until one of them still surviving has been corrupted. That upsets the delicate balance. What I think happened was, Fra Felipe was murdered diabolically in order to distract us from Holly so the demon would have the time it needed to work on her grief and corrupt her. That way—and only that way—could the forces of evil be sure that the *lamedvovniks* would not be replaced, and they could kill the rest of the Hidden Saints as they pleased."

"And bring on eternal night," Alex said, swallowing with difficulty.

"Exactly," Derek said. "But that's what we in the Legacy have to prevent. We work to maintain that balance of good in the universe so the Powers of Darkness never get the upper hand. And that's why we'll have to keep watch over Holly."

"But what about the others? There are thirty-five other people out there . . . other Hidden Saints who are in danger and don't even realize it?"

"Goodness is always threatened by Evil. They all know that," Derek said.

There was a trace of terrible sadness and resignation in his voice that saddened Alex.

"I know," she said, yawning again as a strong wave of sleepiness took hold of her. "You're absolutely right."

It was an effort to keep her eyes open and focused.

"Thanks for calling, Derek. I'll talk to you later."

"Take care of yourself . . . and Holly," Derek said. "I'm glad all of you are all right. We'll talk again soon."

With that, he broke the connection.

Alex snapped off the cell phone and placed it on the nightstand beside her bed. She glanced over at Holly again, grateful to see that she was still sleeping soundly. She smiled at Nick and Rachel, who were watching her with expressions of deep concern and affection.

A jab of pain hit Alex's left shoulder when she leaned back onto the bed.

She felt weak, totally wrung out. And really sleepy.

The doctor was right, she thought.

She really did need some rest. Just knowing that Derek, Rachel, and Nick were with her in this fight was enough to allow her to relax, at least until she recovered her strength enough for the next fight.

"We'll let you get some rest now," Rachel said softly as she stood up and smiled at Alex. She touched her lightly, reassuringly on the hand.

Alex was about to protest their leaving, but then she thought better of it and nodded sleepily.

"Yeah . . . thanks," she said, licking her lips. They felt dry again, but she didn't even have the strength to lift up the glass of water for a sip.

"Don't worry," Nick said with a warm smile. "We'll be right outside the door here, keeping an eye on both of you."

"Thanks," Alex murmured, and that was all she managed before closing her eyes and settling down.

The last thing she heard before she drifted off to sleep was the soft click the door made as Rachel and Nick closed it behind them.

EPILOGUE

Holly's eyes were closed, and she was staring into a rich, pulsating darkness as she drifted in and out of awareness and listened to Alex's voice as she spoke with Derek on the phone. She wasn't sure when she first became aware of another voice speaking. It drifted so subtly into her awareness that she realized she had been listening to it for quite a while before acknowledging that it wasn't Alex, Nick, or Rachel.

It was someone else.

The paper-thin whisper teased at the edge of her awareness, and she found that the more intently she listened to it, the fainter it became. It was only when she let herself go, when she surrendered to the dense charcoal darkness that surrounded her that the voice became clearer, although she could never make out more than a few words and phrases.

The sound of the voice was soothing, with no sense of threat or danger. It reminded her of the sound she might hear in a field in the middle of a lazy, summer day . . . the faint buzzing of bees . . . the soft, steady chirring of crickets and grasshoppers . . . the gentle sighing of the wind ruffling through the grass. The image was so vivid that Holly could practically smell the summer day, and she was filled with a deep contentment she hadn't known since . . .

. . . since Evan had died, certainly, she thought . . . maybe a lot longer.

The thought that her son was dead—truly dead and gone from her forever—filled her with a swelling sadness, but for the first time since Evan had died, it was a dull sense of deep longing, not the sharp, bitter sting of life's finality.

It wasn't you speaking to me, was it, Evan? It never was, she thought, but the thought seemed louder inside her head than the voice to which she was listening.

The whole time . . . it was that beast . . . that monster that was posing as Hunter telling me what to do . . . trying to get me to kill someone . . . either him or myself . . . That was it, wasn't it?

She didn't receive an answer, at least not directly, but she was filled with such a wonderful sense of her son's immediate presence that somewhere, deep in her heart, she knew that he was not truly gone from her. As long as she held onto the love she had felt for him and the love he had given her, he would never be far away from her.

Holly didn't even consider whether or not she and Evan would ever be reunited in some form of afterlife.

It didn't matter.

She felt his presence now, and it was warm and rich and wonderful. She became aware of the soft flutter of her pulse in her chest and neck, the faint stirring of cool air entering her lungs as she took a breath, and the thought that she was alive filled her with inexpressible joy.

And she knew that the joy she was feeling was shared with Evan as well as with Alex and Nick and everyone else she knew in her life.

Love never really dies, does it? she thought, and once again, she didn't get or really need a reply.

She already knew the answer.

But her awareness of her own heart beating brought her closer to wakefulness. She left the comfortable zone where she was drifting and once again could hear the voices in her room . . . Alex and Nick's voices.

"Don't worry," she heard Nick say.

She could imagine the tender smile he must be wearing as he looked at his friend—and her friend—Alex with concern and genuine affection.

"We'll be right outside the door here, keeping an eye on both of you."

Knowing that Nick was there with them gave Holly a feeling of security that she hadn't felt in a long while.

"Thanks," she heard Alex reply, and then, very faintly, Holly heard their footsteps as Nick and Rachel left the room and closed the door behind them.

It could have been moments or hours later that she opened her eyes to narrow slits and looked around at her surroundings.

For a moment or two, her vision was blurred, but she wasn't surprised to see that she was lying in a bed in a hospital room.

She had expected that.

What surprised her was the subdued glow of light that filled the room. Through the wide window, she could see that the sun was setting. It sent out wide rays of light as it dropped below a raft of clouds on the distant western horizon. The room was suffused by a vibrant orange glow that coated everything with a powdery texture. Ever so slowly, the sunlight deepened to red, and the clouds blended from gray to deep purple and black.

But in the middle of a beam of light that shot like a lance through the window, Holly saw something that made her throat catch.

Suspended a few feet above the floor, at the foot of the bed, was a single, downy white feather.

For a moment, Holly thought this was a defect in her

vision; but the longer she stared at it, the clearer it became. In the warm glow of sunlight, she could see the thin, curved shaft of the feather and the gently coiling barbs. Every detail stood out in amazingly sharp detail.

Holly didn't dare breathe as she studied the feather. She was afraid that even the faintest puff of breath would blow it away.

After what seemed like a timeless, dreamy moment, the feather began to move.

But it didn't drift to the floor.

Instead, it moved slowly in a straight, steady line toward the window. It seemed to pass effortlessly through the solid glass, and Holly watched it until she lost sight of it in the blazing red glare of the setting sun.

Then and only then did she let out the breath she'd been holding. Smiling and feeling deeply at peace with herself, knowing that she could live beyond her tragic loss, she closed her eyes and let her head sink back onto the pillow. She was smiling as she drifted off into a deep, restful sleep.